IN A WORLD OF SORCERY ONLY ONE WILL RISE

Saranon clung on as Mitch commanded the dragon to turn in the night sky. He remained silent. She was about to speak as the blast of wizardry seared overhead. The display crackled through the night air. 'I thought they were expecting us,' she snapped.

The outer shield flared as she made contact. 'Stay where you are,' Captain Argaston shouted.

The dragon struck his claws deep into the ground. The shield lowered and let them through. Her sorcery surged from within, and she winced with the pain. There was no way to hide it as she fell to the ground.

Enter an epic tale of sword and sorcery. More than two hundred years ago a powerful sorceress freed her people then vanished. As time passed truth turned into myth and myth became legend. The time has come again. Saranon must claim her rightful place before Zyanthia falls.

www.chantellegriffin.com

RUNNING THROUGH THE RISING TIDE

THE LEGACY OF ZYANTHIA BOOK TWO

CHANTELLE GRIFFIN

First published by Publicious Pty Ltd in 2013
Second edition 2017
by Chantelle Griffin

Interior layout by Chantelle Griffin
www.chantellegriffin.com

Cover artwork by Matthew K. Hoddy
www.spacepyrates.com

Catalogue-in-Publication details available
from the National Library of Australia

paperback ISBN: 978-0-9943921-2-1

Also available in ebook
ebook ISBN: 978-0-9943921-3-8

For my sister

For all that has been before, for all the pain and sorrow, may you rise above them all. For the path less travelled brings hardship, adventure and triumph.

THE ZYANTHIAN REGION, TORDOREN

CHAPTER ONE

The trouble with Magladen

Deep on the plains the shadows grew dark across the sky, Mitch was itching to be off but Saranon was not so sure. Normisia had provided sanctuary. Every day the northern border drew nearer she became more agitated. It was not so much that she did not like the place, but it felt odd. The dust crept into her boots making her feet grubby every time she went outside. The strange warm wind blew her hair into her face and became a continual source of frustration. The sky was even a different colour of blue and the land was poor with few people working the browning fields. The grounds around the Keep Zaidek had been lush and plentiful in contrast. Even though Saranon was not afraid the image loomed in her mind and played havoc with her internal thoughts.

The northern border was harsh and unforgiving; it

would be easier to follow the river up through Magladen. Mitch kicked the dirt beside him and grunted, his top which looked one size too small made his muscular arms stand out. Saranon could not help a small chuckle. He would be missed by a few of the ladies at Eggleston. A plain yet well sized Keep, blending into the background of the earthy hills. This was as far north toward Magladen as any Keep had been and withstood the elements which simmered across the border.

'Have you finished admiring the view?' Mitch spoke with a straight voice.

'Hardly, how do you feel about leaving tomorrow?'

Mitch just smiled and went inside, he did not seem adverse to adventure but she doubted the journey ahead. She needed to make it to Serenphel in time for the next calling that was weeks away. Then to get this far had been more than half a year, soon it would be her birthday and then the anniversary of Tasha's death. Her old friend still beckoned to her in her sleep and woke her at night.

She turned back to Brett the Captain of Eggleston Keep and her new friend Ingrid smiled. 'I'm afraid we can't go with you but I will help you make your way across. The people there are peaceful, but they keep to themselves.'

Saranon knew she was right; Ingrid had taken her along the border before. There had been little conversation and not much could be fathomed from the exchange. Yet try as she might, her dreams were going to be filled with the large forests that hid Magladen from the world outside. The pillow was soft as she settled down with one arm hanging out in Mitch's direction as he slept in the dark.

No sooner had she closed her eyes than Tasha was in her dream clutching at her hand, pulling her in haste. She almost tripped on the path wavering in front of her, we have to go. She knew her old friend was right even if her way ahead would not be easy. The first rays of light shining through the window touched her open hand. Something moved at the corner of her eye and Mitch was standing ready to leave. He knelt down and helped her up, not that Saranon needed help, but she had been dithering somewhat the last few days. He could see it written all over her face.

Brett held the horses at bay to let them pass through the ranks without a sound. As much as she wanted to take Katholomu he would draw attention and it was easier for the sly black dragon to fly alone. The border coming up was the easy part as they passed through the check point and into a windy dense oblivion. 'You seem right at home?' She asked.

Mitch did not answer, he was busy making ground. They could both travel using the lay-lines but the paths were vague and muddy, weakening at points and that was what she was unsure of. If they lost their way it could take ages to get back again.

The dense swampy land let out the odd dull sound from behind the undergrowth. Mitch had stopped up ahead. 'What is it?' Saranon whispered.

He signalled for quiet. She stood beside him and he pointed but she could see nothing. 'I don't see,' she whispered.

'Over there,' he whispered back.

She gave him a disgruntled look. She had a more detailed scan of her surroundings but drew a blank. She was starting to wonder if he was making things up. 'Look between the trees past that rock,' Mitch pointed.

She gave a sigh of exasperation and he added, 'They're clinging to the trunk.'

Saranon squinted and could just make out some odd shapes. That looked more like large stick forms wrapped together. Mitch whispered, 'They are firmadicide.'

'Oh,' her powers of observation were slipping. She wondered how she was meant to feel. She felt calm, which was strange at the moment given the presence of such a dangerous predator. She was thankful the odd gigantic stick creatures kept to themselves unless disturbed. A thought occurred to her, 'Are we encroaching on its space?'

He clutched her shoulder urging her to move on while he shook his head in mute disbelief.

'I was being serious,' she exclaimed.

He gave in, 'See over there are the nefrelle. We'll be fine as long as we stay close.'

'Are you sure about that, because I don't see how we could be safe…' She replied.

Mitch had picked up speed, no doubt to avoid the conversation which left her having to almost run to catch up. After a while he slowed his pace without missing a beat. Saranon was fit but her new found friend made the journey look effortless. His pace was sturdy over the lay-line which covered the ill trodden ground. She was thankful they had not reached the gap, which would be near night fall and she hastened her speed.

There was no sign of Katholomu but unlike people, dragons did not find the dense forest country heavy going. Instead it was a well-known sanctuary and if rumours were believed a place for larger dragons to hang out.She had spotted a few but they were different in build and looked a bit rough around the edges in an unwelcoming way. She felt as though eyes were watching her, then tripped over something running across her path. Mitch stopped her fall and the nefrelle ran out of sight, 'Can they do that?'

Mitch stayed close, 'Be careful.'

'I plan to,' she retorted.

The small furry thing was meant to have claws, small but sharp. As Saranon looked down she noticed a small scrape across her boot, 'Great.'

If that happened again, knowing her luck, it would tear a hole and she would have to mend it. They were trying to stay low as much as possible, at first she thought that would be easy. Yet lately she had been letting in to her energy in her sleep. Having to concentrate during the night was beginning to wear her patience, not that there was much to begin with.

A strange wave came over her and Saranon moved back near the middle of the lay-line, the distraction had taken her too close to the edge. The sun was setting on a warm day; she could feel the sweat drip down her back more from the effort of keeping up than the heat. Mitch was already making camp with a wry smile; he had not said anything about her clumsiness. The place had a good view, but tomorrow meant clambering over boulders and away from the lay-line. She felt calm near its edge but the thought made her shudder. At least she did not have to deal with people out here. The people of Magladen were a hard, down to earth kind. It was more the next stage that gave her a nervous stare into the beyond.

'You're scaring the wildlife,' he remarked.

'What?' She stared down to see the energy build-up underneath her hand. Several worried nefrelle peered at her in the distance.

Saranon calmed down, it was no use getting worked up before she had even started. The blankets they had packed were nice and soft and the calm night meant they could stay in the open. Mitch had mastered protection spells with years of practice that made her jealous. She gave him a look and he refused to be drawn in. The nefrelle kept a small and respectable distance before settling down for the night. When curled up they looked like small balls of fluff with silk soft fur. It was amazing to think that these tiny creatures could take on firmadicide.

A cool wind was creeping up from around the hill carrying a faint growling sound. Before she spoke Mitch did, 'Go to sleep.'

The growling sound continued in the background as she fell into a murky dream of being chased by firmadicide. The light filled the air and cast a shadow from his bulky figure. She scrambled up to find the campsite had already been cleared away and placed her hands on her hips in a huff. She was beginning to understand why sorcerers grumbled about wizards. She crammed her belongings in her small bag. The ground was not too moist underfoot as they began their slow climb over the rocky hills.

For once Saranon could show off, bouncing over the rocks as he struggled to keep up. She glimpsed Stragnar in the distance. Her heart pounded with excitement that was over the halfway mark through Magladen. The wind brushed across her sweaty skin bubbling with fresh hopes and ideas. A muffled sound clambered up her back, she turned around and she could not see Mitch. For a moment she forgot to breathe as she pummelled back to where he had been and almost tripped into the gaping hole. 'Are you all right?' She shouted there was no reply.

How on earth could she loose a wizard? She grumbled to herself. She shone a small light and could make out Mitch's tracker on a ledge, as she groaned.

Saranon latched a strong yet thin rope around a nice piece of sturdy rock. She tried to think of where she preferred to be at this moment, having a nice warm meal at a cosy tavern in Stragnar. The grime was sticking to her sweaty garments not that it mattered, a strange sweet smell began wafting up from the depths. She made herself comfortable on a small ledge and shone her light brighter in to the darkness. 'Oh,' was all she could manage as she found her lost wizard. He was huddled in a calm stance so as not to disturb the firmadicide in their nest. She took a deep breath, trying not to panic as she had been in worse situations. While standing with one foot on one ledge and one foot on another she made a strong hold for another rope to go down. She dangled it between her fumbling hands.

Mitch stood up with all the grace he could muster. He raised himself up, he reached up as if to hug Saranon, then dashed up past her. Leaving her last to get out, she put one hand on her hip in annoyance and started gathering the rope. She felt a small tug and yanked without thinking, a noise grew beneath her and she realised what she had done. She scrambled out grabbing chunks of dirt on her way out. 'Run,' she did not need to say it, as he was already someway ahead.

So much for getting a thank you, she thought to herself. The rustling sound grew behind her…it gathered momentum into a low chirping with hundreds of voices chiming in.

Mitch was using his wizardry to build-up speed, as she looked behind her the firmadicide were catching up. As Saranon was running she eyed a nefrelle stronghold ahead on the left. She was running out of options and slid down the hill straight into them. The firmadicide followed at pace and crashed right into the nefrelle. The two massive groups mingled back and forth. She was too worried at what she had done to look. Then she heard some awful munching sounds. She peered out from her hiding spot to see that the nefrelle were chomping away on a few firmadicide. The idea of watching made her stomach churn, so she backed away and pretended that nothing had happened.

At least this time it was not her fault. Mitch

was catching his breath in the clearing and waved in recognition. She wanted to scream, how could you do that, but the words would not roll off her tongue. So instead she resorted to an annoyed glare that did not phase him one bit. At least the next lay-line was close by or Saranon would be finding her voice after all that. To make matters worse, Mitch appeared to be laughing at her. The unusual pair made their way down along the windy path with time to spare as the afternoon sun shone on their backs. The way ahead broke into patches of fields as they drew toward the city of Stragnar. She could see signs of civilisation on the outskirts, 'What do you think they're like?' She asked.

'The patrol knows we're coming,' he commented.

'Just when were you going to tell me that?' She grumbled.

Mitch shook his head and moved on. For some reason the last league seemed to drag on forever. By the time they reached the small party of troops the last rays of sun were stretching over the hill tops. An officer by the name of Haywood was leaning up against a muddy old vehicle that had seen better days. 'You two took your time, were you thinking of bringing the locals as well?'

He seemed friendly enough and Mitch spoke for a while before they moved away into the Keep Karaden.

It was a smooth but fast drive with the occasional bump from the gravel road. 'So what brings you to these parts?' Haywood glanced at her.

She looked at Mitch for guidance but he was giving no hints away. She hesitated, 'We are on our way to Indarin.'

'Are you sure that's what you want?' Haywood asked.

Saranon did not understand the question, 'I don't know of any alternative.'

'It's all right; I just meant it's dangerous to be travelling that far,' he replied.

'I will keep that in mind,' she spoke.

'She doesn't have a sense of humour?' He spoke to Mitch.

'Hardly,' he remarked.

Great, thought Saranon, why do wizards have to think the same way even across the border? She muted a grumble under her breath, now she had two wizards smiling at her expense. The night time was creeping in with odd sounds through the darkness as they made their way into the Keep. Karaden made up the corner stone which protected the city of Stragnar; it was impressive in size. Haywood led them around the building to a large black sleeping dragon making happy snorts as he breathed. 'I believe this belongs to you.'

Katholomu looked cosy and almost gentle, curled up on a well-worn piece of ground in the courtyard. As she walked closer she wriggled her nose from the smell, the big dragon stank. She bumped into Haywood while trying to escape the smell. 'Don't look at me, we tried to wash him but he wanted to wait for you,' he grinned.

She turned toward Mitch. 'Hey, don't look at me either. He's your dragon.'

'Oh,' she exclaimed while scrunching up her face in disgust.

It was not the greatest experience Saranon had. She walked closer to the wonderful smell of food wafting out from the hall. She felt the warmth on her hands from the fire having Katholomu turn up unexpected did not seem so bad. She sat down on the cosy couch and scoffed down tea, as Mitch and Haywood spoke. Mitch stared as she slurped her soup and she tried not to make a sound, this was going to be a long trip. The calm night blew a gentle breeze through the open window. Even though she could still smell the muck off Katholomu on her hands, she was too tired to let it worry her.

The whirring of the great central core mumbled into a soft whisper as it reached the walls of the corridor. Saranon caressed the wall and the Keep seemed to respond underneath her touch. She let go and looked out to see no trace of the great black dragon. She was not surprised but a little disheartened. If she flew by dragon now she would stand out and dragons were few in Balquene. Mitch was looking unorganised and relaxed for a short stay, 'Are you missing something?'

She could not see his backpack anywhere as she snooped around the corner staring straight at a room full of busy people.

He smiled, 'We're not leaving today.'

As he spoke the clouds turned dark and a deep low rustle swirled toward them on the wind from the dark forest to the northeast. Saranon let out her own grumble in frustration. That meant it would not be safe to travel the lay-lines for at least a few days. 'You could have told me!'

She walked off in a grump and went down to investigate the surroundings.

The dragon had left his marks by flattening a few bushes and bending a young tree to breaking point where he had slept. One of the local drezen dragons, smaller in size, was pawing and sniffing at the ground before she curled up. Tassle looked tiny taking up less than half the space, they were quite strong and compact, purpose built for the rough terrain.

She was not so convinced about the wildlife blocking their path. From where she stood it looked peaceful. The Keep had dealt well with hazards but as she walked through the scrub she was less convinced. The path beneath her led on to the Pheneadin sorcerers' cove residing on the large estate. She had been informed that they were quite content to co-exist with the local Eudarin wizards. Yet the Pheneadin preferred to keep their own space in the giant shadow of the Keep. 'Hello there, we were wondering when you would arrive,' Elise spoke with a pleasant smile. She was a few years older than her.

Saranon looked up with a baffled gaze, for some reason having an inconspicuous approach did not work in Magladen.

The sorcerers had a beautiful set up, it was so light and airy compared to the heart of the Keep and large inside. As she stepped around with Elise guiding her way, she noticed how busy and tense people were. 'It's all right we're just getting ready in case the triden stampede,' her new friend explained.

Elise said it in such a calm voice that Saranon thought she misheard, 'The what?'

'Oh you haven't experienced that they tend to run in every direction except south over the border. If you stay long enough you'll get to see one?'

She opened her mouth in amazement but stayed mute. The thought of staying long enough to see a stampede of anything was not on her list of things she wanted to do. She wondered if Mitch had heard of such a thing. Around her a whooshing noise sprang up from beneath with a loud gush of warm wind. 'We are just making a few adjustments so the Keep will be ready, but you shouldn't have anything to fear.'

Fear was not what Saranon was thinking about, rather how long she was going to have to stay. 'When this stampede thing happens, how long does it take for the lay-lines to clear?'

Elise gave a soft laugh, 'Oh you will be able leave soon enough, besides you only just arrived.'

Elise took her down to meet some of her friends who were helping make final adjustments. As they worked, the sky grew grey drawing long dark shadows, the lights flickered in response. 'You will need to head back,' Elise spoke in a serious tone.

She did not need any convincing to go, the wind was picking up outside hurting her ears before she covered them. There was no sign of Tassle or any other dragons out in the courtyard as she looked ahead. The path gave views back up to the hills she felt a strange calming sensation from underneath the ground where the central core lay.

Something in the distance, a speck or two on the horizon caught her eye. She walked forward against the wind's steady breeze blowing at her hair. She placed her hands on her hips as she gazed at the dotted line. 'So you are, what is keeping me from my path.'

Saranon spoke underneath her breath in cold defiance, how such a beast could cause so much trouble. The triden were a large overgrown crab-like thing with fur on its back. Its dark muddy brown colour blended into the background, and the darkness swallowing the calm blue sky.

She stood alone as the others had already gone inside and shuttered up the grand old building. The leaves blew around her. The Keep stirred below thumping underneath her like a dampened drum chiming with her heartbeat in the small of her ear. Then it stopped and the ground cracked beneath her with a whip of excitement. Her blood stirred the Keep opened up in anticipation of attack. She scrambled for her talik as Mitch called, 'Are you going to come inside?'

'Why, are you scared?' She asked and there was no reply, 'I take that as a "no".'

Mitch was good at intruding on her thoughts. As the rising wind swept the ground around her, she wondered if it was all a lot of fuss over nothing. The Keep did not think so with a cold shudder deep from within. The might of the central core sparked upward through the great claws around her. Arching into the sky above, her scepticism was waning as the small dark dots on the horizon began to grow in number. The dots formed a patchy line along the otherwise peaceful hillside. The wind began to drop away and for a moment Saranon thought it was for nothing. The Keep took on an odd view with the barricades and the silence. The shadows broke to let in blue sky and she ventured out past the claws of the Keep into the meadow below.

It was a searing rumble that pummelled the ground as she looked up and saw what she had been waiting for. It felt like forever as the great dark mass heaved in slow motion caressing the lower hillside in a dark embrace and spewing forward. The temptation was too great as the excitement drew her in. All she could think of was that she wanted to be part of it and for the moment the part of her brain that kept her safe was staying silent. She lunged forward at pace letting her sorcery grab hold of her. She jumped up and rode a triden driving it forward with such exaltation she forgot all about the safety of the Keep.

Saranon rode hard, spurring the triden on to the head of the mass and leading it around into the dense forest beyond. She rode with all her might as the great tide of triden kept pace behind and around her. The great beasts stopped to catch their breath in a clearing and she almost felt disappointed it was over. Her hands were white with excitement and from holding on so hard. Her back felt sore, but as she walked away she still could not understand what all the fuss was about.

CHAPTER TWO

Hiding the Angeon

The rush of excitement still filled Saranon's veins as she left the mounting numbers of triden behind her. It had been breathtaking but now she had to get back to the Keep and some sort of normality. She looked in the direction of Karaden that from a distance did not appear to be affected. She shook her head in bewilderment. She wondered if it was just her who found the whole event rather strange and lacking in severity. The thought was not long to be pondered, as she was soon joined by Haywood who drove by. He was silent but not in a bad way, she figured there would be plenty of work waiting back at the Keep.

Haywood looked at her as if expecting her to say something, but Saranon was in one of her moods. 'You are full of surprises for one so young,' he smiled.

She did not know what he meant, 'Next time can we

avoid the whole incident?'

Haywood laughed but he did not say anything, she could see Mitch waiting as they returned. She strode toward him and in a matter of fact tone stated, 'I don't think I like triden, and they smell.'

Mitch kept a straight face as Haywood chuckled behind her, 'I don't like them either.'

Haywood came over and patted her on the back, 'You're more than welcome here anytime,' and with that he left her in peace.

'Is he all right?' Saranon asked Mitch.

'Yes,' he replied.

She was about to ask another question but had second thoughts it had been a strange day already and she had had enough of the wildlife. A nice hearty meal sounded good right now.

The Keep showed signs of strain as they walked along the main hall. It was more artificial and could be fixed which was just as well because she liked the Keep. It had a nice hum that reminded her of Darkonia and hoped that all her efforts would lead her back home. At the moment, that seemed a long way away and she sighed almost in disbelief. The food was good and the Eudarin wizards knew how to have a feast. Her normal response was to shy away but today it felt like a welcoming hug at the end of a hard day. Karaden hummed away underneath her fingers as she went to bed, tomorrow with any luck they would be on their way.

The first rays of sun hit the floor radiant and bright.

The excitement that had washed over Saranon had now been replaced with grumbling. She packed away her belongings for a second time, hoping for an early start to the day. The sunlight shimmered on the courtyard and this time Mitch was ready to go, finally she sighed in relief, 'Did I get it right this time?'

Mitch beckoned her on before Haywood could answer. A little further down the track Mitch explained that the young sorceress had managed to make a grand impression. She could see that he knew it was more by accident than by design. 'Well,' she said. 'I will take compliments even if it was an accident.'

The journey was easy going and the warm weather enjoyable for the rest of the way as they strode into their last stop. Before stepping over into what she had been informed was some sort of medium chaos. Mitch was becoming serious underneath his dark brow and she noticed he was tense. She had been given a set of instructions before making it thus far. She rambled about in her papers as they sat in the small courtyard of the last destination in Magladen. 'You won't need that paper in Balquene,' Mitch sounded much surer than he looked.

The tidings were small and neat. They reassembled their luggage including a few items that had been prepared at Haywood's request. Saranon heaved on a formal coat that felt almost weightless and tried on a few other garments to the guards' bemusement. She had not bothered with looking like a sorceress much anywhere, because she had not felt like one. It was an odd thought but the more time she spent travelling, the more she felt comfortable with herself. The ride on the triden had settled her dreams and she had slept well, it was a shame that would not last.

Tellembre that had remained silent by her side, was worn with ease. She was quite used to the two bond-breakers now, but still kept Corsavere hidden away. It resembled a small elegant dagger when at peace, but she knew it to be a tyrant when called. Through the whole journey Pennie had remained out of reach, but that meant her old friend was busy and did not want to intrude. Things were different in the morning, Mitch woke up a completely different person. His face was stern and he hung in the background, for the first time since Saranon had known him. It was amazing to think such a large man could do that, but he did so without effort.

They checked in to Balquene. Everything seemed perfect but the undercurrent was there, filling her senses. It had been a while since she had been under such tight scrutiny with such little interaction. The air smelled thicker with a whiff of distrust and she wondered if it would be like that for whole journey until Serenphel. As they left, a scene broke out behind her, something had happened and the guards circled in. She did not need to say anything as Mitch followed with haste. The lay-lines were well used and looked after as they arrived at the town of Salby and she breathed a sigh of relief. The mid-afternoon heat creased the sky as they trudged on through the dusty streets. The place was filled with a stale smell that cluttered the air around them.

For once Saranon did not seem to be the centre of attention, as a few stares found their way toward Mitch, who for the most part remained silent. The city on the fringes was well used to travellers as she made her way into the tavern. She was used to speaking for herself, but the calm acceptance felt odd as Mitch stayed in her shadow. It was a cool relief to move out of the warm sun. She toyed with her drink before saying something, 'It's my birthday today.'

'Pennie told me,' he said.

He produced a small bundle and passed it to her. Inside was a beautiful hair piece that reminded her of home as she held it tight in the palm of her hand.

In the evening the noise of the tavern began to grow and reminded her more of Normisia which put her at ease. She did not think she would ever be excited by the merriness of rowdy voices. She saw a few glances from a friendly looking face of a wizardess but appeared not to notice Mitch by her side. Saranon warmed to her company as Gezelda asked her where she was headed. That was an easy answer as Balquene was used to its sorcerers travelling to Serenphel for training. She glanced at Mitch every now and then but he looked relaxed. The sensation crept up her arm but she pretended not to notice. It was too soon after the triden for her power to surge again, yet another thing for her to worry about as she clenched her fist.

She needed some fresh air and Mitch left his place to join her outside, they moved away and he could see the look on her face. He went to say something but it was too late. The air moved around them and they had company. The wizards circled in with trained ability, she tried to reach out to Mitch but they had already taken him. She sped after them down the street and out of sight, sliding fast into the shadows as the energy within her surged with delight. The Angeon beckoned underneath her skin and it gripped tight from within her soul, burning her eyes. She could sense Mitch being hurt and she was taking too long to catch up.

Saranon moved further into the old Keep, near the north of the city. It had been built around but the disguise fell apart as her senses reached out. She was so close to Mitch now but still too far. The wizards were well locked around him as she cringed with the surge of the energy making its way up to her throat. She tried to hold it down knowing it would only delay the inevitable. As she listened to the voices, it became clear that Mitch was not welcome, she should have left him behind. The energy churned up inside her making her head spin, now was not the time to lose control.

Mitch was cornered in the darkness of the Keep and the deep murky edge of the sheal lapping up against the open floor. The intense energy burnt like fire up her throat and she ran in searing agony to the liquid edge, letting the Keep suck the excess energy out. The voices of the shocked disgruntlement of the wizards she had knocked aside in the process, sounded far away. Saranon took a step back and gasped as she broke away from the Keep and stumbled around to see stunned faces. That was not exactly what she had planned. An older wizard Bohdan spoke up in the array of silence, 'I think that is enough for now.'

His greying eyes stared down the fierce competition that had left Mitch with a few extra bruises. She stood beside her wizard, she felt a great weight had lifted off her soul but this soon filled with annoyance. Her sixteenth birthday was ruined, she grumbled as the events of the evening were forgotten under the docile faces. For once she was envious of Mitch who played along in a brilliant manner. It felt like she was the only one who was dismayed by spending time with wizards who could change their mood quicker than she could. In the large gathering room Saranon spotted Gezelda. Before she made herself hesitate, Mitch pushed her forward. He whispered in her ear, 'It's all right.'

Strange words from someone who was going to have a black eye tomorrow, she was in no frame of mind to argue, this got her nowhere with wizards. The light shone warm and lit up the room. Gezelda looked past her and for the first time noticed her companion, 'You chose strange company.'

'You have an odd way of greeting people, but I would prefer to enjoy the rest of my birthday in peace,' She remarked.

Gezelda smiled, she had not given much away. She wondered what would have happened otherwise. As if knowing Gezelda responded with an apology, 'We thought Mitch was travelling alone.'

The answer was unsatisfactory to her ears but Mitch

was making every effort to shrug off the chain of events. So she tried her best to put her sentiments aside. It was a shallow attempt, but he did not say anything. Saranon shivered as she looked on even though she did not want to fall asleep, her eyelids were falling as she grew tired. He put an arm around her and took her up to bed. The room was strange but large and well furnished, 'I don't want to go to sleep.' She spoke as she fell asleep in Mitch's arms.

The morning's first ray brought with it a massive headache, it pounded down the side of her face. He closed the curtains again, 'It's all right, I don't think the light is going to make any difference.'

He let the light in, 'That's good because you may want to see the view.'

Saranon clambered over to look down at the bustle and further onto the heart of Thaldar. They were on the outskirts of the city, but high up. 'How did we get here?'

Mitch did not answer as she sat on the large window sill peering down; the place was immense and alive with people.

She started counting, 'There are a lot of bond-breakers down there.'

'I know,' he replied.

A knock came from the door as Gezelda entered, 'A bit different from home.'

Saranon thought in a strange way it reminded her of home. Darkonia had entire cities filled with sorcerers and wizards, not that she had seen much. The wizard Keep Thrakin was almost dwarfed in the size of the city, which spread farther than she could see. The headache dispersed as they walked out through the maze of people, Gezelda had been polite but to the point. They could stay but the wizard clan could not help her through the maze of Balquene.

There were too many unknowns for a sorceress and it would be easier if they went alone. It was a bitter cop out, but one she was happy to accept, she did not want to travel with the people who had harmed Mitch for whatever the reason. The wizard had taken the whole ordeal in his stride much to her annoyance. The city was grubby, but full of life, as they walked through. She was still feeling miserable, caught up in her own thoughts, when a crowd drew thick around an open square. To her amazement she could see sorcerers using bond-breakers as she dodged being shoved to the outer rim. Mitch whispered, 'Perhaps you could give that a go.'

Saranon glared at him, then tried to peer closer as the noise of the cheers increased. Her breath slowed as she peered on, the whole thought of using bond-breakers for show had not even crossed her mind. Mitch grunted as she lost her balance and stepped on his foot, the thought brought her right back down to earth as she cringed. It was an unusual sight as they made their way through. The misquew kept on the edge of town, with so many sorcerers they shied away from the inner hub preferring to keep to themselves. She understood how they felt; the boastfulness and open displays of sorcery for fun were starting to get to her. She kept the only bond-breaker she had on her belt wrapped underneath her coat just in case a passer-by was tempted to ask her to show off.

The outer city came like a breath of fresh air on her dusty shoulders. The soft comfort of the misquew felt like home underneath her finger-tips. For once she did not mind the grime that came off the sleek animal's coat of silky dark fur. The northern outskirts of Thaldar turned into a more familiar green background. The forest rising up around the two as they rode inland. Away from the populated coast to the west, it was a small detour but Saranon wanted to stay as far away from attention here as possible. Balquene could be rather cumbersome to new travellers. The night was warm and kind with a cool breeze sweeping her hair back from her face.

She stood up on a pile of rocks as Mitch made camp in the open; it was a beautiful night so far from home. She could feel a small tear trickle down her cheek; it dried in the wind before she could wipe it away. The road was well used and she could hear some voices in the distance. 'Are you going to make some company?' He asked in a casual tone.

'What?' She asked.

Before she had a chance to turn back around, Maya made her presence known with Helen standing with pride beside her. The two sorceresses were not much older than she was. They were from Balquene, but grateful to the have another sorceress in their midst to talk too.

The pair had entered the Reanval competition in Craiden for the first time. Saranon tried to smile and sound enthusiastic. She sighed with relief that she was a year too young to enter the competition. Mitch gave her a funny look from the side lines, 'Yes, Saranon is most looking forward to when she will be old enough to join in.'

That started them chatting away and volunteering to help her with her skills. She wanted to kick Mitch, but he was too far away, if he thought he was being funny she did not appreciate it.

Knowing the basics would not be so bad and Craiden was on their path. She disliked, it but she knew Mitch was right, he groaned as they talked into the night which was fair justice in her mind. It was a distant mix of emotions that swept into her dreams. All she could see was Tasha in the empty square back at Thaldar holding up the bond-breaker, Attourin, she had given Pennie. She had Tellembre tight in her hand and they fought to see who was stronger. In her dream the air electrified around her as they clashed. Tasha matched her in strength and agility urging her on through the sweet warm night.

The morning felt strange with the fresh air blowing against her skin. Mitch had managed to distance himself from the high pitched giggling that followed soon after. It was odd to feel at ease laughing, but this was so far from the life Saranon had known, that she let herself relax. The cool water from the stream was a welcome relief from the heat rising over the hills and filling the clear blue sky. Helen watched Mitch with intrigue then giggled, as her faced turned red when their eyes met. Saranon's mouth opened in astonishment but before she could speak Maya did. 'It's all right, Helen already has a boyfriend you'll meet him at Craiden.'

Helen stood beside her and peered up ahead. Not another soul appeared but there was movement on the horizon as the company rode on with Mitch looking on from behind. She could not help but turn to check but he gave no sign, he was so quiet that she was starting to get worried. Silence was not the Mitch she knew from Normisia. Three groups passed them by. Each time their eyes met Helen and Maya it was as though a secret code had been exchanged and they went by their way. Each time Saranon wondered a little more about her new friends who were filled with excitement.

As the afternoon grew too warm for comfort they came to halt. This gave her a perfect opportunity to quiz Mitch who was reluctant to oblige by dodging her first approach. 'So what do you think?' She asked.

'I think that you've just made friends with Lady Davene's daughter,' he replied.

'You mean after all this time we could have avoided Magladen?' She said under her breath.'

Saranon gave him such a stare that he let out a small laugh of satisfaction for managing to annoy the young sorceress yet again. 'You and I both know the answer, now get to know your friends so we can have an easy trip back.'

She thought to herself, as if that was going to happen. If anything life had just become more complicated but they were travelling the same way. So it made sense to blend in, she was enjoying the company. Maya and Helen were content practising without any regard to the energy they were using. It splayed off the blades and every now and then part of the energy would escape past the shield. A rock blew past Saranon just missing her face, she turned to see both sorceresses gasp then giggle in all the excitement. Maya invited her into the circle and helped her go through the basics. She could feel her heart beat with excitement at the chance of learning and became embarrassed at showing off. Her cheeks grew red and felt hot as she tried to hide her nervousness.

The amount of concentration was draining, but deep down she was happy as it made it easy to skim away from the edge of becoming the Angeon. Here in Balquene she preferred to keep that knowledge to herself for as long as she could. As her mind turned to thinking she let go a little. Maya fell back and both girls rushed toward her, Saranon breathed a sigh of relief as she knelt down. For a moment her heart felt like it was going to beat through her chest. The small bruise healed as they watched but it was a sign that she was happy to accept. She banished herself to the sidelines to watch for the rest of the early afternoon.

The scenery changed as they moved further north following the lay-lines. Less people travelled along the alternate path, which made for good time as they arrived in the evening at Reneby. It lay on the verge of the great forest stretching east. Whereas to the west grew sprawls of civilisation meshing into large towns rising up from the cultivated dirt. It was an eye catching moment as they all stood on an outlook part way up the hill. The landscape appeared with a strange beauty as it filled Saranon with excitement, she had managed to make it this far.

As the night set in she could hear rowdy voices in the distance. The disturbance annoyed her but Helen and Maya did not appear worried so she tried to ignore it. Mitch was quiet in the background but every now and then she caught a glimpse of him looking up. The ground was hard underneath and she was left lying awake, wondering how lucky she had been not to cause serious harm to Maya. She knew that was the real reason she could not sleep, but blaming the ground was easier. Mitch reached over and patted her arm as if in acknowledgement of what she was thinking. The wind blew calm and the voices with them fraying into the back ground, at last thought Saranon, a little bit of quiet.

Something brushed against her skin and she expanded her senses as she turned out of her sleep in annoyance. The misquew made a funny low sound and she stood in a fluid motion. As her energy awakened with her it was easy to tell that they had company. Helen and Maya were still asleep but Mitch had crept over to wake them. The misquew felt uneasy, as she waded her hand through its soft fur she could feel the skin grow tense. A shuffle rang through into the clearing as an ominous sound reached her ears. Several figures dispersed and she ran between them and her wizard. Not thinking, as she slipped into the ever growing Angeon that came to surface with the thrill of excitement.

The Angeon gripped at the edges of the energy, heading towards them like a rushing wave. She ripped it to shreds, knocking the intruders back from the clearing. She chased, forgetting the need to hide. A heavy blow flew out from the side towards her as Saranon fought back through the night her energy strengthening in response. She chased to the edges of the wood none the wiser. Their faces were clear, but whoever the five sorcerers had been this place was well known to them. She could feel the sting of cold sweat drip down her neck. She changed back to find the misquew standing on edge in a large group as if to say 'and don't come back'.

She laughed then she reminded herself of what she had done now there were two sorceresses who had seen the Angeon. Her shoulders shrank low as she headed back riding a misquew in cold relief. It was little comfort to her self-pity. Of all the things Saranon had been told to avoid and she had walked straight into that one. She could see the clearing up ahead and Mitch waiting as he came over she spoke, 'I stuffed up didn't I?'

'No, but you may want to reassure your friends,' he replied.

CHAPTER THREE

On the path to Craiden

The three young sorceresses and Mitch clung to the path. They made their way straight for the big city of Craiden looking around them in a nervous manner. The bright warm day gave no inclination of the trouble the night before, as if mocking their uneasiness. For once he was in the lead, she threw a small pebble close by to get his attention and he did not seem bothered. Helen was still quivering from knowing their attackers, at least it was not Saranon who had attracted trouble this time. In some way it was a relief after bruising Maya, it would have been a fine start to a short friendship.

The subject changed to Mitch as she cringed. 'So how did you two meet?' Maya asked.

'I thought we were discussing the attack,' she responded.

'Ooh, it sounds like someone's avoiding the question,' Maya spoke and Helen chimed in.

Helen was still looking shaken, so Saranon gave in as she spoke of Cornell the Dihan who had tried to kill her and skipped over the location. She was aware that Normisia and Balquene had an awkward relationship and it would be better for Mitch if he came from the country side.

She could see him shake his head, 'And what happened after that?'

He spoke from ahead enjoying this version of events.

'Why is Mitch laughing?' Helen enquired with concern.

'I fell into the water in the Keep during the ceremony.'

The two sorceresses roared with laughter. 'I didn't think it was that funny,' Saranon commented.

'No, you're right it isn't.' Maya spoke trying to stop giggling.

Saranon felt like she had just dobbed herself in. For a moment she missed the fact that Mitch had stopped over to the right, it made Helen feel uneasy. 'I thought I heard something,' he waited for a while then continued on.

'The sooner we make it to Craiden the better,' she spoke her thoughts aloud.

'I agree,' Maya said by her side.

The eerie feeling returned, she was not sure if it was just her imagination as it pulled at the edges of reality. The thought played with her mind and put her out of the good mood she had been in. A storm grew overhead with one more night before Craiden it was not looking pleasant.

Helen and Maya led them to more comfortable quarters in a small town that was used to visitors. Saranon was relieved that the place was busy with tourists and people travelling to Craiden. She noticed Maya was still tense, 'Is everything all right?'

Maya whispered, 'We are still vulnerable until we reach Craiden.'

She knew what she meant but was hoping to relax, the food was much better and Mitch had pre-empted by ordering tea for her. As she took the tray the storm broke outside thrashing against the window and she was glad to be inside.

For all her ability Saranon did not like sleeping in the rain, the warm hearth in a dry crowded room was welcoming as she ate. Helen smiled as Saranon scoffed the food down in chunky pieces and without thinking tapped her on the hand to slow down. It was an old habit she was finding hard to break, but after the camps good food was appetising. Looking through the window Saranon thought she saw a shadow dart across in the gloom outside. When she looked closer she saw nothing and shrugged her shoulders. She licked the juice off her fingers at the same time. Instead of being disgusted Helen understood, 'I'm amazed so many survived the camps.'

She swallowed her food in one gulp as Mitch replied, 'We are fortunate that Saranon made it to Normisia.'

She coughed in disbelief. After the reception she received from the Cryzinelan it was strange hearing the words come from his mouth. The tavern was well set up for the weary traveller with the comforts of home. It was then that she realised that Maya was Helen's bodyguard. For a moment she felt clueless, with a stunned look on her face. Maya just gave her a knowing smile as she walked across the room getting organised for bed.

The company stayed together as neither one thought it safe to split up. Maya had the same uneasy look about her that Saranon felt earlier. A noise crept from the window near where Mitch was sitting, all three sorceresses jumped and he gave them a disgruntled look. The idea of travelling with adolescent girls that had been spooked by the wind did not impress him. She tried to make it sound more serious but he only grunted at her. The night was filled with sweet smells and music wafting up from below in the warm room. She pulled the blanket up she opened her eyes, there was a hand moving near the window.

She shook Maya's shoulder as she headed near Mitch who had fallen asleep on the long couch. She crept over, but before she could reach it the window blew open and an assailant crashed through onto the floor. Mitch moved at the same time in a cold embrace and held the young man pinned down on the floor. She stepped onto the couch with Tellembre ready in her hand but the night gave away nothing more. Behind her the room had become quite crowded as Lady Davene's guards had arrived. They came with the first rays of light breaking across the ground and bleeding into the room. For a moment Saranon was annoyed by the inconvenience. Then she saw Mitch's strained expression as one of the guard's carted the unwelcome intruder away.

He stood up straight beside her and dwarfed the other two men in the room. 'We came as soon as we could Miss,' spoke Tyron, his hair was still damp from riding through the rain.

As Helen spoke, Mitch led Saranon outside to where a fleet of dragons rested. The rozzen dragons shone with their well-kept coats gleaming in the early morning sun. 'I think you're new friend was out of her depth, she reminds me of you.'

'Gee thanks, that's reassuring,' she examined his arm, 'So how are you?'

'I'm fine,' he said.

Mitch's subtlety was lost on the young sorceress as she went up and inspected the dragon. Maggard turned his head toward her and rubbed it against the outstretched palm of her hand. The gentle giant was happy to see Helen as she approached them, 'I am sorry to have caused you so much trouble.'

She spoke with a mild sadness in her voice. She was about to say that she was all right but Mitch got in first. He smooth talked his way into hitching a ride with Lady Davene's daughter. Saranon was speechless and annoyed at him at the same time.

Afterward when they had a moment she took him aside, 'What are doing?' She exclaimed in total frustration.

'It would be easier if we travelled with Helen,' he answered.

'How? Have you thought this through? Why would I want to travel with someone who doesn't fess up about how much trouble she's in?'

Mitch gave her a sarcastic look but did not respond, so she continued. 'This is different, if I knew what sort of trouble I was in I would say something. I don't think it would help but I would tell you.'

'Really,' he smiled in surprise, 'I'll remember that.'

It had been an unusual day, Saranon was quite happy not being the centre of attention but she had been irritable. She chose to ride with Maya on the misquew rather than fly on the dragons with Helen. Riding a dragon had a different meaning in Balquene and she was not convinced that it was the right time to send that message. The well-built road was filled with travellers and unanswered questions of the night before. She could sense Mitch was already having doubts, but she did not have any other ideas. Maya reminded her a little of Pennie back home, interested in details and the way she held herself with confidence. Like her old friend, Maya was not one for giving too much away and expected Saranon to go with the flow. She knew how that had gone with Pennie in Normisia.

As the great gates of Craiden loomed overhead she finally thought of an excuse to part ways. Mitch had promised to check in with the local wizard clan, he gave her a grumpy look as she tried to remain serious and hold onto her tone of voice. As chance would have it, she did not have to wait long. She could feel her whole body breathe a sigh of relief as a familiar face came over. Fiona, Gezelda's older sister came to meet them. Parting them from the group, She could sense the urgency but Mitch stood back until she reached for his hand.

Saranon went to thank her and brushed her arm. Fiona jolted back in shock, 'Sorry you startled me,' she explained.

'There's no need to apologise,' Saranon did not want to disclose what she had felt. Fiona had been hurt and she knew that feeling too well. It stayed with her for a while and Mitch stepped closer, her palm was sweating and she let him go. News had travelled of her accidental union with Thrakin Keep through the wizard world, much to her bewilderment. For her it was just part of being who she was. Mitch warmed to Fiona but it was an uneasy truce, she poked him in the back and he was still tense.

After Normisia being in a wizard Keep did not appear strange, so when Fiona offered she accepted without hesitation. It was Mitch's turn to be annoyed, but she did not mind. There was something about Helen that she could sense in a few quick glimpses. They had been brief but all too familiar from her past. When they were alone Mitch slammed the door, 'What were you thinking?'

Saranon nudged the angry wizard away, 'Fine, you wander around here and if you want we will leave.'

'Is this pay back?' He asked.

She did not know how to respond so she left Mitch to check out the Keep alone. She held her head in her hands in disbelief then tried to get up.

The world became blurry and she knew it was the Angeon from deep within wanting to resurface, only this time was different. She would have to ask Andon Keep for help and leave Mitch for a while. Either way she was not looking forward to the next few days as the queasiness came over her in bouts. Her heartbeat pounded in her ears as she stumbled downward into the heart of the Keep. Andon was welcoming and Saranon figured it must be because of Thrakin. It would not be the first time she had heard of Keeps communicating to one another. Underneath the whirling buzz of people the energy struck through webbing over the surface of her skin. She would have to go down even deeper.

It was a long road down, the Keep was helping her but then she slipped into a hole which felt familiar and her thoughts turned to Odana Temple. Andon pulled her down deep into the heart below the chambers and straight down into the central core. The whirring sound was less intense as Odana, but familiar just the same. The tendrils pulled back and she floated. This time she was not in shock at the unnatural sight within the giant circular core ebbing downwards into nothing. In the glowing darkness the Angeon changed, forming new pathways across and within her. She let herself go floating above the great core which sparked with excitement in response. The core sent great shards of energy up to the surface.

The queasy sensation took over as she transformed and the Keep repaid her kindness to Thrakin. Inside the central core the mighty surging energy of the Angeon, paralleled the core within. The great walls were well fortified to absorb excess energy and hide the transformation. Saranon was not sure her nerves would hold up but from a distance she could hear the Keep soothing her thoughts. It was not the first time the central core in Andon had met an Angeon. The process took days to complete but Andon was pleased with his work, not that the world outside knew it yet. The energy settled with the pathways complete running without an undesired short circuit. That had been causing her so much trouble. It was a calmness that she enjoyed in the lulling hub reaching from below.

The climb to the surface was a grateful relief. She had all but forgotten about Mitch, the Keep told her that he was still around and the thought did not stop her from fretting. She went straight to where Mitch was and found herself heading toward the outdoor pool. That was not like him at all, so she ventured forward watching her step. Saranon could sense the laughter as she moved closer and realised she was stupid to think that he had been in trouble. Mitch splashed water at her from the pool and she stopped it without thinking. The droplets fell on the ground from mid-air. He looked at her from the water's edge, 'You've changed.'

'So have you,' she replied.

She approached Fiona sitting at the other end of the pool, 'How did you manage to get Mitch to relax?'

Fiona's face flushed with embarrassment. 'Ooh, right,' Saranon spoke, she should have known.

That explained why the Keep was not worried about Mitch when she had asked him. Now was not a good time to tell Fiona that he had a lady waiting for him back in Normisia? She took a mental note to remind him of this when she started dating. At least she would not have to worry about having an argument over staying at Andon Keep.

The Reanval competition would be soon, she thought of leaving while the roads were void of traffic. Yet a sorceress not wanting to see the Reanval would attract attention. In some ways it was a relief to have the decision made for her, but waiting gave her time for her thoughts to run idle. Mitch was occupied which gave her time to search the city. The place was fast becoming a beacon for sorcerers from the furthest ends of Balquene and tensions were beginning to flare. Saranon ducked out of an angry dispute not far from the Keep. She made her way to the Haveena Stadium where preparations were taking place.

As she moved among the slow moving throng of enthusiasm she heard a familiar voice. 'I thought I would find you here,' Maya spoke with an open smile.

The two of them talked as Maya showed her around and introduced her. It was strange spectacle with strong shields protecting onlookers from any mishaps. The thought of one failing, gave Saranon an uneasy feeling. It was not something she was accustomed to and trusting it did not feel right. She had two days of indecisiveness before she had to make up her mind to attend. Yet it sounded like Maya had already worked that part of her calendar. The flow of excitement illuminated around her and she was happy to take a step back.

She felt like she had to find her feet again after everything that had happened at Andon. She blamed it on the long journey when Maya noticed she was tired. She did not mind the company but the thought of attracting more unwanted attention after Reneby did not appeal to her. So she was quite content to be staying with wizards. After Normisia it was becoming a recurring theme for the young sorceress. Maya introduced Saranon to her cousin Kadin in the practice area. He was not much older and sweat poured off him as he held out his hand to shake hers.

She wiped her hand afterward but Kadin had a welcoming warmth about him. 'Maya tells me you had some fun on the way up,' he spoke.

She began to feel meek in his presence, 'Yes,' was all she could manage.

Afterward Maya burst out laughing, 'That's the first time I've heard you lost for words. If it means anything I think he likes you too.'

Saranon was trying hard not to blush in the confusion she had not expected to feel that way and returned to Andon not knowing what to say.

She almost bumped into Mitch while attempting to sneak in. The tall wizard stood in a casual manner blocking her way, 'Where have you been?'

'Haveena,' she said as she gained her balance.

He looked down at her in deep thought, 'I think we need to have a chat.'

The young sorceress was taken aback when she realised that Mitch meant a chat about boys. With all the travel Saranon thought it was a bit late. She could not help but see the irony in having him try to explain boys. It was all she could do not to cringe while he spoke.

She tried to change the subject, 'So how are you and Fiona?'

'What?' Mitch grumbled to himself without answering the question.

She giggled to herself it was enough to get him to leave her be. She could feel the buzz of excitement growing around the city and penetrating the atmosphere of the Keep as she slept. The glowing in her dream grew with the voice of the Keep and it woke her in the warm muggy night. She could feel a sharp pain running up through the walls hurtling from outside. If Saranon had to make a guess she thought the Keep was under attack. She raced downstairs and Mitch blocked her path, she almost leaped on him to get past but he pushed her back, 'Stay out of it.'

Every essence in her body was telling her she had to do something. Then having him looming over her creating an obstacle compelled her to wait. The force knocked several wizards down as she squirmed in frustration. She was not about to take Mitch on, especially when wizards were involved. The attack died down with the surge of energy from the central core strengthening the protection shields. He loosened his grip on her in resignation. Saranon slipped out of his arm and rushed down into the chaos. There were two blankets hiding the losses lying on the floor, as she glared back up at him in annoyance.

'Don't blame Mitch, he was trying to help. The Immaron would have increased their attack if they had known you were here.' Fiona spoke as she attended to some of the wounded.

Saranon felt useless for a moment before Fiona suggested that she assist with the wounded. It was not something she had experience with and her awkwardness showed. To her amazement it had a calming effect and she shook her head, it was going to take a long time to understand wizards.

Andon Keep hummed with delight as the sun broke into a bright warm day, sweeping away the pain of the night before. Saranon's frustration still creased her brow as she strode around the Keep checking the shield. Mitch spoke with a sigh, 'Why don't you visit Haveena? We can manage here.'

She was hesitant to leave but he shuffled her outside and she was not about to argue. She suspected the wizards were up to something and she knew her goal was Indarin so she went. The streets were void of any sign of disturbance. After a resounding huff she made her way up the slope to the grand Haveena Stadium looming over the productive city.

Kadin spied her as he was warming up with friends, Saranon had been looking for Maya but the distraction was welcome. The place was full of excitement and yet again she wondered if she would ever feel at ease with the display of raw power. She did not have time to think long as Kadin chatted away. He was quite at home with the prospect that she had travelled from Darkonia. This was much at odds with some of the strange looks she was picking up from the periphery. She was distracted by his smile as a surge of sorcery came down behind her. She turned and shattered the strange bond-breaker into obliteration with hers. Piping hot sparks flew into the air and around as Kadin stood transfixed in silence.

The show was over as soon as it had begun, as the sorcerer who had attacked her fled. Saranon pulled him down and pinned him against the floor, her temper plain on her face. The slow deadly embrace came to a halt with Maya screaming from the distance and she let go pulling back her energy. Regardless of what anyone thought, the blow would have knocked her out and it was not to be scoffed at. She seethed underneath the surface. It was ironic that everyone was rushing to the other sorcerer's aide but she felt little pity.

'You could have killed him,' Maya screamed at her.

'The feeling was mutual.'

Maya was astounded that Saranon had not faltered and stood her ground. The presence of the younger sorceress washed over the bewilderment. It transformed the small arena with a sense of awe. Kadin rushed from the side, 'Three of the shields are down,' then changed the subject, 'How strong are you?' He asked.

'One thing's for sure you won't be able to enter the Reanval.' Maya spoke as she picked up a broken shard from the bond-breaker. She peered at it in a frightened fascination.

Saranon shrugged as her attempt to stay out of the way soon vanished. Fear turned to excitement as Kadin's older brother Reece began organising the clean-up. He grumbled about the lack of time before the start of the competition. She stood watching him, not sure if she was welcome, but the sorcerer did not mind. 'Thought you'd bring some excitement to the arena for the day? I've been waiting for that to happen, the Immaron have been looking for a fight all week.' Reece commented.

Saranon was not sure what to say, she had been attacked and then berated for defending herself. No wonder Mitch had been so keen for her to stay away.

She had felt like she had taken one step forward and one step back. Reece could read her frustration and told her where she could find Kadin and Maya. It was a strange sensation as she walked inside the old stadium. It was as if time stood still inside the walls with the bright flags highlighting different areas and patrons. Saranon breathed a little sigh to herself and was about to knock when Kadin opened the door, 'I thought I would see you again.'

She became speechless and in the awkward silence he let her in. The room was filled with three other sorcerers of similar age preparing their gear in a relaxed manner.

It had not occurred to her that she had reduced tomorrow's competition. As the sorcerer who had attacked her was in no condition to perform and the sorcerers were happy with better odds. She was still calming down and talking about the Reanval was a pleasant distraction. This time she managed not to blush in Kadin's presence as she had the image of Mitch telling her to be careful, stuck in her mind. Saranon went to say something as she left but Kadin kissed her on the lips. She was so shocked that she scrambled back to Andon without saying goodbye. Her heart was still pounding in her ears as she entered inside the Keep.

CHAPTER FOUR

The Reanval competition

On the day of the Reanval competition the streets burst into celebration. It appeared that everyone was up carly, just when Saranon felt like sleeping in. Mitch had urged her out of bed so she would not miss a thing. She was beginning to get jealous of the fact that he could sit this excursion out. His happy whistling did nothing to ease her mood. 'You look beautiful,' were not the words she expected to hear from him as she showed him her outfit.

She gave him a grumpy look as he continued, 'So what did you get up to yesterday?'

She was about to respond when he went on, 'I hear you had a lovely evening with a young man. Is there anything I should be aware of?'

'No,' she said in a meek voice.

'I told you to be careful didn't I?' He reminded her.

'Yes,' Saranon did not think this was fair, given that it was obvious Mitch was sharing his bed. Yet she was not about to say that and scampered off before he could say anything more.

It was easy to blend in, as she became swept along in the cheering crowd heading for the stadium. With many colours present denoting the popularity of the event. She was gliding along amongst all the excitement with a smooth stride all the way to the stadium. The second main arena was filling fast and she could just make out Kadin and Maya in all the commotion. The events were soon being called and the crowd settled in excited anticipation. For all Saranon's lack of understanding, the sparring was professional. She watched in bewildered awe at the sport. Kadin made third place in his rank which he earned with a swift graceful air. Yet the strength of his opponent in the last round had been exceptional. The crowd cheered with tense excitement the whole way through.

Maya had not been so lucky, making eleventh place with Helen making ninth. The two were competitive, but all that was put aside as they greeted each other after the game. The main stadium was reserved for the experienced. In amongst the games the lightning showed with energy glimmering off the vast array of shields. The sparks crackling at the edges made Saranon feel uncomfortable, but the people in the stadium shown no sign of distress. As Helen left the arena she used it as a quiet excuse to move inside but even that was packed. She waited a moment in two frames of mind wondering if she should see Kadin again when Maya caught her arms and beckoned her. Before she had time to ask, a thunder of energy ran through the place with a jolt, it shook the ground with such force then another. 'It's Reece,' Maya panted through her breath.

She looked up at the doors to the main stadium where they were headed and froze. She did not have much time to think as Maya urged her forward through to the arena. The noise was immense; it hit her ear drums with a tumultuous roar. People were already scampering in disbelief and running for the exits almost no one was left. If anything sorcerers could be counted on, it was for making a quick escape when not at the centre of the dispute. The shields were only just holding. She knew Reece did not have long as he struggled with every bit of his energy to hold of his attacker, this was not part of the show. At first Saranon was daunted by the task, but the sorcerer was losing ground and she had to try something.

In the chaos the glow came like a small ember folding in on itself with strength as it grew with immense force. She lunged forward with speed, breaking the hold over Reece. The ground shook with an all mighty rumble, the energy that flew out broke all the shields around the arena. The sorcerer ran, then tumbled as the air shook with the energy. He was pounced on and led away as Kadin rushed in to help his brother. A few brave people who had remained came out of their hiding places and cheered in relief. As she stayed by Reece's side watching him on the stretcher he spoke to lighten the mood, 'I think you've got a fan club.'

'I still don't get it,' Saranon spoke, and he laughed.

It felt like a long evening that dragged on before she went to see Reece with Maya.

The sorcerer looked much better than he had a few hours before. She breathed a heavy sigh of relief, for a moment she thought he would be lost. It was still a blur with the adrenalin running. Kadin had stayed by his side and as Maya, left she found herself speechless. It was strange to think that she had saved someone's life and she felt awkward sitting beside him in an odd silence. Kadin wanted her to stay and she was not sure whether to be flattered or embarrassed. Maya came by again, 'Well I think Reece is right.'

'What do you mean?' She asked.

'I think you've got a fan club. I've already heard at least two stories of a how a great sorceress saved the day.'

All Saranon could think about was how Mitch would react when he found out. She stood up, 'I'm sorry but I need to go, it's getting late…'

'You don't need to make excuses,' Reece said as he thanked her.

It was dark as she managed to make her way back unnoticed. What would Mitch think? She was starting to panic as she crept inside and almost made it to her room as she heard a familiar sound of footsteps beside her. 'Did you have an eventful day?'

Saranon could feel herself cringe 'I… there was an emergency… and…'

Mitch stared at her with his big brown eyes, 'So much for a peaceful journey.'

'I guess you heard,' she replied.

'And the rest of the neighbourhood, I thought the aim was to be quiet,' he remarked.

'Well, I didn't say much,' Saranon said.

'Hmm, I don't think you need to. Now come downstairs and eat something, while you tell me how you defeated an Immaron,' he suggested.

Mitch was patient but she could tell he was not impressed. 'Learning restraint is difficult, but it is an important skill to have. Make sure you think next time.'

He removed himself from any further questioning. He left her with that thought as she became annoyed with him, but then she had expected as much from the soldier within.

Saranon was still seething as she slept in the next morning, Mitch had not come along to rush her and she was thankful. She had too much to be thinking about after last night with Reece. It was going to be awkward attending the Reanval competition after that. It would be a relief when the four days of the competition came to a close. Not thinking she ran downstairs and almost tripped over Mitch startling both of them. He had been crying and her heart sank, 'I will try to be careful today.'

He looked at her in surprise, 'Fiona's missing.'

That had not been what Saranon was expecting and it took her a moment to digest what he was saying then let out a long sigh. She looked around at the panic that was beginning to envelope the clan. The competition would have to wait. Mitch dragged her along and into the thick of the search party getting ready, with the assumption that she would be going with him. She was about to remind him of their previous conversation, but he shot her a serious look and she held back. The competition had begun and there was almost no one on the street. At first she thought they were going to question people but no, that would be too easy.

As she ran to catch up she had the distinct feeling they were heading straight into trouble. The feeling crawling up her spine only added to the thought as Mitch slipped out of sight and Saranon had to find him again. It all felt like a lot of nonsense as she lost track of him again, she tried searching and could not find him. 'Oh, for love of Odana,' she exclaimed.

How could she lose a wizard? She thought to herself. The whole situation was beginning to wear her patience as her frustration grew. She knew what she needed to do but she was not ready to go there after yesterday and she felt trapped by her indecision. She stayed with the search party as they honed in on an area. She wondered if she was doing the right thing as she let the wizards lead.

It was the cold that struck her first after such heat outside in the midday sun. This time, Saranon showed no fear, as she was still bound by her confusion. In the dark she could tell what was happening and did not reach out as she heard Mitch's words deep from within. Corsavere had lain dormant for so long on her journey she almost forgot what it felt like in the palm of her hand as she grasped it. The edges of the trap rose. It unravelled just as fast as

Corsavere's blade sliced with such ease through the invisible edges. She thrust out her hand parting the grey mist as she latched onto an Immaron and held him down. The cold anger raged at the edges of her mind trying to break free as she held on.

Mitch's voice broke her concentration, 'You can let go now.'

She looked up and realised that the hard work had been done and all the wizards, bar Mitch had left. Saranon let go and the sorcerer ran without looking back, she was relieved to find her way out in the warm afternoon sun again with Mitch. For a moment there she had not been sure what to do if she had lost him, Captain Mirshendy would not be a forgiving person. As they made their way back to the safety of Andon Keep, she relaxed. Before Mitch reminded her that she would be missed from the Reanval if she did not attend the last part for the day. She only wanted to relax and calm herself after what had happened but she went.

The light warmed her heart as she grew excited to see Kadin again. She was still unsure what to do; Craiden was a confusing place to be. Saranon made it in time to see the last game and that the shields had all been fixed, Maya came looking for her, 'Are you all right?'

'Yes, I'm just a bit tired from yesterday,' she replied.

'No wonder, that was awesome.'

That was not the word she would have used. Yet she was not about to argue as they went back to celebrate with the other participating sorcerers for the evening. Reece was looking better as he sat in the corner and beckoned for her to come over. The sorcerer still looked pale and shaken in the evening light, Saranon felt out of place and Reece gave her a reassuring smile. 'I hear you had some more trouble with the Immaron.'

'It wasn't much,' she spoke.

'If you travel north through Estrard you will avoid most of them, few Immaron go there because of the Evergeldy.'

She was not sure what to think of going through Estrard, but was grateful for some friendly advice. Mitch had mentioned it before in passing. There were two main gates to Serenphel and the western gate could be found there. It was closer to Indarin but not the most popular travelled. Either way Saranon's excitement at the end of the Reanval approaching was fast fading with the sunlight. It was a long walk home and full of strange disappointment. She had not seen much of Kadin but then it was good since she would be leaving soon. Andon lay peaceful as she started to pack in the glimmering light. It let out a happy small humming sound that faded into the background as if thanking her from a distance.

She would miss the Keep after its most precious gift even though she did not know what to do with it. At least there was no longer the need to worry about ridding herself of an unwanted build-up of energy. She examined her hands, no marks yet, she was complete, her sorcery running well through her body for the first time. It was a grand sixteenth birthday present as she smiled in gratitude.

Now she just needed to find Mitch. He was in the Keep somewhere and was good at shading his exact whereabouts, if only she had such luck. In the wizard Keep, Saranon stood out straight away as she searched, it was tolerable given she was a visitor.

She rushed by to find him kneeling down in the garden and for the moment she thought Fiona had died. 'It's all right.' He spoke without turning. 'I think I owe you an apology.'

She sat beside him; in her heart she knew why Mitch was so solemn. She reached over and patted him on the shoulder. 'We have a long way to go and I need a companion.'

'If we were in Normisia…'

'But we're not,' she replied.

He appeared more at ease as Saranon wondered if it had been the right thing to ask Mitch to go with her to Serenphel. Then it was too late to begin doubting that decision. He leaned over and gave her a quick hug, before he disappeared walking off inside the Keep. Again leaving her even more bewildered than before. For a long time her dreams had been filled with the normal unravelling of thoughts. As she drifted off to sleep she could feel her old friend Tasha tugging at her arm, trying to get her to move. As she opened her eyes to the dream she could see Tasha urging her on into the darkness of the unknown. The light shone off her golden brown hair. Her friend pushed Saranon into the great shadows of grey swirling up ahead and colouring the ground beneath.

She gasped as she woke throwing her arms up and latching onto Mitch with stunned surprise. She could see he had brought her breakfast and that softened her mood. 'If you want to leave we can.'

'What about the Reanval?'

'We've stayed long enough,' he replied.

She agreed with him, as much as she was grateful for the last few days, Balquene did not sit easy in her thoughts.

The pair slipped away with Andon growing smaller in the distance. It dawned on Saranon that he had been rather keen to leave. When she quizzed him he confessed that Fiona had wanted to marry him. She burst out roaring with laughter as she almost lost her balance. Mitch gave her a filthy look. 'And you were worried about me.' She stated as she calmed herself down.

He grumbled under his breath as they travelled north on the misquew and she tried her best not to laugh every time she looked at him.

Half of her wanted to know what happened and the other half thought that it would just annoy Mitch if she asked. This left her with a small smirk across her face. The journey was so peaceful with almost no people travelling by. She was amazed when greeted by a few wizards going about their business with ease. A cool breeze came across and swept along to the west bringing with it small clouds crowding up the sky. Perhaps Tasha had just been referring to the weather in her dream it was a nice thought anyway. Mitch had setting up camp for the night down to an art. Her efforts took at least twice as long between grumbling and his mood lifted as she grew crankier.

She finally gave up and set up the tent with her sorcery. It seemed like a waste but her frustration was crowding her mood and if he grinned at her one more time she was going to snap. He handed her a warm cup of soup as he sprawled out the map and made notes, in theory they were running on schedule. Saranon grew excited at the distance they had travelled already her heart pounding in her chest. They moved further north and closer to land ruled by sorcery. That placed him out of his comfort zone and she was still finding her feet. They had been lucky so far even with Mitch's love entanglement, she laughed to herself one wizard was enough to look out for.

He peered up from the paper as if reading her thoughts yet another annoying aspect of wizardry she thought. Wizards were blessed with the skill, even though it was not her strength it did not stop her from trying. Mitch laughed off her pathetic attempt as the bond between them only gave him greater protection against her. Saranon's efforts amounted to naught. At Craiden he had communicated with the people at the great Indarin. The response to her struggle had been underwhelming. They had expected as much from a Keep as far away as she could imagine or at least as far as she ever wanted to travel.

As the night closed in her curiosity kept her awake, 'Mitch?' She asked.

'It's private,' he responded as if knowing her thoughts.

'How did you know what I was going to say?'

'Go to sleep,' he replied.

She giggled to herself in the dark and snuggled into the warm sleeping bag. In the morning light she could make out Faldarin Keep at Estrard in the distance. The city was a rising monument to the old capital that once ruled over Balquene and Serenphel.

An ancient rival to the old Zyanthia that Odana had been built to protect. It still shone as glorious as ever in a light misty haze forming from the night before. At the northern most edge she could make out dragons on the horizon and wondered if Katholomu had followed them this far. Large rozzen dragons with graceful elegant wings glided through the sky. She counted the silhouettes of two riders and grew excited at the thought of being among dragons again. She turned in a rush to leave and saw Mitch's worried look, 'They're scouting.'

'Oh,' Saranon's heart sank as she realised she had missed the obvious and let out a disgruntled huff.

She stayed close to him on the misquew. Then he told her to look where she was going for the second time after becoming too absorbed in the dragons flying past. Instead she sat up straight and concentrated on being inconspicuous. Mitch just shook his head as they moved on. The inner hub of the city had a different feel from the nice clean streets of Craiden. It was not exactly dirty, just old, but it made Saranon feel weary as they walked along. They had arrived at the southern rim in good time. The city sprawled out for a long distance on all sides with centuries of uneven growth making it look like a maze up close. He brushed up against her as he peered around a corner and moved away.

He said nothing and Saranon followed him as two sorcerers walked past with a purposeful gait. His mood had changed and after they left he whispered, 'They are looking for someone.'

With that her thoughts of an easy path into Serenphel began to wear thin. She wondered if dealing with the Immaron would have been a better alternative. The idea dissipated as the day grew brighter and the city opened itself up with an array of shops for much needed supplies. After their quick exit she had packed little and with Mitch spending more than her she guessed he had done the same.

She peered over at someone running past out of the corner of her eye and followed down an unmarked street. She was left wondering why she had considered it important as she turned around and saw nothing. As her footstep marked the pavement to go back, she heard voices raised and knew that it was Mitch. The scene happened so fast that she only just had time to see the sorcerers disappear with him. Saranon could sense the massive force around them and it was all she could do to watch. She wanted to do something but the tone of the conversation she picked up in the upheaval only reinforced the need to stay away. As the people around her steadied themselves back to normal, the shopkeeper spoke to her but with fear in the edge of his voice.

It was all she could do to stand still without quivering and she felt ready to burst into tears inside. It would be no use to Mitch now as she had to figure out how to get him back. Her heart plummeted to her feet in dismay as she felt like she was the only one who cared enough to sort this mess out. She felt numb as she went around trying to piece things together without being too nosy. In her case this was rather difficult and time consuming. She sighed in her own thoughts near the grounds surrounding the great Keep Faldarin. She could sense nothing and that was what worried her to the core. The Keep was not the kind of place for a wizard, even Mitch and she had to get him back, after all she was supposed to look after him.

The thought of failure hit her like a brutal force sneaking up behind her and churning her gut. The queasy feeling was the least of her troubles as she pondered what to do. The idea that the Immaron could cause trouble even from this distance did not please her but all she wanted to do was find him and leave. The glamour of the Reanval competition had worn off and had been replaced with a hard chilling edge. The great Keep's slow hum could just be heard above the silent sunset, sealing the sadness inside her heart at Mitch's absence. For everything Saranon had come from and everything she was going to be. She took a deep breath and entered the outer perimeter of Faldarin.

The outer area was teaming with wildlife that resided where people were not welcome. The smell of kultier rose ever sicklier from the depths. It was not a grand way to enter as she began wading through the sludge. Yet a direct confrontation without knowing the Keep was a risk she was not yet ready for. The large old tunnels with their worn inscriptions reminded her of Odana with the colour long faded. It was a beautiful site in an array of mess and stench as Saranon trundled through.

The haze and stench was all too familiar as she strived to find a connection to the Keep. It was old and well-fortified as she clung to the edge of the path rimming around a hollow pit. The light from above glimmered on the writhing bodies of the kultier below bouncing off the shiny scales from their shells. The hum grew louder a she approached the pit and held onto the slippery side walls layered with grime. As the central core roared from the depths below, the sound faltered just for moment then returned to a smooth rumble. Saranon looked down as she smiled to herself, if there was one thing it had in common with other large old Keeps it was the need for maintenance.

CHAPTER FIVE

Meeting the Evergeldy

The ravenous creatures ruled over the lower areas writhing along the walls. They crawled at any angle seeming weightless as they ran by. Saranon moved across as she felt something she had feared, it was Mitch and the sensation made her all the more frantic. She stopped a moment to calm her thoughts, she moved on trudging through the crowded tunnels. She noticed voices bellowing down from above in murmured tones. The sound ripped past her ears as the roar of anger and sorcery only just missed knocking her to the side it was all she could do to hang on. There in the silence lay her answer as she came to grips with the need to force her way in.

The Keep hummed with the absorption of the energy as it dissipated into the cavernous holes below. She reached to her energy within letting it saturate the surface as it glimmered in the dark. The magnification blocked the next blow and she could hear the voices in the distance move further back. The excitement ran a trail of sweat from her shoulder slipping down her back as she shivered. A window of hope opened as she managed to gain ground moving past the threshold of the Keep. Saranon stood just above the crossover. A bolt thundered from deep within only just giving her enough notice to duck as she clung to the ledge trying not to lose her grip.

She steadied herself just out of sight. Every breath raging in her lungs from the crackling energy left hanging in the air. In the darkness she soared and gave aim up ahead, her energy rippled through the halls. The response came loud and calculated in return, knocking Saranon back in full fury. The force catapulted her hurtling at great speed. She flew straight down into the murky undercurrent. In stark shock at receiving the force full blow the liquid sheal began to solidify. The substance bounded her with great strength back into the world of the living. The waves of the energy hitting the wall of moving sheal echoed with the sounds of chaos through the far reaching Keep.

Her energy magnified in the recourse and spun like a fine web around lifting her up. The Angeon inside her had changed growing into what she would become. The spark blew out into a dazzling light, outshining the Keep in the dim haze bringing with it the immense power of the Angeon. The roar shattered through the open air of the Keep. Bellowing as the old cylinder, one of twelve that had been holding on for so long broke in the impact.

She rose to the surface as the ash suffocated the clean air whisping through the tunnels. As the Angeon, she touched the surface of the main courtyard outside. The occupants of the building had already begun rushing out and as she looked upon them Mitch came running in her direction. He grabbed her arm and spoke, 'Move, just move.'

Saranon looked once more over her shoulder to see the Evergeldy glaring at her in a silent truce. She returned to normal as she ran by his side. She was beginning to doubt if he knew where he was going but she was not about to argue. He found a tavern on the edge of the city to spend the night, even after her hesitation. She was not about to argue as Mitch lay down on the soft bed and rested. His exhausted body soon drifted off to sleep. Leaving her peering out the window pondering what had happened.

Saranon stayed up with the energy still slowing down inside her body, she was not ready to rest. She could see one of the sorcerers below in the street looking up at her, out of habit she waved and he waved back. For a moment she froze still she had not expected that and Mitch was asleep leaving her in a quandary. She was mixed between guilt and excitement. She smiled at him at least someone would be getting some well-deserved rest. As the moon hid behind the moving clouds in the night sky, she lied down and fell asleep with the hum of the Keep still whirring in her mind. It was Mitch who woke first to the cool morning light. He snuck downstairs for a hearty meal, returning with a second breakfast as he nudged her awake.

Saranon placed her pillow over her head in protest at

the disturbance. Her muscles remained half asleep so Mitch put the warm scrambled eggs near her nose. 'I thought you were supposed to be sleeping in.'

'You have a new boyfriend,' he commented

'A what?' She asked.

She jumped up and slammed the pillow into Mitch for giving her such a start. She peered out the window and the sorcerer was still there, he looked up at her and waved then left. 'I do not have a boyfriend,' she glared at him and then felt pity for him, he was pale and weary.

She did not want to ask him about Faldarin as her heart sank knowing he had been hurt. She leaned forward and gave him a hug. Saranon closed the door as Mitch went back to sleep. He had assured her that he was fine and she was not going to argue, he was already cranky. The end of the Reanval had marked an end to the hot weather. The air still had warmth in it under the midday sun and the cool breeze was welcome relief to a muggy climate. The streets were filled with people and she could sense no sign of any sorcerers paying attention to her. This did not mean much, but today Saranon was not in mood for company as she strolled along.

The place reminded her of Gosbin with the Palascene and she wondered what Tasha would have made of it. Her arms itched and she stopped for a moment, the force from rebounding off the sheal in the Keep had left small grazes along her skin. Raynard stood beside her at a distance. The sorcerer commented on her arms and she looked up startled and annoyed at the same time. The Evergeldy knew who she was and she felt awkward not knowing what happened to Mitch. The sorcerer was not much older than she and held himself with a steady grace, almost in awe of her. They were caught in a moment each not knowing what to say. Then a gruff voice called for Raynard and Saranon said, 'It was nice meeting you.'

It sounded daft after she watched the sorcerer run off and felt her cheeks grow hot. If Mitch had not stirred her she would have been less embarrassed. This was not what she had expected as the rest of the day became ordinary in comparison. She hoped he was having a better day. As she went upstairs with her days pickings, Mitch was more alert, 'So how was Raynard?'

Saranon grumbled in annoyance, 'You didn't tell me you two had met and he is not my boyfriend.'

She placed the emphasis on 'not' as he passed her a letter, the invite was short and curt. 'So we will be going to Faldarin?' she asked.

'No, you will be,' he replied.

She frowned at him not saying anything, Mitch's look told her he did not have the patience to visit Faldarin again. She wanted to do the same and sighed knowing that could not be. The weather mirror imaged her frustration. The sky poured down with tepid rain tapping on the window sill. 'I'm sorry I cannot help you,' Mitch spoke.

The large gates of Faldarin loomed overhead as Saranon approached the Keep through the front entrance. This was a novelty after the last occasion. Before she had time to speak the gates were opened for her. The warm fresh breeze carried the moisture from the night glistening in the sun. The first glimpse was disturbed only by the lull in the hum of the Keep from the broken cylinder deep below. It mattered little to Faldarin who still had eleven remaining, to pick up the load but a nuisance nonetheless. The courtyard was calm as she strode up the steps to where Ardagh rose to greet her. Raynard's uncle welcomed her into the grand hall. The natural light shone through illuminating the peaceful surroundings with a white warm glow.

It was a tempered greeting as Saranon made her presence known and the air filled with a hint of reluctance. Afterward Raynard and his young sister Melissa came to show her around. She was left feeling as though the main question on the lips of her new acquaintances had not been asked. Melissa looked up to her with unwavering awe and kindness. It was flattering and made her feel awkward at the same time. In a quiet moment the young girl asked, 'Are you going to help fix the Keep?'

She smiled as the innocent question hit home and she knew it had meant to be asked all along, 'I will try.'

The recognition of her response spread across Raynard's face. He was about to say something, then refrained not wanting to disturb the moment. Melissa captured Saranon's attention guiding her from place to place. Melissa was busting with excitement as she introduced her new friend. Ahead of her lay a daunting task as the Keep gave up one of its secrets. The vast size of the broken cylinder laid beneath her as she peered down over the gloomy edge. Years of grime had smothered it with a slippery surface and the sight did not appeal to her. Underneath ran a myriad of cracks circling downward as the muck shifted revealing the rough broken lines.

It was hideous to think the Keep had been left teetering on the brink, perhaps it had been a blessing to occur now. The Evergeldy stayed out of her way except for Raynard whose interest kept him close, by his fidgeting it was clear he wanted to help. Between them they managed to set out a path and equipment for the gigantic task. Saranon groaned in anguish as it became clear she would lose several days off her journey. Melissa greeted them as she tried to sneak out the door and she felt she owed the girl an explanation. 'My wizard will be wondering where I am.'

'You'll be back tomorrow?' Melissa asked.

She thought that was a given, 'Yes.'

Melissa's eyes lit up with delight as she ran off with excitement.

Saranon's weary limbs carried her back to the tavern where she found Mitch who had already ordered tea. He looked up with a wry smile and shook his head at the sight of her slumping in the chair. 'You can always come with me tomorrow,' she suggested.

'No,' he said.

Mitch was in no mood to go there and she did not blame him, she was relieved to see him enjoying himself again. He was acting rather carefree and she suspected he knew something as she studied his face.

'You still can't read my mind,' he said in a matter of

fact tone as he ate a large warm meal.

Saranon was growing tired and had no patience for guessing games while she scoffed down her food in chunks. He motioned for her to slow down as she let out a noisy burp it was an old habit that stayed with her. The night was far more peaceful as she fell into a deep sleep and the turmoil of Faldarin faded. As the clouds of the dream world entered her mind she could see Tasha's hand reaching for her up out of the hazy mist. She leant down and grabbed hold, not wanting to let go as the spirit of her old friend reached toward her.

As she heaved Tasha out of the maze below it came together. She unravelled the whirring mass until she was peering down at the broken cylinder in the Keep. Tasha stood beside her enshrined in a glow of light. Now you know, with that her spirit vanished and she was left peering down at the gloomy depths of the broken cylinder. The darkness wrapped around her until a slight movement brought her awake, it was just Mitch so she drifted back to sleep. As she rose early in the morning he helped her prepared for the day with a worried look, 'Are you all right?' He asked.

Saranon replied but he was not convinced as he gazed at her with stern eyes then let her be.

He was avoiding asking her too many questions. Not wanting to be roped into an undesirable and awkward visit to the Keep. It mattered not with the task ahead looming over her as she focused on the image in her dream and hoped that it would be enough. If it had not been for Mitch the

Keep would be a comforting place, but the sorrow filled its walls soaking into the ground and covering her mood. The look in Raynard's face echoed her thoughts as he greeted her with a calm tone and a hint of prior frustration. As they left the habitable areas of the Keep, Saranon could see why the situation had become strained.

She peered over the edge and it was as though no work had been done. The weight of Raynard's gaze made her hesitate. In the moment, part of her wanted to rush in and the other wanted to pull back, not knowing what had caused it. The setback would be compounded if it happened again. She was about to drudge through the mess when Raynard pointed up in silence to one of the Evergeldy. She thought that he could have timed the interruption better before her hand squelched in the muck. They watched the sorcerer dart off and shared a silent moment of disgust as the events became all too clear. If Saranon was going to have any luck, it would mean completing the task in one long stretch. A friendly gesture of kindness was starting to fray her nerves.

She reached within and focused on unravelling the images behind her dream with her old friend in the quiet. Raynard left her to preside over the ever reaching darkness below. Faldarin preferred the silence as it hummed in relief. It had suffered and calling out a faint simple message beckoned to her for help. Saranon calmed her mind and then catapulted herself off. She hurtled at great speed off the ledge and into the soft thin web still gracing the inside of the cylinder as the Keep clung on in desperation. She slowed her descent into the darkness as the sparks of energy from Faldarin fell into place and held her in mid-air. The light glimmered in tiny droplets embracing her body.

The formation sealed the links in the cylinder sending it into a slow spin. Building up the energy inside, until it became so unbearable that she had difficulty clinging on. The burning sensation shifted along her arms. With a shattering of the tiny webs the force blew out sparking a massive expulsion. She shot up into the open air way beyond the confines of the Keep. Stunned silence racked her frame as it took a while for the air to fill her lungs. The crackling sensation of the fine energy particles dissipated into the sky. The Keep reached out its strength and grasped. It yanked her down ebbing off the flow in a fluid motion, leaving in its wake the figure of the great Angeon.

Raynard and Melissa stood out in the open courtyard on the steps. Their lone silent stand spoke volumes for the protection of their Keep. Saranon returned the energy inside her as she left the Angeon and Faldarin behind. The Keep whirred in gratitude with the mild hum piercing through the surface. She rose with the morning light with their belongings packed by the cheerful wizard the night before. It lifted her spirits to see Mitch in a pleasant mood. He was not the only one glad to leave Estrard. The calm cool weather spread across her face, as they glided through the quiet streets in haste to avoid too many onlookers.

Even as the two reached the northern edge, the peace brought forth by the morning remained uninterrupted. A familiar rustle ebbed from the thick vegetation on the outskirts of the city, followed by a deep grumbling sound. Katholomu reared his majestic head high above the trees. The beautiful sleek black dragon eyed Saranon without a hint of remorse for leaving them so long. He shook off the leaves and half a bush that became entangled around his hind leg. Then the dragon lowered his head, underneath her hand, letting out a low short purr before ending with a blast of air through his nostrils. Before she had a chance to ask, Mitch had already hauled himself up on the great giant. The dragon held out his arm for her to climb on, as she wondered where he had been.

The powerful hind legs leaped as they lunged into the air holding on with Katholomu fast gaining speed. The last of Balquene withered away beneath them, as they flew across the border gripping on tight as Saranon laughed in delight. The great beast did not understand the meaning of slow as he kept at full pace. He powered straight for Indarin leaving her to ponder if the dragon could have offered this before now. As the Keep drew near she remembered one problem, landing. The dragon was so big that the standard landing strip was far too small and heaving all that strength to a stop, was by no means elegant. She motioned for Mitch to stay down close to the dragon's thick soft skin underneath his scales and fur.

The dragon, Katholomu, hit the ground ripping up the dirt in a mighty spray and summersaulted with both riders clinging on. Kat landed on all fours with a pounding in the outer courtyard. The sharp talon in his wing scraped the side of the building with a horrible jarring. Running the length of Saranon's spine as she squeezed her eyes closed in a grimace. The open courtyard soon filled with onlookers as she felt her cheeks grow red. Mitch slid off with ease and greeted a wizard as though they were old friends leaving her feeling foolish on her own. The spin made her descent awkward as her shoe wedged between the scales and she gripped the dragon in a half fall on her way down.

The marmoz dragon eye-balled two wizards hoping to move him on until Mitch stepped in and explained. Ryan stood next to her motioning her inside and away from Mitch. She tried her best to compose herself. Her ears were still ringing from the tumble after Katholomu's spectacular landing. The crowd was slow to disperse leaving her in an annoyed state, grumbling as she went down the hall. It had not been the entrance she had hoped for and she shied away from the attention carrying forward with the occasional laugh. The greeting further inside the Keep was more sombre as Saranon breathed a short sigh of relief.

The Armythral were all too familiar with faraway guests. She felt as though she had missed out on the previous discussion. She had banked all her hopes on travelling to Serenphel. At least now the journey through Balquene had given her more than anything she had hoped. It made no difference as she met the Armythral. As a few remained unconvinced and her inability to show the finer points of what they were expecting only made the decision firm. She was granted access to Indarin just as any other and no more was spoken of the Angeon raging in the quiet inside. Saranon did well to restrain herself and hide her frustration as she thanked the Armythral for allowing her to stay.

She strode in a far corner of the Keep in sullen silence. Her temper flared beneath her skin and itched along her arms only recently healed from the Faldarin Keep. The Keep was bustling with sorcerers, including the non-habitable areas, as she travelled down. It was a calming blessing to know she was not alone and smiled in friendship as she strode past two sorcerers busy with repairs. She felt the humming of the central core below and moved further away. She slipped in the distance downward to the vast core hiding in the darkness. Indarin was bemused by the tiny visitor as Saranon glanced around the core. It was showing far more signs of wear than Odana for such a young Keep, in comparison.

The exclusion of sounds other than the whirring of the monumental core filled her with a calm sensation. She had been searching for this, as her body and mind relaxed into the Angeon. It did not last long as the Keep was interested in communicating with her. This time she was only too glad to talk to someone that listened. If anything, she knew she had made a friend out into the ever reaching darkness, as Indarin chatted away in a place where few had been. She felt at ease, away from prying eyes, even if the return journey meant re-joining the world above.

The quiet night up above saw many a person packed away in the habitable area. Except for a jovial soul by the name of Larry who had stayed behind to tidy up. 'You were gone a long time. Checking out the place?' He asked.

'Yes,' Saranon was not sure how to answer as she side

stepped the question.

The sorcerer smiled as he wiped the grime off his hands and followed her to the surface, 'So where are you headed?'

'I'm not sure yet,' she responded.

'I see, come with me.'

Larry showed her to the small reception that looked more like a casual meet and greet as he waved goodbye. She was unsure what she was meant to be asking but Sandra did not give her time to speak. 'So you'll be wanting keys to your room then,' she whisked around the desk and walked at a brisk pace.

She rushed after her up the stairs as the lights lit up the hallway with a warm glow. Sandra gave her a quick tour with all the grace of having done the same many times before. She left Saranon on her own to meet her flatmates. She felt like the odd one out, as it became clear from Todd's reading material, that all the others were studying the same course.

She went straight into her room taking a deep breath. Gathering her thoughts it had been a long time since she had lived with other sorcerers and part of her wanted to run and find Mitch. Her mind filled with images of Pennie and Tasha in the camps, as they came rushing to the surface. She wondered if it would be rude just to go back down to the central core and disappear for a while longer. After a while she opened her eyes where she sat. She peered out the door opening to the balcony which wrapped around a great many rooms. All leading out to a sunny courtyard with raised garden beds below. Todd popped his head out the window beside her, 'Are you going to come inside?'

Saranon knew he was just trying to be pleasant but at the same time it was overwhelming.

CHAPTER SIX

Dragon reunion

Saranon rushed out of the study to meet the snoring dragon cuddled up on the hillside with his head snuggled down in his powerful wing. After being so long without him, the attraction of the stubborn marmoz had not worn off. Katholomu lifted his tail, knocking over a large metal tin that flew high into the air. The tin rolled, clanging along the ground, as it tumbled. He rubbed his head up against her in acknowledgement. He raised his body from the ground, steadying himself with one foot on the side of the hill. If there was one thing the dragon could do, it was making everything else look miniature in comparison. She swayed while rubbing his head, as the dragon tried not to move in excitement.

It was a clumsy compromise and the humour was not lost on Mitch who looked on with a wry grin. She motioned with her arm for Mitch to come closer, but he was not tempted. He kept a respectful distance from the friendly giant. With a slight heave Katholomu almost toppled her over and she knew it meant he wanted to ride. This time Saranon lifted herself up not wanting to make the same mistake, with a great thump and whoosh they were off into the deep blue sky. The dragon soared through the ice cold clouds as they went. It was just what she needed after a frustrating day where she had almost torn her hair out. After being on her own for so long, the idea of dreary old text books and listening to a monotone voice did not engage her enthusiasm.

The only delight was that the work had not been difficult and with any luck she could move on after the unit was finished. The dragon provided a perfect excuse to let off some of her energy. As if reading her thoughts Katholomu dipped down near the edge of the Keep landing, near an outpost. As Saranon's feet touched solid ground she turned to the great beast, 'Now if only you'd done that the first time.'

He scattered off in offense, not wanting to stay for a scalding. The dragon was too big to chastise, as she watched him try to hide his bulk, then give up with an air of disgust.

The outpost, an end node with a direct link back to the central core, lay silent on natural ground blending into the scenery. Saranon stood within the short walls rising up at the corners creating a mental enclosure around the hard floor. It took greater concentration to engage the Keep at such a distance, but well worthwhile. As she gripped the rising energy with her own and immersed herself in its warmth. The walk back was a quiet one, until the thud of Katholomu's great feet shook the ground as he caught up and passed her making it a race. The dragon bent down for her to ruffle her arms around his chin. Scratching a cumbersome itch, then he leaped up deciding that was enough.

She shook her head in disbelief at the occasional agility the dragon displayed. After the brief introductions at her apartment, Saranon felt more comfortable. Yet she was still at odds with having to catch up on the basics that seemed to dull her mind. The Keep was not concerned, as it continued moving. Her knowledge grew through the central core and people business was not something Indarin was in tune with. She had already begun collecting a few handy resources suggested by the Keep. This had gained some puzzled looks when she asked for them, but nothing more. She noted in a small book the occurrences of the day building up a collection to take with her back home.

The next day brought with it a loud knock, as Hailey woke her up from a turbulent sleep emanating from her dreams. Hailey was kind and came from a family near the coast where her older brother and father trained dragons. Seth was much older than his sister and eager to meet the sly Katholomu who had formed his own reputation in the brief time they had stayed. The sleek black dragon was in the middle of rubbing himself in the dirt showing his soft silky belly for all to see. Seth kept his distance at first, then approached the great dark beast as Kat let out a loud snort, holding out his head in greeting.

To Saranon's annoyance the dragon urged Seth to climb on and leaped up in the sky leaving her speechless. Hailey burst into giggles beside her, she tried to talk and Hailey laughed louder. She went back and found Rasputen climbing on and rushing into the sky chasing Katholomu in a speedy haste. The large rozzen dragon was eager to keep up, exerting a great amount of strength with pride. Ahead she could see Kat was starting to play up and she urged Rasputen into a high dive speeding up as he flew. As they crossed paths Saranon let go and almost felt her heart go through her chest as it pounded. Before grabbing hold of Katholomu's shoulder and taking him down in a controlled glide.

The impact of the landing threw her straight into Seth's back as they both clung on. In the silence that followed they clambered down, Seth steadied himself then smiled, 'Can we do that again?'

Her mouth dropped wide open in disbelief, as he burst out laughing and patted her on the back. 'It's all right, I was joking,' he smiled.

A disgruntled Kat stared them off as they both flew back on the more dependable Rasputen. Who took advantage of the situation, by showing off. As she looked back she knew the grumpy dragon was going to be her problem later.

As they ventured down toward Indarin, Kat was already curled up pretending to sleep as though nothing had happened. Rasputen let out a snort and a low roar in protest, as he eyed the other dragon. Hailey rushed over as Seth told the tale and repeated it over lunch in the courtyard for any one passing to hear. Saranon was not sure whether to hide but her new friends urged her to stay. The thought of hiding underneath the table sounded enticing. 'Well,' exclaimed Hailey. 'At least you won't have to worry about what anybody thinks of your dragon skills after that.'

She sighed to herself and hoped it was true, but the grand entrance was going to be hard to forget. She was almost certain the dragon had done it on purpose. A steady breeze kicked up in the latter half of the day as she strode out of site to an end node and connected with the Keep. The first time had been awkward, but with every effort she was becoming familiar and Indarin was a gracious teacher. Saranon listened with care to every signal that hummed from the depths. It was a lonely challenge she had set herself and the Keep was willing to help.

The exertion aligned the Keep and distilled the sheal into its final form. Allowing the Keep to run and concentrate on other matters, like the state of the central core. Power diverted there could smooth over the superficial damage. For that the Keep was more than willing to oblige her. After all it was Saranon who was using her energy rather than Indarin's. As she slept that night a soft thud pattered across her window bringing her out of her sleep. She rose knocking a glass on the floor, Katholomu's eye levelled with her through the railing of the balcony and she climbed on. The dragon swished with timely grace making little sound in the heavy night air clouding the Keep.

The brilliant moon rose above hiding nothing under its warm grey light. Bursting down upon the dragons as Katholomu flew to greet them. It was then that she felt that she had been coaxed into something by the great dragon. She thanked herself for remembering to take her bond-breakers. There was no time like the middle of the night to get acquainted to the dragon elite. Holding nothing back, the dragons flew on with great speed through the spell of the dark. Flying fast into Espony and danger harrowing into the target with such force, Saranon had little time to brace herself.

She immersed herself in a solid wall of protection. Enveloping the group as Katholomu took the signal as his queue to plough hard into the building. The impact sprayed an explosion of bricks and concrete. That shattered into dust clouds in a harsh gust, wiping out the surrounds with a blistering force. The ground thundered with a concentrated energy, exploding on impact. All the dragons escaped from the rubble, fleeing away from sight. Leaving Saranon wondering what she had just been involved in. The dragon provided little comfort as he set her down in the courtyard. She thought of waking Mitch, but then that would need an explanation, one that she did not want to answer.

She could still smell the dust as she woke in the morning to a loud noise, for a moment thinking it was the dragon, as she readied herself. She made a small entrance, trying to discern what had happened catching fragments, as she walked to class. By the end of the evening it had become clear that there was no way anyone thought a person had been riding with the dragons. She breathed a quiet sigh of relief. If only Mitch would be that forgiving, she made her way to the northern wing and knocked on the door as he opened it. He was about to say something, then changed his mind after a moment, letting her through the organised mess. Mitch tried not to laugh as her tension slipped away into annoyance at the look of the bemused wizard.

Saranon was going to have to figure out how to deal with Katholomu on her own. She found the dragon curled up purring away with not a hint of acknowledgement of the incident at Espony. She sat near his arm staring at his sleeping face as the giant opened one eyelid. As much as she was agreeable to rescuing dragons from harm's way, she preferred to know. Rather than get taken along for the ride and dumped in the middle. She leant over almost falling as she hugged the warm tender dragon, he winked and her heart melted. The final exams of her first units came around quicker than she anticipated as Saranon fumbled dropping her sova bag as she went.

It was a relief to think that after this, she could start moving into the general subjects. Hailey had already suggested one that she and Todd were doing. Either way she would have to get through the next few days and she beamed with excitement. She joined the throng of many anxious sorcerers rushing in the hallway. The light filled the walls as she waited, her stomach feeling queasy, then her worrying faded as she flew through the tests. A small part of her wondered if Ryan had been right, but then the doubt fled her mind, in her heart she knew she was the Angeon. She breathed a sigh of relief with a few days off, Seth and Hailey had invited her to stay with them near Lethrill Bay.

The place was not far even though she would be taking Katholomu with her, she thought the company would keep the dragon out of trouble. Hailey rode with her brother Seth on Rasputen as she geared up to go on Kat, the head start did not bother her with the dragon's speed. The air was still warm in the autumn breeze as the dragon glided in, excited by the company, he stumbled before coming to a halt. The glimmering light sparkled across the water as Katholomu trampled in. The commotion brought Seth's team out from behind the cliffs. As the guards landed their dragons up on the grassy fields making their way down to greet them.

Kat shook himself off, blasting a fine spray over everyone before bounding over to nudge each of the five dragons. He skittered around Rasputen before flopping on his side. Saranon ran ahead with Hailey to her family's Keep, it was small in comparison to Indarin as the two settled in. The night sky stretched across the day. She joined Hailey and Seth for a late flight with the dragons, out across the cliff face. They flew over the regular rush of the waves breaking along the sandy shore. She loved the feel of the sharp night air brushing against her cheeks and neck as the last glows of the sun lit up the land below.

She could understand why Seth had chosen a life with

the dragons, as the feeling of freedom washed through her soul and tingled in her feet. Katholomu was more than eager to show off, swooping around and back, almost losing height as he heaved himself upwards. She laughed with excitement as his strong wings flexed in the wind. The beautiful promise of a new start from Indarin filled Saranon's heart with hope as she enjoyed the time away. The lights beamed in a line leading them home as her heart pounded loud in her chest from exuberance.

It was a swift come down with an exhausted thudding on the ground from Katholomu who walked off, leaving her for a nice warm grassy bed. She went inside to the warm cosy fire, shedding cool air from her skin. Hailey was too excited to eat as she stopped half way through to show her their proud ancestral home. The halls were garnished with elegant paintings and artefacts like a miniature museum. The history of Hailey's family made Saranon think of her own, a hazy labyrinth lay between then and now, clouding her mind. An absent tear trickled down her face before she wiped it away.

The night was filled with laughter, she and Hailey tried to stop but the more they giggled. Making small plumes of light then blowing them up into the air like tiny fireworks. For some reason green was a difficult colour to produce for her. It kept going purple or blue as she whined in disappointment. The small show lit up the open courtyard as Seth made an attempt to give advice from below. The sorcerer stayed near the light of the open doors, where he and Darren were cleaning their gear. Hailey only giggled even more when the next attempt failed and Saranon was just thankful it was not a serious matter.

In the distant dark Katholomu's head appeared around the corner with a low calm growl letting them know he wanted his rest. The girls ran inside squealing and giggling at the same time. She had not had so much fun in ages and fell into a contented sleep. The brightness of the day filled the room with warmth she had not felt in ages as she rushed outside, with Hailey showing her the way. An empty spot of crushed grass remained denoting Katholomu's presence nearby. The girls went to the shore to watch the dragons gleaming in the morning sun, as they fished. Kat had his head down on the rocks, scoffing a large fish while holding one end in his claws.

Seth was waiting near the cliff face and Saranon tip-toed toward him. Rasputen dipped his head to let the two small riders on as they flew north to the heart of the dragons' domain. It was difficult for her to grasp the concept that something so small and fluffy grew into a large scaly, grump of a dragon. The soft little creatures darted around their mother in the distance. Rasputen greeted the closest male baring his chest with friendly pride. The large male was not impressed about having young dragons bounding too close. He snorted, warning them to stay clear. The little ones were inquisitive with sharp teeth to match as she stayed out of the way.

Saranon was grateful for their kindness, as they showed no care at having people so close. A rustle up ahead sent a small alarm through the dragons and Seth motioned for them to leave. The sorcerer waited for Rasputen to take them up into the air before leaving a distance behind. The dragon flew fast with the skill of experience leading the girls straight home. As Hailey climbed down and looked back she could see no sign of her brother. She started to panic and Saranon jumped back on Rasputen flicking back into the air. At first all she could see were dragons below and wondered as the large dragon eyeballed the scene from a distance. Rushing in close to the wounded dragon Seth had been on. Taking her down hard for the ride, swooping in an outstretched form there was still no sign of Seth.

She could not return without him and jumped down not far from the wounded dragon. As Rasputen leaped up, the pelt of energy fired and as her stomach churned, she let out a massive shield blocking the move and providing Rasputen with safe passage as he flew behind her. The tips of the scrub caught alight with the roar of another blast and Saranon pounded it down in frustration. She was about to run after the culprit and almost missed seeing the guards swoop in with ferocity, lifting the air up in a great gust overhead. Rasputen roared with delight, as his fellow dragons flew past, rustling his mane up with all the fierceness he could muster.

Seth ran toward them and jumped on the dragon wasting no time grabbing the agitated sorceress in his arms, as they flew off. She was not impressed about being hauled off in midstream, trying to break free of his grip without falling off Rasputen. Both she and the dragon snorted in disgust at the same time, causing Seth to laugh and shake his head. As they landed back at Armeria, the sorcerer let her down then flew away leaving Saranon to grumble and shout after him. 'He won't listen,' Hailey spoke as she rushed to meet her.

She knew that Hailey was right as she shrugged her shoulders in annoyance at being dragged out of the scuffle.

It was a long and harrowing wait, wearing at her patience, as she stepped with a heavy stride across the open courtyard. She caught site of the great dragons coming in to land. Relief lifted the weight off her shoulders and Hailey rushed out with open arms to greet Seth. The weary travellers returned hiding their hard faces. Saranon looked Darren in the eye and saw a glint of something she knew all too well, she was about to speak but thought better of it. In the brief instant the guard picked up on her staunch stand and waited for Hailey to leave. The sorcerers sat around resting their aching muscles in the lounge near the courtyard, with the open fire warming the room.

Darren gazed in thought at her before asking the question burning through his mind. 'I get the feeling you have already seen death.'

Seth shot her an astonished look as she answered dispelling the illusion of innocence. A silence hung over the room as she hoped she would not have to explain, the momentary pause brought no relief racking at her nerves. With no way out trapped by her friendship with Hailey. She made a short response, admitting to her part in the fall of the Arthrose. After the words left her mouth, Saranon could not bear to stay a moment longer, the awkward stares were not what she had come to Armeria for.

She had come to Serenphel to move forward and her mind ran free with a mountain of turmoil. She strode with haste out in the calm night air to Katholomu who gazed at her stern brow. The great dragon had no intention of sticking his head into her problems but then he had included her in his. The dragon lay down his head beckoning her on board and they flew in the grey light of darkness showering over the land. The fierce mood of frustration covering Saranon seemed to leak its way into his thoughts. Katholomu led her far north into the tip of the dragon colony reaching into Espony. In the darkness she watched as the grip of the fallout from the fight lay wanton on the land.

In empathy she shed a tear in disgrace at the scene underneath the starlight and wondered if this would be her future. Without hesitation she glided off the dragon, Kat, with ease. She strode with all the magnificence hidden beneath the surface as the Angeon rose within. Moving out her energy struck itself deep into the damaged ground. Binding it together and reshaping the malformed land. The energy soared creating a rocky alcove emblemizing the northern boundary of the dragon colony. Noises drifted on the winds suggesting she would soon have company. She took flight on Katholomu leaving her masterful work for the eyes of the morning light. In the soon approaching dawn that crept ever closer as she flew on.

Saranon's frame of mind was calling out to return to Indarin. Yet a moving glint in the first rays of dawn caught her eye, as Hailey waved her downward. Katholomu rested a short distance walking to a stop beside her. Hailey rushed up and grabbed her arm. 'You didn't have to leave, Seth can be like that but I need to ask, did you see anything happen near Espony?'

Saranon leaned close, 'That's where I was.'

Hailey's mind ticked away as it came to bare on the same thought, 'It's going to be an interesting time at Indarin.'

Seth and his fellow guards were out busy for the day. This suited her, as she was finally able to rest her weary head in a stagnant dream, replaying the night's events. The sorcerer was waiting in the courtyard when she woke in the afternoon. His expression still glum and Hailey's mood was serious. 'Did you bring back the old ridge line?' He asked.

Saranon sighed in acknowledgement that this was a good time to leave. 'Yes,' with that she turned to face Hailey, 'I will see you back at Indarin.'

'Wait,' Hailey called out.

Saranon turned back as she was walking, to let Hailey finish.

'What he meant was, thanks for helping,' Hailey explained.

Seth's facial expression showed no sign of change. Even though it was a kind thought, at least she had not ruined her new friendship. Katholomu waited for her arrival near the front entrance eager to be off into the sky. The dragon took her back at a cracking pace across the warm afternoon curling into a cool breeze. Kat swooped over the crescent of the great Keep, shining the sun's rays off his wings at full spread, as he passed the tip. As the light faded Saranon felt a blast roaring from the depths sprawling upwards at such a speed.

She pelted her energy downward with intense frustration at being interrupted. Her annoyance steamed through the air. The marmoz dragon did not miss a beat nor flexed his muscles in shock as he landed in smooth formation and pride. Todd rushed out to greet her flinging his arms in excitement. 'Were you showing off?' He shouted over the rumble of the Keep, as it slowed down to a low hum.

'Of course not,' Saranon said in annoyance and the sorcerer burst out laughing in response.

CHAPTER SEVEN

Welcome to Serenphel

Saranon's grumbling mirror imaged the Keep's mood as she followed Todd in through the hall. The place seemed quiet as the sorcerer explained they had been trying to repair the Keep. An argument had broken out on how best to fix it, just before her arrival. She did not think much of the excuse for a jettison of raw energy flying at full pelt out of Indarin with impeccable timing. Todd saw she was not impressed, as he realised how lame it sounded. 'I'll go down and have look,' she grumbled.

'No, I don't think you should,' Todd exclaimed.

'If I have to put up with almost getting fried, I'm going to have a look,' she continued.

'Really I don't think…'

Saranon stared at him in disbelief…she was not about to argue with a friend and glared at him daring the sorcerer to continue. The lights flickered as she walked past down the flight of stairs. She stepped into the dim shallow light parading at intervals along the walls. After having to deal with the mess at Armeria she was in no mood to be told otherwise from a friend. She leaped into a flurry of shouting and animosity. The Armythral did not look at all impressed with her arrival. If that was how they treated guests, she was not sure if she wanted to know them on a bad day. As she stomped through making her presence felt. With one swift motion she walked straight through the sealed door sensing the astonished voices behind her.

The first glimpse did not appear to be as much. As she began trudging further in a close sound sparked her attention. Larry walked through the closed door behind her, 'Trying to beat me to it?'

'If I was going to end up toast I've earned the right to check it out,' she commented.

'Get a move on then,' Larry walked past her carrying his tool kit.

The sorcerer was unfazed by having a companion and had little hesitation giving Saranon tasks. She reminded him that she had come to observe first and moved in to see remnants of the overloaded line.

She peered down the giant crater emanating through the cracks in the floor to the giant hole below and clambered in. Larry made no effort to stop her as he worked away the tunnel was dark and deep, caked with the remains of charred ash sticking to her boots. The hole was enormous and she could hear the growl of the central core rising up through the Keep. Larry popped his head over the edge and shouted, 'We're about to get visitors, a few of the labs have gone off line.'

'I thought that was a good thing,' Saranon said.

Thinking that the Keep diverted power to support the damaged area would help make the repairs quicker.

Larry stopped a moment, 'You're definitely new around here.'

She liked the sorcerer, he had an odd simple charm about him but she did not want to find out what he meant as she examined the left over rubble. If time was short then it left her in a bind and the Keep cranky under her feet. She rose with that thought in mind raising the Angeon inside and spreading her energy out to sense the Keep. The energy burned, wanting to be let out in full force but Saranon hung on. Weaving it and wrapping it around the Keep and bringing the great line up through the floor as the Keep extended it upward with her help. The two worked as one to place the line back into its rightful position.

The section locked into the duct without a trace or seam showing on the surface. The keep glistened in excitement pulsating underneath. The energy ran warm straight from the central core up the line, just as a great noise overhead boomed. Larry held out his hand to haul her up and they ducked back through the sealed door without a trace. They stood in silence as the thudding and shouting grew louder, reverberating through the wall. Saranon stood for a moment waiting, but the shouting did not interest her and the Keep had settled. She turned to leave and Elliot stormed through unlocking the seal and opening the door.

'It's about time someone fixed that,' Larry spoke up.

'What?' Elliot asked.

'The door, I couldn't for the life of me work it out.'

Elliot gave him a strange stare, then walked on, after the sorcerer had left Larry spoke, 'It happens all the time.'

The whole event did not make sense and as she was about to say something the others giggled at more shouting coming from through the wall. 'You have a strange way of doing things,' Saranon exclaimed and Larry laughed.

She stood there not sure what to say as Larry composed himself wiping his gruff hands on the sides of his trousers. 'So who taught you to repair the Keep?' He asked.

Saranon hesitated wondering if he was serious, 'No one.'

Todd laughed then stopped as both glared at him, 'I mean there's no way you could have done that.'

She sighed in exasperation at the thought of a long night ahead. The older sorcerer eased off as though sensing her mood and she was not prepared to hang around.

The shores of Lethrill Bay had worn her out. A conversation was the last thing on her mind, as the image of a nice warm soft bed after a big meal popped into her thoughts. The sea floated in her dreams and the sandy shore reaching up out of the water. The Keep seeped through her memories, intruding on her inner most thoughts, murmuring thank you. The words struck into her mind compelling her to wake. It was a deep low rhythm that reached her fingertips as she caressed the wall with her hand. As Saranon opened her eyes she could see the cool rays of light dipping past the edges of the curtains and grumbled at the end to her sleep.

It was difficult to think of anything as she heard Hailey's voice and rushed out to meet her. She stopped in her tracks as she caught sight of Seth standing in the door. For all its grandeur and size, Indarin was becoming far too small for her liking. The sorcerer paused and then apologised as her legs almost collapsed underneath her in disbelief. She knew it would have taken a great deal of convincing for Seth to say those words and accepted his apology in a haze of embarrassment. It had not been the start to the day that Saranon had expected. She was left floundering through a haze of thoughts as she bounded straight into Gwen on her way to class.

The shock reverberated through her as she gave her a dark stare before moving on. A flash of images entered her head and she dropped to the floor, relief flooded through her as she checked to make sure no one had seen. She dashed in and plonked herself down near Todd, the only familiar face in the room paying no attention to his friend. 'Aren't you going to say hello?' Theron asked.

The question woke Saranon from her bumbling, 'Hello.'

Theron was expecting a longer conversation and Todd exclaimed, 'She doesn't know.'

She let out a big huff realising she was the last to know something and Todd let her out of her misery, 'Theron is a Prophet.'

'Yes,' Saranon exclaimed anticipating more of an explanation.

Todd laughed and shook his head just before the class began, leaving her annoyed for the entire lesson. She snuck away early rushing toward the library. The encounter with Gwen had ruffled her and she knew there was something she had missed.

The image haunted her in the dry stale air as her fingers fumbled along the spines of the books. Until she found the Eskardy, the sorcerer clan from Espony further north. She heard a shuffle behind her and jumped, almost dropping the book, to see Theron standing behind her. She peered around the corner, wondering how she had missed seeing him. 'Do you want to know what you are looking for?' Theron asked.

'No, I will find this myself thank you.'

'Are you sure about that?' He asked.

'Yes, thank you,' she replied.

'Do you know what I am?' Theron asked.

She thought it was a silly question given that she was an Angeon, 'Would you like to know?'

Theron was not impressed by her response, he was not used to other people having knowledge like his. Saranon did not have time to talk riddles, so she said it straight. 'You are the strongest Prophet at Indarin, now if you don't mind I would like to search for the information myself.'

With that she sat down and began flicking through the pages. Theron sat beside her, 'Are you sure there is nothing you want to know?'

'I'm positive,' she replied.

She smiled to herself as he left, while turning the page. Her thoughts were interrupted by a sorcerer grumbling at the Prophet for running off. The novelty of meeting him was lost on her. Saranon was not sure why and paid it no more attention as she read further back into the past of the Eskardy. As she read of a hidden time, she found the link she was looking for, a connection with the Angeon. If there was one image that Gwen had brought back to life it was from home. She closed her eyes to a faded memory from her distant past wrapped behind a wall of pain. She had too much to be concerned with to be awed by a Prophet with an attitude, if anything she found Theron annoying.

The only reason why she had refrained from being rude is because she knew what it was like to feel alone. She found herself wandering down to see Katholomu. Who was rolling around rubbing his back against a large sandstone rock with satisfaction. Mitch snuck up around the corner catching his breath, 'I heard you met Theron.'

Saranon shrugged in disbelief at all the fuss, 'Yes,' she said in a strained voice.

'I didn't think you would be over awed,' he commented

'Hardly,' she spoke and Mitch laughed.

Saranon's mind was still clouded with Gwen. She flew up into the still afternoon air with the fine breeze beckoning across a clear blue sky. The dragon had a purpose in mind and took her deep into the heart of Espony. He staked his claim by flexing his large graceful wings casting a shadow increasing over the land with the setting sun. She looked deep down upon the land in a sweeping gaze. It was hard to think the last Angeon had been here many years before. The hour was growing late and she had to return, something inside told her not to stay. The last rays of light beamed golden behind her as Katholomu jolted into the air with a mighty leap. He flew far too close to several buildings showing his massive span, before reaching for the heavens.

Her skin prickled with a strange delight. If Indarin was not forthcoming with answers, perhaps Espony held the key she had been searching for. As she clung onto the dragon, the night closed in around them and the great lights of the Keep guided them in with a brightness she had not yet seen. Kat kept to the outer boundary, as she strode in to see Seth, who had just flown in earlier. The sorcerer stepped aside to let her pass. This was not the Indarin she remembered. The Keep hummed running warm under her fingertips. 'What do you think?' Seth asked.

'What's going on?'

Seth explained that the Keep was being geared up for the next round of training.

Saranon was not impressed. She soon realised this would mean a barrage of sorcerers wanting to use the outer areas, including the end nodes. She grumbled underneath her breath as she went upstairs slamming the door behind her. 'Are you all right?' Hailey asked as she looked up from her studying.

She acknowledged her, as she searched through the books she had gathered in her room. To see if there was something she had missed. She was in need of another venue within the Keep, apart from the central core. This time she would have to look within the gaps as she grumbled to herself. One of the least disruptive places would bring her close to the Prophets' quarters. A scowl creased her forehead whilst in thought.

She stood up and took a deep breath at the uncomfortable change. The restrictions of learning were tiresome, she was going to need somewhere else to unwind. Saranon began tapping her fingers on the small desk in annoyance before drifting off to sleep. It took a few times for the message to sink in with her new friend Theron, that foresight was not something she considered to be a gift. The sorcerer was amused by her abrupt reluctance to ask him for anything, including a spare pen, just in case he misinterpreted. They had been practicing concentrating their energy to hone it in on a marker.

Todd knew it was Theron's weakness which was why he enrolled in the unit. For Saranon it was tedious and both her friends were getting frustrated. 'Why don't you try?' Todd asked.

She did not see any harm in helping Theron, so she walked down to the floor of the purpose built court. She stepped in front of the young Prophet who smiled at her and she whispered, 'If you know, don't ruin it for everyone.'

He smiled and shook his head. She unfolded her energy then compressed it down into a fine tube. She hurled it at break neck speed at the absorption pit at the other end.

The court flashed with the sparks of light, flickering

with intense heat. The dense padding in the pit lit up with a warm orange glow soon fading down to red and darker. She turned to Theron and said, 'Now it's your turn.'

'No, I don't think so,' he spoke.

The sorcerer was about to take a step back, but she grabbed his arm and stood behind him. Theron's nerves were starting to show as he gulped, she guided him wrapping her energy around his, for support. The sorcerer closed his eyes in concentration and then let go at the same time Saranon boosted his efforts.

The energy shone like a thick electric bolt arching across the room, thundering with a grand roar that shook the walls as it went. 'There,' Saranon stated as though the outcome were a given.

Theron stood in awe as their teacher Anne rushed down in shock. 'You didn't see that one did you?' He said.

The Prophet gave her an annoyed look as Anne met them in a flurry of speechlessness, as the three friends stared in stunned silence. Saranon made a poor attempt at guessing charades. That was met with a stern look by the older sorceress as the other two snorted back laughter.

'You are not supposed to exert yourself,' Anne stared at her.

'I wasn't.'

'She's right,' Theron backed her up.

Saranon glared at the Prophet, 'I do not need your help.'

'Well I could have gone further.'

'No!' She shouted.

The pair argued as Anne watched on in astonishment. Before finding a calm moment to change the subject, 'Someone needs to clean up this mess.'

She was referring to the excess energy now stored in the pit and Saranon knew it would have to be filtered into the Keep. Without hesitation she held out a web of energy opening the pores allowing the energy to drip-feed through. In a rather stubborn tone she spoke aloud, 'I have other things to do,' and with that she turned and left in a huff.

The arguing had wasted precious time alone with the Keep. She was not willing to stay around for the stunned silence that followed. Being taught at a slow pace was one thing. Yet, having someone tell her she was about to exhaust her energy when she was far from it, only darkened her mood.

The inner gaps within the Keep provided her with ample space to manoeuver. She wove her thoughts into energy cradling it in a delicate form. It was not the most ideal shape but it met the criteria. The place was an unattractive dead zone as it did not receive the full energy spiralling up through the Keep from the central core. It did not matter to her, who saw it as a large space to show off and relax without distraction. The small sound of her talik cut through the air interrupting her peaceful thoughts. As Hailey broke the silence and brought her back to reality. Saranon shrugged her shoulders and left the tranquillity for the busy habitable area of the Keep.

Hailey beamed with excitement as she greeted her at

the door, 'There is an Angeon at the Keep.'

'Really, where?' She asked, bewildered at the thought of another like her.

'I meant you,' Hailey laughed.

Saranon stood completely perplexed, then shrugged it off. Todd explained the three sets of consecutive readings that came from her talik. While helping Theron had verified what she already knew. She thought to herself how long it would have taken to find out otherwise. She left to find Theron as a thought crossed her mind, for a sorcerer he was immature.

As she approached she could hear raised voices and waited. It was not long before she grew impatient and burst in flinging the remnants of the broken seal. She had missed knocking back Ryan with the force in the process. The sorcerer had assumed that Theron had asked Saranon to intervene. Not one to let a friend down she answered 'Yes' before the Prophet could speak. 'Now, I have business to deal with,' Saranon spoke.

She carved through the web of sorcery covering the room with such force it startled everyone including Theron.

'You can't do that,' gasped Ryan.

'I never did understand that word,' she spoke as Sandra urged Ryan out of the room leaving Theron and her alone.

'Do you know what you've done?' Theron asked.

'Something you should have done a long time ago,' she spoke with annoyance. The young Prophet nodded as if reminiscing and she continued, 'No offence but can you leave that for later.'

'I thought that was what you were after?' He asked.

'No,' Saranon replied. She did not think she needed to explain herself but Theron's look said otherwise, 'I prefer to make my own mistakes.'

He laughed as though a big weight had been lifted from his shoulders.

'What I came to say is you did well today,' she exclaimed.

At first the sorcerer was a little quizzical, but he soon felt Saranon's steadfast response and became more serious. He sat down in thought, 'So do you think you will find what you need here?'

She was not sure what Theron was searching, for but answered, 'I already have what I need.'

Deep down she knew what she said was true, if she left today she would find a way to manage, it would not be perfect but it would be enough.

Her response unnerved the Prophet. She wondered if he could see everything while her sceptical mind answered for her. She peered around the room as they spoke, it was much larger than her own, a book caught her attention as she opened it and Theron stopped.

'You won't find anything about the Angeon in there.'

Saranon turned the page she was looking at and moved it towards him placing it down on the table, 'I was not looking for me.'

Theron read closer, 'I misjudged you.'

She wondered if the young man before, her ever had a friend, the Prophet stared at her but said nothing. If she wanted to there were a hundred questions she could have asked. Something inside told her that no answer would bring her any closer to the energy within. The understanding was mutual, if just a little awkward, as she left Theron in peace albeit temporary. As Saranon peered back over her shoulder, she knew there was one big unspoken difference between the two. There were a lot of prophets in the world of sorcery. She was left feeling alone as she vacated the inner sanctum of the prophets.

The Keep hummed in tune mirroring her thoughts of satisfaction at knowing all along the Angeon had come to stay. She laughed as she went down the hall. It left a bittersweet taste in her mouth, with one large unanswered questioned hanging over her, like a dark shadow. What was gained by not recognising the Angeon within? Saranon did not think the Armythral were the kind to concern themselves with fear of retribution. The sorcerers had placed great emphasis on her lack of significance in the world. Even now the fuss was muted within the Keep Indarin, as she pondered the thought late into the night.

The great Katholomu had curled himself up into a comfortable ball. He stayed a respectable distance from the glowing embers of the fire shooting up across the courtyard. The dragon was too big to sleep inside. If he concentrated, he could, but the moment he stretched his large heavy muscles the space would become far too small. She made a comfortable seat on his hind leg as she sat down facing his half buried head. Katholomu looked up and rubbed his cheek down her side in a welcoming embrace. While she patted him deep in thought, Mitch made his way toward her and the dragon moved his head away. 'Do you like Theron?' He asked.

'He's just a friend,' before she had time to add more Mitch was off again.

She thought of wandering after him in annoyance, but stayed in the dragon's calming presence, fuming to herself. He had a habit of picking the most inappropriate moment to intrude on her thoughts. The dragon's face creased with a slow smile rising up from the corner of his mouth. 'Don't you start,' Saranon whispered in disgruntlement as she stroked his head.

The night stars shone bright above her in a clear sky as she strode past listening to laughter escape through the dragon pens.

He caught up with her reaching for her arm, 'There's a rumour going around that you and Theron are…'

'What!' She roared across the crystal clear night air.

'I'm sure it's nothing,' with that he left.

Katholomu let out a muffled grunt that sounded like a short laugh, covering his eyes with his tail. She grumbled almost stumbling in agitation as her annoyance at living in a large community grew. If there was any comfort with luck her time here would be short lived and she could return home to her own muddled life.

Helping the young Prophet earlier had left her muscles aching and it came back to haunt her while trying sleep. At the time Saranon had not taken much notice. Whatever had laid its path around Theron, was stronger than she had anticipated, not that it made much difference. She could already tell knowing Theron was going to be a nuisance and she laughed to herself thinking the Prophet could say the same of her. As sleep swept in an old dream returned. Before the image of Tasha and Pennie entered her mind she heard a woman's voice ruffling on the wind. It called across the breeze from the depths of home in Darkonia, a faded memory lost in the depths of her mind.

CHAPTER EIGHT

A new beginning

The morning began with the usual rush out the door and last check to make sure Saranon had everything. As she sat in her normal place near Todd, she followed his gaze to their teacher. Anne was fumbling with nerves and with all eyes focussed on her, she dropped the dragon sphere from the desk. As it teetered on the edge in slow motion she blew across the table. Letting out small glimmers of energy sparkling in the air, holding the Orb as it floated to the ground. 'Show off,' Todd whispered, and they all laughed.

As Anne gathered her composure, the rest of the lesson went uninterrupted. Saranon thought she was alone as she scampered off after class. Yet the heavy footsteps speeding up behind her, said otherwise.

She slowed down to let Theron catch up as Mitch's words from last night stuck in her head. 'I thought I might walk with you,' Theron gestured.

'I'm going to the dead zone,' she replied.

The Prophet stopped a moment. 'You are welcome,' Saranon said not wanting to miss a beat.

The sorcerer walked with caution by her side, as though in deep thought. The place was just as she had left it, with a few sounds echoing through from the rooms nearby. An awkward shaped space left over with pipes running through it, packed close to the walls.

It dipped down with different levels providing a flat platform where Theron sat with his study book in hand. She beckoned him down further to no avail. As the Prophet watched on, she called up the power from deep within transforming into the Angeon. Theron's patience was remarkable as he stood up afterward, 'Do you know what I think?'

'I would prefer not to,' Saranon spoke, 'I like to leave the future where it belongs.'

'Fair enough,' he spoke before he left.

She watched, staring at him as if warning him not to say any more, Theron only smiled in return. After the sorcerer was gone, she practiced alone. A few strange noises carried through the small vents breaking her concentration. Indarin still hummed in a smooth tone so she pretended to ignore the racket. She pressed on concentrating deeper. The Keep greeted the surge of energy with satisfaction and delight as it whirred away from beneath. As if in seconds, the power of the central core roared up around her in a massive whirlpool of strength. Saranon shot up floating above the ground, as the great mass of liquid sheal swirled around with great force.

The spasm of energy leaped around in shear tentacles sparkling with light, as the gas particles rose up from the heat. The Angeon embraced the strength of the Keep wrapping it around and through, as it spiralled higher. Then she turned it back down into the depths with such force, that it sealed cold across the floor. Whoever had summoned the Keep's energy, it had not been meant for her. The hall was quiet as she raced away and in no mood to find out what had happened. The light shimmered across as the great form of the large dragon brushed across the window. Katholomu nudged at the door with agitation as Saranon held out her hand. She clambered on, as he took off, whisking her up into the air without a moment's notice.

A storm was brewing in the clouds above, closing in on the sun in a slow elegant dance across the sky. The wind whipped down her arms as she clung on, while the great beast gathered speed, heading north. She cringed in disgust at the dragon's choice of direction. As if sensing her mood, he grumbled, heading downward near the steps of the cliff face enveloping the city below. This time Katholomu remained silent among the backdrop. As he urged Saranon down the hill with gentle encouragement. A glimmer came across the street, catching her eye as she strode down, the sun shone off the edges of a great building holding her attention.

The great hall rose above her having lived through the

time of Zeralden Hadenvar the last Angeon. The building showed its age well. The warm outdoor lights began to flicker and glow as she approached. The light illuminated her shadow across the courtyard. A small yet familiar pattern caught her sight near the entrance, reminding her of Odana Temple. A small shy voice spoke behind her, 'It's beautiful isn't it?' Kera stood smiling.

Saranon turned in surprise to see she peering over her shoulder. It was good to make a friend in such a strange place, as the two chatted away underneath the fading sky.

As she waved goodbye and made her way back, the streets were filled with a hub of night life. The casual conversations floating by reached her ears. Carrying with it the words that made her stop, she lingered thinking she had misheard but it was spoken again. The night was young and she need not be anywhere as she mingled among the Eskardy who were used to visitors from Indarin. If anything, the night allowed her a freedom she had not enjoyed at the Keep. In the excitement, she dropped her small sova bag, before she could pick it up, Gresham knelt down and handed it to her. She blushed with embarrassment as he smiled and left through the crowd.

The night gathered momentum and Saranon slipped away in the darkness. Finding the sleeping dragon curled up where he had landed. The thought of another Angeon rocked her to the core. As she rushed back to Indarin she wondered if the great dragon had meant her to find out. The cold brushed along her arms giving her solace, as the idea settled in, making her feel uneasy. The night wrapped around her as Katholomu landed with a thud across the courtyard. He bounded along melding into the dark background as he let his small traveller down. Why had she not been told of the other Angeon? The thought made her skin crawl, as she turned to see Mitch heading towards her with an unimpressed frown.

The wizard had stayed away while they had been at Indarin Keep even though she had missed his company, 'Something's going on.'

'What isn't?' She exclaimed.

'Are you all right?' He asked.

'There's another Angeon.'

Mitch stood there in shock at the thought of a second Saranon then regained his composure. 'So you've had an interesting day too,' she remarked.

'Part of the indolin chambers was flooded,' he explained.

She pondered a moment on what he had said and thought of the sheal coming up through the dead zone earlier. It made sense, but she had not paid it much thought. 'Did you want to stay in the wizard quarters, it's getting a bit crowded where you are?' He asked.

'I'll think about it.'

Saranon went to find Todd and Hailey, who were busy chatting with some of the lecturers and more experienced sorcerers, who were moving into the vacant rooms next to them. Chilcott was helping Anne move in two doors down. The thought of having her lecturer down the hall was not lost on the other two either, as Saranon tried to hide her annoyance.

'I know,' whispered Hailey in agreement.

The noise meant an early night was out of the question but her mind was running in all directions at the moment. Her eyes focused on Chilcott, one of the more experienced sorcerers and revered for his ability to break up fights. The older sorcerer stared straight at her with piercing hard eyes and an emotionless stare. She had seen him before, down in the imbenik chambers, but did not consider stopping to chat.

'What happened?' Saranon asked.

Anne spoke for him, 'The side wall of one of the eastern labs blew out and the blast broke the pipes. The area is being drained, but the clean-up will take a while, so here we are. Where have you been?'

'Espony,' she replied.

Anne froze, 'That was quick.'

'Katholomu wanted to go for a ride,' she explained.

'So you've been in Espony all this time?' Anne asked.

'I was with Theron beforehand, why?'

'We thought the habitable area was going to be flooded, but then it hit something and stopped. You wouldn't happen to know anything?' Anne enquired.

Saranon knew what the older sorceress was talking about as she left her and Chilcott alone. Todd ran after her smiling out of breath, 'So you met Chilcott, he's not big on words. So how did you stop the sheal?'

'What?' She was astonished.

'Hailey and I knew it was you as soon as we realised

where it was,' Todd explained.

She was beginning to wonder if it had been too obvious and Todd shook his head as if reading her thoughts. Hailey joined them a little way out, 'Sorry it took me a while to get away. Come on you have got to see this.'

The three avoided the main crowd gathering around the eastern section with a crew already well underway. Hailey moved forward to a staircase hidden in plain view in the wall near the side entrance and they snuck down out of sight. A tremble curled its way up Saranon's spine and she could see that Todd was not much braver, but curiosity kept him moving forward.

The voices dimmed as they moved along. The sheal had already started to retreat with signs playing across the floor beneath. Small amounts of sheal posed no harm to sorcerers, especially when detached from its source. They strode across without fear. The slow methodical lapping of the vibrant liquid penetrated through the room. They did not get far, as the sheal lay close to the underside of the floor, holding them back with a deep murky edge. Todd was disappointed, as he poked around to see if there was anything below the surface. The sheal gave nothing up as Saranon gazed around and through a small alcove. As she peered through Hailey let out a tremendous scream and she bumped her head hard.

The sorcerer looked alien all geared up knee deep in the water. Larry lifted his head piece up, 'What are you lot doing down here?' he asked, then spied Saranon. 'Get a suit on then come around, what are you waiting for?'

She and her friends were speechless. Todd grabbed her shoulder and urged them back up. She peered back as Larry sank back in the sheal without a trace. Her head still throbbed as she stopped short of running straight into Chilcott at the top of the stairs who stepped aside.

They joined the main crew as Chilcott spoke to Larry when he resurfaced sitting for a rest, 'I don't want any of them going down there.'

'The Angeon will be fine,' Larry spoke as he rested.

Chilcott stared at her with deep concern, 'I do not think you are the Angeon.'

Larry almost laughed, 'Come on Tony, she saved your hide earlier. Who do you think was in the dead zone?'

Saranon answered for him, 'Your fairy godmother.'

Larry burst out laughing as Chilcott look confused, 'That wasn't you.'

'Give it a break and let the girl suit up,' Larry said as he stood up.

When she came back Chilcott was gone, she let out a deep sigh. Larry heard her and spoke. 'He's had a couple of hopefuls let him down over the years, all talk and no spark. Come on I'll show you something.'

Hailey and Todd watched in pure amazement as she followed Larry down into the depths. The sheal made a strange gulping sound as it wrapped around her. It was eerie and silent, as Larry's form lit up in a small warm glow up ahead moving with ease as though it were second nature. It did not take long to find the problem with Saranon almost tripping into the gaping whole, as Larry held her back from the edge.

They walked along and she made out many tiny punctures across the surface, it had not taken much for the pressure to blow. Larry's voice came through loud and clear, 'I can mend it, but it would take me and a team ages, I thought you might like to have ago. Once it's sealed, we would have time to get a good look around before tinsel toes starts poking his head in.'

Saranon smiled knowing exactly what he meant. The sorcerer had always been kind and accepted her without prejudice. She set to work, while Larry stayed close pruning the area as the sheal slipped away.

Soon the liquid was well below her shoulder, as she opened her head piece the line slid below her waist and continued edging downward. In the distance she could hear shouting. She peered around the corner just in time to see Chilcott heave a blinding punch into Purton, who fell back against the wall. Chilcott caught her eye and stopped striding out with the sheal lapping at knee deep. He tripped and almost fell, regaining his balance in time for Purton rushing towards him. She stood there speechless as Purton tried to shove the other sorcerer under. She need not have worried, as Chilcott held his own soon gripping Purton's head under his clenched arm. Larry placed a hand on her arm and she jumped in her skin with fright.

'What's going on?' She whispered.

Larry spoke, 'We think Purton may have done it.'

'I doubt it,' she replied.

Chilcott looked at her, as Purton twisted his head out

of the close embrace. She finished her sentence, 'Not unless he's Eskardy.'

Larry spoke in a slow voice, 'Are you sure?'

'See for yourself,' she pointed.

Chilcott followed behind as they examined the underneath of the pipe Saranon had just mended. The jagged outlined still showed as a discoloured silhouette, he ran his hand along the line. 'Now do you believe me?' Purton said puffing as he steadied himself against the door.

Chilcott said nothing and the other sorcerer left wiping the blood off his face. 'I think you owe him an apology,' Larry spoke.

'Later,' said Chilcott.

'You do speak,' Saranon exclaimed.

Chilcott stared at her.

'You can't blame the kid,' Larry commented.

Chilcott tapped his fingers along the pipe in deep thought as he spoke, 'You are not the only Angeon.'

'Now, you don't break it to a kid like that,' Larry spoke.

'It's all right I know,' she interrupted.

'Did Theron tell you?' Larry asked.

'No.'

Larry smiled and nudged her out of the room while Chilcott examined the damage. They both heard him say, 'How could I have missed that?'

Larry let out a small laugh as he waved Saranon goodbye at the top of the stairs and went back to clean up. She was in two minds about going or following Larry then a voice spoke behind her. 'I wouldn't do that if I were you,' Purton was standing behind her, his face showed no sign of his earlier dispute. 'I owe you thanks,' he shook her hand in a gesture of gratitude.

Something almost no one had done, in that instance the energy still flickering in immensity reached out in a gentle caress. By the sorcerer's look of astonishment he had felt it. 'Chilcott's the one you want to teach you, I'll ask him when he's settled down.'

'Thanks,' Saranon was not sure whether she wanted to be residing next to two of her teachers, one was more than enough. Hailey rushed up to her, 'Wow, did you miss some action?'

'I saw enough,' she said.

Hailey was still dazzled by the fight as they found Todd sitting in the lounge with a glum look on his face. 'Purton is Todd's uncle,' Hailey explained.

Saranon stared in surprise, 'He's all right.'

'Are you sure?' Todd asked.

'Yeah, it looks like the sorcery used was from an Eskardy and he was fine when we spoke a moment a go.'

Todd was still stressed, even when he relaxed and she felt sorry for him as they stayed up chatting.

She placed her empty cup on the sink, it had been a long day and an even longer night as she wondered what Purton had meant. Things were beginning to get complicated; she tapped her fingers on the bench, the others had long gone to bed. 'You're picking up my bad habit,' the sorcerer spoke behind her.

Saranon turned to see Chilcott standing in the doorway, 'So you talk after midnight.'

She gibed as he continued. 'I'm swapping you over to my class, from Braxton's.'

The sorcerer left before she could speak again. Not that she thought much of Braxton's class, but the fact that Chilcott had known about the other Angeon annoyed her.

Then it occurred to her, she now had two of her teachers living next to her unit. Saranon groaned, too many people to ask questions when she wandered off. The silence the Keep had offered, was beginning to look a little frayed around the edges as she heaped up the covers and drifted off to sleep. Saranon's head throbbed as someone knocked on her door, in all the commotion, she had forgotten about hitting her head. Todd crammed his head around the door, 'Purton just said you got switched to Chilcott's class.'

'Yes.'

'Get up or you'll be late.'

'Oh no!' Saranon rushed grabbing her books and then wondered if she would need them. She hesitated a moment then left rushing straight past Chilcott. 'You're in hurry to get somewhere.'

She stopped and turned, falling into line with the sorcerer's graceful stride. He was a mirror of calm after the night before, unlike Saranon, who showed signs of lack of sleep. As soon as the lesson started she knew it would be no easy ride. She felt like she had just been flung up a few levels and had some catching up to do. Chilcott handed her a new text book without a second glance, it was twice as thick as her last and she let out a small sigh.

Hailey tapped her on the shoulder and pointed her to the page they were up to. She thanked the fact that her friend was already taking the class. At the end Chilcott spoke up in a monotone voice, 'Vandragamond, I want to speak with you.'

It took a moment for her to realise that was her, as the others piled out the door, he looked up with a steady eye. 'Purton thinks you are worth spending time on, you are not the first Angeon I have taught.'

He let the words sink in before he continued, 'Merrick Calthazard left a mess behind him.'

Chilcott rolled up his sleeve revealing a long scar running up his arm. 'You do this and I will have you kicked out of Indarin quicker than Katholomu can fly you to Espony, understood.'

Saranon was speechless, as the sorcerer gestured the meeting was over and she sprinted from the room. Hailey grabbed her arm as she spun around the corner, 'Hey.'

Hailey continued, 'I thought he knew something but I didn't want to say, I hope you don't mind.'

'No,' she replied.

The eastern wing of the Keep was still a shambles, as the last of the sheal was swept away leaving a shiny clean edge to the old surface. It was difficult for her to think that one substance could cause so much trouble. She strode down the open stairway to find Larry taking a break. 'I'm sorry I didn't tell you earlier,' he said.

It had not occurred to Saranon that he knew about

Merrick, but she accepted the apology. Thinking aloud she spoke, 'Chilcott said he made a mess.'

'Sure did, Tony was lucky to get out alive. The lad almost brought the house down, he was too hot headed and wanted everything now, but I'm sure you know the type.'

There went her plans of having a friendly meeting as the thought showed on her face. She did not doubt the finality in Larry's words as he stood up and went back to work. She peered through the door and noticed that someone had smoothed out her rough job on the pipe. Any signs of the cracks had disappeared on the gleaming surface. The old sorcerer smiled and said nothing as he saw her mind ticking away. The man hesitated with words on the edge of his tongue then stopped himself short. A sound came whistling up from the lower ground as Saranon stuck her head around the corner and she left the sorcerer alone. The steps were new as she entered a part of the Keep that would have been well occupied.

She marvelled at the detailed space below. The door of the lab was open so she let herself in, almost tripping over Purton's feet in the process. The sorcerer was busy fixing something behind the wall, 'Greetings Saranon.'

He called out without stopping. She assumed that gave her an open invitation to look around. As she traipsed through the large space picking up objects as she went. 'Can you pass me the kedril on the right?'

She handed it to him, 'You could have got it yourself.'

'I know, but I had to find something for you to do,'

he replied.

She gave him a stern look as the sound of footsteps approaching made her jump. She fell with a thump to see Chilcott staring at her. 'What are you doing down here?'

'She's helping me,' Purton explained.

The sorcerer mulled the words over, before moving on without a sound. Getting down to the business of restoring the lab as it had been. Saranon listened to the pair exchange short words and whispered to Purton, 'How do you two work together?'

Chilcott's ears immediately pricked up as his friend answered. 'Rather well.'

The sorcerer spoke without turning around, 'When will the engine be back up Mr Purton.'

'Another day I'm afraid,' he replied.

Chilcott came across to take a look as Saranon skittered out of the way, in his angst he knocked her flying as he pushed past. She slipped on the wet floor crashing to a full stop, slamming with both her hands into the control panel. 'Oh….' She exclaimed as both sorcerers scrambled in desperation to shut down the machine.

The terrible clanging sounded, then slowed as the machine whirred to a stop. Chilcott breathed a massive sigh of relief as he looked down, he had just hurled across the room.

'Why don't you go back upstairs and I'll handle it from here,' Purton suggested.

As Saranon motioned to leave, he added, 'No, I meant you.' He stared at Chilcott who understood and left. 'Sorry about that, he had three months worth of research ruined.'

'I can understand that,' she said as she brushed herself off.

It did not take long for her to discover how talkative Purton was, as she stayed to keep him company. Wondering every now and again when would be the right time to leave, as she kept eyeing off the door. 'It's all right you don't have to stay,' Purton said and she took it as her queue to hurry back upstairs.

The halls glimmered with light in the darkness, with almost no one in sight as she rushed by realising how late it was. The sound of muffled voices wafted through the corridors as she halted in her tracks and listened. It was her old teacher Braxton talking in the darkness. 'They don't suspect a thing, and everybody has been too busy with the clean-up.'

Another voice sprang out of nowhere, 'Then we had better get a move on.'

Saranon wanted to hear more but she could not without making a sound and would rather not have their attention. She crossed the large entrance and scampered to her unit, breathing a small sigh a relief as she reached the door.

CHAPTER NINE

A bloodline of old

The wind whistled in her hair as she saw the ground move beneath her feet, Hailey and Todd could not make sense of what she had heard. In the meantime, Katholomu had begun bending his weight, across the metal banister in agitation. The great dragon had almost taken off in one leap, but now he was rummaging through the clouds. Saranon was hanging on for all she was worth as he sped with all his might. The dragon grinned with excitement and flew faster. Just so she had to cling on the softness of his fur, between the thick folds of scaly skin. The muscles flexed as he pounded down on the side of a hill, skidding before coming to an abrupt stop.

The morning sun shone around Armeria as it glowed with a halo of light as the sun's rays reflected off the surface. Seth had been polite to her after the incident, but the image of a young girl who had not seen hardship, was shattered. After the sorcerer had settled down with that thought, he had become more comfortable. It was a weight off Saranon's shoulders, as Hailey had become a good friend. She could make out their forms in the distance flying high as Katholomu stood up straight. Assessing the dragons they were riding and letting out a low bellow. Rasputen responded with a deep low sound swooping across the valley as Seth glided in and down with the group landing in close.

Darren walked over, 'The place hasn't been the same since you left.'

'Pardon?'

Seth responded, 'He means the rozzen colony is doing well. Your dragon looks like he's itching to go, did you want to fly with us?'

Before she could answer Katholomu had spread his wings in eager anticipation, 'I guess that's a yes.'

No sooner than she had managed to secure a hold around the dragon's shoulders, than he heaved down. He rebounded with a mighty force up into the sky.

The other dragons followed suit catching up and fast taking the lead. Katholomu was more than ecstatic as he stretched himself to fly in perfect motion with deep concentration. The first stop rose up through the landscape as a weary outpost that had seen better days, came into view. It was a decent size as Saranon came into land on the edge, with Katholomu walking over. The dragon acted as though his clumsy landing and larger size were not noticeable.

Almost no attention was paid to such a common site as Darren and Seth checked in at their usual stop before heading further out. She waited outside, warming her face in the sun as her dragon waited. He shifted his weight as he curled his tail around the length of his body.

She left his side as she scurried around the outside to take a closer look. Saranon had not moved far away when the dragon let a loud snort, as if startled. The massive dragon did not have much room to move as she stepped around without seeing anything in sight. She placed a gentle hand on his forearm as the dragon stood poised and strong. Katholomu followed her with his eyes, as she walked away unimpressed at being left alone. As she peered off, she felt something rush past and held out her hand. A piercing jolt ran up her arm in a muted battle before she had it extinguished.

Katholomu jumped up flaring his nostrils to make a point, scanning the area with caution. While stepping forward with one arm poised ready. Saranon's initial shock had worn off as she searched around, wherever it had come from now showed no trace. Seth rushed out toward her, 'Duck!'

'What…' she began.

Another blast came forming out of the corner of her eye. This time she was ready and pulled in hard like a lead getting shorter. Its owner fell from the second storey window on to the muddy ground below.

The force of the impact was minimal as Talmon soon steadied himself. Clearing the dirt off in disgust, the sorcerer showed no sign of remorse. 'Why did you bring them here?'

Seth looked aghast and answered, 'Let's go.'

His face was stern as he stared hard in a silent standoff. She was not sure what was going on but hiked herself up on a full sized Katholomu who was not prepared to show such mercy. As they left, he flicked the sorcerer across the yard with his hind leg slamming him into a wall before darting off. Saranon deflected Talmon's last efforts as the gap between them grew too wide for another round.

The humour was not lost on Darren or Rory, as the first spoke up, 'I've always wanted to do that.'

'I doubt it, your mother would never forgive you,' Rory spoke.

Saranon had become lost part way through the conversation. With good timing Darren responded, 'He's my cousin.'

'Not that it counts for anything,' Rory added.

'I'm yet to be reacquainted with mine, so I wouldn't know,' she said.

Saranon had not meant the comment to carry as much weight as it did in the silence that followed.

Darren interrupted her thoughts, 'Don't worry, I'm sure you'll have at least one like that.'

The day grew bright as they made their way down to the shore. Scanning the far reaching dragon colony for signs of trouble, as Seth took Rasputen low to the ground. The dragon was showing off his might as Katholomu flew low to the ground fast behind and stormed ahead right over the top. Colderay followed with Darren gliding him with little effort. Katholomu grunted in disgust with so much friendly competition. They branched out in a wide formation along the shore. He dove down near Armeria in the cool midday sun breaking through the rising clouds.

Kat arched out stretching his limbs, showing off his full length. He was just a fraction longer than Rasputen, the largest of the group, as they rested. Rasputen flared in silence narrowing his eyes as he pelted Katholomu in the chest. They tumbled in a tight embrace, ending with Rasputen pinning the large dragon to the ground. 'Now you picked that argument, don't expect me to save you,' Saranon grumbled with a harsh edge on her tongue.

Katholomu tried to move, but Rasputen had the upper hand as he gave in and the two became friends. A large dot grew on the horizon as Levette brought Hailey down close next to Rasputen. Seth was about to say something and stopped as he saw his sister approach.

She looked straight past him at Saranon, 'I thought you were here, Talmon didn't waste any time getting sympathy.'

'I hope you didn't believe him,' she responded.

'Of course not,' Hailey rolled her eyes in disbelief. 'It's not the first time Talmon has done that but it might be the last if he has any sense.'

'My cousin, no,' Darren said with much sarcasm.

The company sat as they ate, her eyes were caught by a low glimmer to the south near the rocky coves.

As she turned she saw Seth transfixed in the same

direction in deep thought, 'What is that?'

The sorcerer finished his mouthful and pondered, 'Work. Why don't you stay with Hailey?'

Before Saranon could answer the small group had already risen on their dragons with Seth waving a small goodbye as he flew past. She felt as though she had just been cheated out of the action in her slowness to respond. As if reading her thoughts Hailey explained, 'He meant it.'

Saranon let out a sigh of exasperation at being left behind and tried to hide it with a smile. The pair walked for a small way heading back to Armeria. Katholomu pretended not to notice, after he had snuggled himself into a cosy spot. In a way she was relieved to be spending time with Hailey, it would give her dragon time to calm down as he warmed himself in the sun. The garden emerged up ahead, sprawling out on both sides, as a large thud raked across the ground bringing her to her knees with a heavy weight. Hailey clung to the open gate as she regained her balance, that was not what she had expected. Katholomu rushed in with a mighty leap, flicking Saranon up in a half summersault. As she heaved herself up on his shoulders.

The dragon bounded, twisting his full weight around. So close to Hailey's face the draft brushed across her shoulders. Katholomu flexed his muscles upward as he picked up speed. He flung her straight into the oncoming storm shattering across the darkened sky. The wind turned to greet them head on, as it rained out from the blows of sorcery flashing across the open sky. The ground thudded again with a mighty flash sending chills down her skin. The dragon persisted with his chase, carrying her with him. He began to roar underneath as if egging her on. The energy drew away around her in a massive rush, culminating at one point in the distance.

Saranon allowed her energy to intensify growing ever stronger in the void. She followed through with a mighty sound, as it catapulted at speed crackling through the air as it went. Her energy hit its mark with deadly precision that lit up the sky with a cold burning glow. Katholomu flew with speed knocking the opponent's dragon into the sea she plunged down with him, jumping off at the last minute. She plunged into the icy depths becoming disoriented until she managed to reach the surface. Seth and Rasputen dived down and plucked her with ease from the cold embrace. She clung on as the water below her flurried with dragon blood. Katholomu's head broke the surface as he gasped, treading water before jolting up in the air.

Seth grabbed her hand and pulled Saranon up behind him. He headed straight into Armeria with only four other dragons following. She did a quick head count and saw Rory with Darren on Colderay. 'I would have managed,' Seth spoke as they flew in.

She was speechless but she was not about to argue while riding on Rasputen, that would be asking for trouble. They dived hard into the grounds of Armeria, knocking down a small statue, as they went. Darren immediately slipped off his dragon and came to her side holding out his hand in a gesture of kindness.

She accepted as she looked back, but Katholomu

had long since disappeared. 'Your dragon looked fine. I wouldn't go after him though I couldn't say the same for his temper. So is he your dragon or are you his person?' Darren asked.

'I haven't figured that out yet,' she answered.

Darren's body language blocked Seth from making any more comments as he stood between them. Seth became disinterested and went to reassure Hailey who had come out to greet them. Saranon stood staring out to the distant ocean, absorbing the events and drying off the last of the water from her wet clothes.

'That felt like a different type of sorcery,' she remarked.

'He was using an Orb,' Darren answered.

The concentration of energy made sense though she had not dealt with an Orb since leaving Darkonia. They were difficult to use and viewed more as prized ornaments. The sorcerer noticed her elongated silence, 'Do you know about Orbs?'

'I've used one before in Darkonia,' she responded.

Darren reached into his satchel grasping a thick cloth, it unravelled, revealing a dark murky Orb underneath.

She picked it up in the palms of her hands and it glowed. 'The last one I held was the Eye of Escora, it was so pure that no matter how long I looked at it I could find no blemish.'

She held it up to the light and the clouds of imperfection showed in the faint glowing light from within, 'It looks like it was made in haste.'

'I think you're right,' Darren spoke as he wrapped it

back in thick cloth and carried it in.

As he handed his parcel over, Seth gasped in astonishment holding it up out of way of Hailey's grasp. The tug of war did not last long as Hailey outsmarted her older brother, 'This is the Orb of Throm.' She said as she peered into it.

The visible shock of surprise reverberated across the room missing Saranon completely. As Seth spoke first, 'Are you sure?'

'Yes, we need to return it,' Hailey replied.

'What?' Rory shouted, 'After all that are you serious?'

'I'm afraid so, it belongs to Gresham,' Hailey spoke as Saranon's cheeks grew red with embarrassment.

'How old is he?' She asked.

Seth sighed, 'If you've met him perhaps you'd like to return it?'

'Only briefly.' she spoke trying to side step the issue.

'It's all right, we'll handle it, I wonder if it was stolen?' Darren asked aloud.

'It would seem the case.' Seth said eyeing the Orb over in his hands before putting it away.

Everyone including Saranon was showing signs of a weary day in the afternoon sun. With an odd silence hanging over the sky as though mirroring their mood. It was not until she searched for Katholomu, lying low in the long withered grass, that she understood the extent of the damage. The dragon had a fresh mark from his opponent's claws stretching down his side; she held out her hand and healed the wound.

Katholomu's eyes met hers in a sad deep stare, she rubbed his cheek for comfort and he motioned her up on his shoulders. She took great care as she lifted herself up and he took to the sky turning back into the path of the original attack. He landed with all the grace he could muster, as his body still tingled from the fight. A small ripple of energy floated up from the ground, a left over remnant from the intensity of the energy that had built up towards her. The smell lingered in the air with no real sense of direction. She leant down running her fingers along the ground, sensing the past events with her mind.

A fragile picture flicked across her closed eyes as she scanned the area. Before she could stand again, something moved out of the corner of her eye. Any remnants of the sorcerer she had fought with, were long gone, but she was not alone, with another presence close by. Saranon peered over the top of several large rocks, her heart missing a beat as she recognised Gresham. The wounded sorcerer stared up unsurprised, 'I thought you would return.'

She stood shocked as his words sank in. Then without a second thought she bent down and helped him over to Katholomu, he sat down to rest, 'You got what you wanted?'

She did not like being second-guessed as she held his head in her hands and healed him. His presence muddied the situation, 'How did someone get your Orb?'

Gresham remained silent, so she filled in the gap, 'I have no use for it.'

The sorcerer steadied himself on his feet and climbed

onto Katholomu with Saranon behind him. The dragon was unimpressed at the newcomer, as he moved his head around to glare at the sorcerer. Gresham spoke, 'My friend wanted it.'

'Oh!' her heart sank as she realised whom the other sorcerer had been.

As Katholomu flew in, Gresham spoke under his breath, 'I guess he won't be bothering me anymore.'

The comment only made her feel worse as they landed. Seth relieved himself of the Orb and with it a whole lot of trouble, as Gresham accepted it back in an awkward silence. He led the sorcerer in and away from Saranon as she let out a small sigh of relief afterward. Meeting Gresham again under those circumstances, was not how she had imagined it. The idea perplexed her the more she thought about it. Hailey caught up with her out in garden, while she was brushing down a shabby and disgruntled Katholomu. Who was not sure whether to purr or growl at the attention.

'That went better than I thought,' Hailey said with a deep resounding sigh. 'Gresham is gone now if you want to come inside?'

She hesitated before pondering, 'What were they doing near the cliffs?'

'It's a weak point near Armeria.' Hailey answered.

She stood back from the dragon as Katholomu's patience grew thin. He scampered off in a great heap as she spoke, 'I was hoping it was something innocent.'

'So was I,' Hailey replied.

It was not comforting to know the intention, as

Saranon wondered if there was more going on. It would have been too easy to blame Armeria if Gresham had not made it out alive. Hailey gasped at the notion, before allowing it to sink in, neither was prepared to exclude the possibility. The offer of dinner had been too good to pass up as she sat down to dig into a hearty meal. She competed with Darren and Rory, who had empty pits for stomachs, after using their energy. She was about to say something, but no one was listening. So she gave up, as Darren scoffed a large chuck of bread smeared with the last portions of food from his plate.

As if stirring her he leaned over and said, 'So what were you saying?'

She stared at him in annoyance that was lost as Darren grinned. 'I was just thinking what would have happened if we had lost Gresham?' She asked.

'Then it's a good thing we didn't,' the sorcerer showed reluctance to give a straight answer as he disappeared from the table.

Katholomu was ready and eager for a night flight as the sky darkened around laying shadows on the ground. The dragon's dark colour blended in well as they took to the sky, as the breeze picked up over the ocean and carried its chill across the land.

The wind whipped along Saranon's arms as she went thinking of Indarin. Yet that was not where the dragon was taking her, as he veered to the north. Espony shone in the distance as he landed close in stark silence. She was hesitant to leave, but the dragon urged her on in a firm stance and she knew Katholomu was not about to relent. It did not take long to find Kera in the crowd. Kera spoke, 'Come with me.'

When they were out of the sharp cold air enjoying a nice warm drink, her new friend continued the conversation. 'Gresham said thanks.'

Saranon almost bit her lip in surprise it had not occurred to her, that the two knew each other. Kera explained that Gresham and Soren's family were related. There had been an uneasy resentment when Gresham's uncle had left him the Orb of Throm. She spoke, 'I'm afraid I'm not that familiar with Orbs.'

Kera laughed, 'The Orb is rumoured to be made by one of the strongest sorcerer's Espony has ever had, it's a bit late to want it now.'

She could feel herself blush, 'No, I didn't mean it that way.'

As the night drew on, there was one question that was being avoided by both of them, the other Angeon. It had plagued Saranon's mind earlier. Yet if meeting Merrick had the potential to disrupt her time at Indarin she was not so eager to find him. As she left, Kera spoke behind her, 'You are similar to my brother.'

'Pardon?' She asked.

'The Angeon,' Kera explained.

She looked down at her sitting at the table. For a moment regretted not having Mitch with her, not that he was inclined to say much.

She was speechless as she stared in disbelief at her new

friend. Part of her wanted to run, but curiosity stepped in holding her there in deep thought as Saranon sat down. It was difficult to understand, but it soon became clear that Merrick did not have much to do with his sister. In a way she felt sorry for her being forgotten. Then there were times when not drawing attention was something she craved. Kera smiled, as though in sympathy and appeared embarrassed at what she had just said. 'I thought being related to an Angeon would be a good thing?' She asked.

'He can be reckless,' Kera spoke a familiar tune.

'What do you mean?'

'He knows he's better than everyone else, I think you need to be careful,' Kera warned.

Saranon had grown to like her in the short time they had met and leaving her, carried a reluctant sadness deep within her heart. The cold night air wrapped around her with the clouds sweeping in, it was time to leave. The dragon had a way of letting her know what was going on, as she patted him, climbing up onto his shoulders. Looking back at the peaceful city, a fleet of dragons zoomed in across the sky. Before she had time to react, Katholomu leaped with all his might in the air as fast as he could.

A bolt of energy ran out, Saranon blocked but it fractured across the dragon's left wing. He went down in pain with a small thud, as he regained his composure before hitting the ground. It was all she could do to cling on as she slid sideways with the fall. She gathered her strength, glancing up to see the mighty dragon carrying Merrick. Without a second thought she poured all her energy into catapulting the sorcerer and his dragon as far away as possible. Merrick had not been ready. The force shot him back through the sky with such ferocity, that it left the other sorcerers riding with him in shock. Katholomu did not wait to be told, as he flung himself into the air heading south straight for Indarin.

Saranon's hands went numb as she trembled, still expecting to see something in the sky behind them, as they fled. The dragon landed with such force scraping his claws along the hard surface of the courtyard. Before she had a chance to move Mitch had climbed up yanking her down. They ran inside as Katholomu squeezed under the large opening into the foyer. He manoeuvred his way into the dragon pens before the giant door fell down into place. 'What did you do?' Mitch asked.

'Me?' She exclaimed.

'Well it always has something to do with you,' he responded.

'What about Craiden?' She asked.

'Ah…' He hesitated, 'That was different.'

Saranon scoffed at his remark, as they went further into the heart of the Keep. Her vision moved in slow motion as she noticed a wave of energy rippling through the Keep. 'What's happening?' She asked.

'The shields have gone up,' he replied.

'We're in deep trouble aren't we?' She asked.

Mitch stared at her, 'I'm glad you got the message.'

The walls tingled with a slight tremor. As they ran towards the centre he grabbed hold of her and pushed her towards an open door up ahead. She would not let go and they both hurled over the edge, down into the depths of the Keep below. Their fall slowed before they came to a stop in mid-air. The energy from the Keep provided a plateau, like a hard surface, at the focal point of the massive opening. Mitch took a moment to steady himself as he stood up towering over her, disgruntled by the situation. Indarin mirrored his mood as it readied itself in anticipation. The silence swept down the side of the large vertical tunnel as she tried to reassure herself. She knew he could tell of her immense panic starting to rise within.

CHAPTER TEN

Mercy

The dull thumping reverberated through from the edge of Indarin. It sent small shivers through her spine as Mitch stayed close. His fear crept through his eyes as he breathed. Another dull sound rattled down through the walls of the Keep at an electrifying pace hitting nothing. As he placed a hand on her shoulder, 'You need to stay away from the edge.'

The realisation hit Saranon as she peered upward. It was meant for her then another thought struck her, 'You were going to leave me in here alone.'

He hesitated as if caught out, 'Do I look like I want to be here?'

'And miss all the fun,' she glared at him.

Mitch groaned in response as she went and peered over the end of the platform and down into the dark abyss.

A massive spark of energy ran curling down the outside as the Keep funnelled it down, absorbing its strength along the way. 'Do you think I can do that?' Saranon turned to look up at Mitch for an answer.

'One day but not now,' he said it with finality in his voice.

He looked as though he were about to leap over at any moment and haul her into the middle.

Before waiting long enough to find out she strode the short distance back. As he was thinking aloud, 'Did you do something?'

'I knocked Merrick off his dragon,' she replied.

He cringed, 'I thought you were told to stay away?'

'Look, I'm not having this argument now,' she spoke.

As she stepped away losing her attention of where she was and fell back off the platform.

Mitch lunged, but he was too late and the energy around them was too strong for him to grasp her. She looked up and saw him stranded helpless above. Saranon tried to reach out to the walls, but the remnants of Merrick's energy made it a near impossible task. As she slid even further down only slowing the decline. If she could not go against the flow, there was always another option, as she placed all her energy into speeding up her decent.

She fell straight down to the full force and shield of the central core. If she were unfamiliar to Indarin, it would be a one way trip to oblivion, but the Keep already knew her. The energy seared through her as she plummeted through the shield with a mighty shock. Her energy creased around the giant sphere as she burst through. From the edges of reality Saranon heard the thunderbolt of the other Angeon crashing downward from above. It shook the building and sped down to its destination with precision. The melding of her energy with the central core spread far too slow. As she watched in horror as the bolt blasted its way through, just before she secured the central core.

The pain ripped through her mind as the Keep reeled from the shock and the ground above grew silent. The central core shone in disgust, flickering in the distance between its usual calm and irritation. Reaching up and increasing its efforts to heal the open wound. The fine cracks spread far, reaching out from the point of impact just above Saranon's head. The pounding had stopped as she tried to get out. Slamming her energy up against a hard surface that was not willing to give, or let her out. Panic started to cross through her mind as she remained calm on the outside and tried to think. The core was old and began healing the wound from within. Then it sent her hurtling up through a separate exit in the Keep.

She glided straight up through an opening leading to a familiar place, Purton and Chilcott's lab. The floor opened up with the raw stallic energy spewing forth, shocking Purton in place as he stood. The large gust was absorbed back into the Keep leaving Saranon lying on the hard cool floor in its wake. There was no denying the magnitude of the energy that flowed from deep within Indarin, it stained up the walls in a thin light spray. She took a deep breath and her lungs filled with pain from the harsh intrusion as she gasped. Purton found the strength to haul her up and he ran down to greet her calling for help as he went. He picked her up and rested her arm on his shoulder taking her above to the habitable area.

Anne was waiting and checked her over before letting her go into the waiting arms of Mitch, who was still distraught at what had happened. His face was pale with fright and Saranon knew he thought he had lost her. It was a sobering thought as she let him take her away from the growing excitement. She made out Hailey's face in the crowd and gave a tired recognition, she smiled in return. It was a fine mess, but she was glad to be out of the central core, as Mitch placed her down on a large couch in his room. The soft silence was a welcome relief as her ears still tingled from the harshness of the whirring, far below.

He sat beside her with both the colour and relief returning to his face. She smiled, but her voice betrayed her not making a sound. There was a small knock at the door that startled him. Saranon could sense who it was. Theron entered, skimming around the surprised wizard; he leaned over and said, 'I'm sorry.'

She smiled and managed a whisper, 'I've been through more than that.'

'She's right,' explained Mitch. 'You should've seen what she did in Normisia.'

The Prophet looked up as though he missed something important, then let it be. She knew that even Prophets could not see everything but with Theron, she would not want to guess how far that went.

He spoke, 'I asked the Keep to help you.'

'Thanks,' she was not sure what Theron meant, but she was grateful for any help she could get.

He left her in peace, but Mitch looked like he was going nowhere as though she would disappear if he left. She could not blame him and held out her hand, he grasped it between his hands until she fell asleep. It had taken all his strength not to dive in afterward, but he knew it would have been an almost certain death. His only hope was that Saranon had visited a central core before, a place he could only dream of going.

Mitch had left her too long in the care of the Armythral and if she had to stay at Indarin any longer, things would have to change. Part of him felt like he had failed but he knew for the Angeon, it was different and he would not be able to keep her safe. He picked up another blanket and placed it over the sleeping sorceress. He tried not to disturb her as he went to his own bed too weary to keep his eyes open any longer. The morning brought a loud harsh thud at the door after Mitch had been up for an hour. Chilcott stuck his head around to see if he had woken her up. 'I need a few helpers to mend the Keep and seeing as you are in my class now I thought you might like to volunteer.'

It was a lame excuse to see if she was all right, but Saranon did not mind, she had recovered and it gave her some normality to return to. Either way it was going to be a busy day. She ran downstairs past the dragon pens and through the main entrance to find her class already waiting. She was hoping to make a quiet entrance, but as she skidded through the door, that was the last possible thing she could do. Hailey handed her a spare kit. 'What's this for?' She asked.

'You'll see,' smiled Hailey.

They made their way through to one of the outer control rooms where Chilcott produced a series of large maps. Her heart sank as she realised they would be going around checking and replacing the small pieces that had been damaged. Saranon was about to roll her eyes in disgust, but thought better of it, the rest set to work without hesitation. She knew that if everyone helped the task would be done and the Keep would return to its old self. Rather than making the irritable humming noise that hung in her head, like a bad tune that would not go away. The door swung open and Purton came through with a large set of kedrils and a face that meant business. He yanked off one of the rear panels and checked the conduits behind the walls.

As she turned back, she could see Hailey beginning to lean forward near the main controls. She caught a small glimmer of a spark and yelled out. Hailey looked around in surprise. Chilcott noticed and grabbed a thick rag like shield. Throwing it over the broken tablet and disconnected it from the source. It glowed hot on the ground with a sharp, charred smell hitting the room. They piled out to let the air clear, it was a poor start to the day, but it gave Saranon a chance to look around as work progressed. Chilcott was undeterred as he motioned everyone back in. Without hesitation he went up to where Purton had turned his attention to the primary control panel.

Leaning over they yanked it apart, the pieces inside had corroded and Purton let out a small groan. The task was fast growing well out of their expectations and the frustration on Chilcott's face showed. As he turned to Saranon, 'The sooner you return to Darkonia the better.'

The words hit her hard as stone, she ran out of the room not thinking of where she was going. Within a short space of time it felt like everything she had worked toward was fast unravelling before her. She ran down to her retreat and almost slammed straight into Theron. The sorcerer looked as though he had been waiting for some time, his face showed great sorrow running deep mirroring the Keep.

'Do you know what happens next?' The Prophet asked.

'We are going to fix the Keep,' Saranon spoke with deflated enthusiasm.

Theron smiled, 'You understand.'

She had built up a short yet extensive knowledge of working with Keeps. Her practical skills showed as she began directing Theron. It was a long slow preparation, but they both knew it had to be done. They opened a small entrance down to the depths of the inner workings of the Keep. She had chosen the site well with easy access for one with experience. They climbed down into the ill-fitting tunnels holding the large conduits running downward.

As they looked along the length the damage was immense, it kept on running along and down the sides. For Saranon it would be tedious rather than complicated.

With the most pressing problem the exposure and leaks in the massive cables. Yet, if repaired it would reduce the damage. She groaned knowing she would need to do most of the work, 'Remind me to return the favour to Merrick one day.'

'Do you want to do that?' Theron asked.

'Probably not,' she half spoke to herself.

She headed down to where the ideal location would be. As they neared it, the sounds of voices travelled up, showing signs of fraying frustration. After Chilcott's cold remark, she did not think walking straight into that would be of any use. So they travelled to the second ideal location underneath. Theron inspected her choice, 'Are you sure about this?'

'It's a bit late to start having doubts,' she spoke as the young Prophet shook his head.

Saranon slipped down and the Keep wrapped around her on the soft stone bed, she could see Theron beginning to do the same.

'Are you sure you want to do this?' She asked.

'I know what I'm doing,' he replied.

She was not convinced, but she was not about to turn away his help either as the Keep recognised them both. It soon became clear that Theron was out of his depth although she did not mind. He had a calming effect on Indarin that made her wonder how long it would have taken her had he not been there. The true frustration of the attempt above came through as a fleeting glance. As she sped further down in the heart of the Keep with her energy trying to stay in balance.

The great central core whirred below in anticipation. She could sense Theron trying to reach out, but the pressure was too great and Saranon led him down with ease. She felt like a great connector linking Theron with Indarin deep underneath. She waited for him to catch up before leaping far ahead and straight into the task at hand, smiling at his surprised shock. This was a journey she had done many times before in the sanctuary of the Keep. The Prophet needed little encouragement but in comparison, he was leagues behind. Indarin did not appear to notice as it worked to mend the bulk of the damage left in the other Angeon's wake. The noise above them faded into a soft quietness enveloping the whole building.

Saranon's energy intertwined with the Keeps in a warm careful embrace. A jolt shuddered through separating the link to both of them. Theron gasped, the sharpness of the pain as it hit home before fading away. She did not show any sign of discomfort as her annoyance numbed the sensation. She sensed the sealed door and spoke, 'Someone's out there.'

'What?' He asked.

'They're trying to get in.'

Theron froze beside her looking around for another way out. Then he grabbed hold of her, jerking her backward before she regained her balance. The two ran as the seal began to give way, Saranon's heart thudding hard, whoever it was had been hidden from their senses. She grumbled at the thought of being stuck with a Prophet who was beginning to panic, as she tried to calm herself. She had managed to seal off another area as Theron knelt down on the floor not making a sound. It was difficult to tell how close the other sorcerers were, but for some strange reason she did not want to break the silence of her friend.

The Keep gave little away and for once she found herself wanting to ask Theron with the words sitting inside her mouth. Just as the words were ready to be said, she could sense the danger leaving and let out a frustrated sigh. All the while the sorcerer watched her as if knowing with his eyes, holding an uneasy truce waiting for the next step. Saranon moved over near the open door at the other end of the room. As she did, a surge of energy reached around with such force taking her by surprise. She reacted with the full might of the Angeon incinerating three sorcerers before she had time to gasp and take it all in.

She moved forward around the corner as her senses pricked up. It screamed through her body and her mind as she held back her energy at the last second. Chilcott flew around the corner straight into her path as her palms were still burning hot. The cloth on his arm seared away leaving a large gap, without a trace, on his skin. Theron came running to see the consequences and stopped short when he saw Chilcott alive. 'You knew,' Saranon spoke through gritted teeth.

'Excuse me but I was the one you almost killed,' Chilcott interrupted.

'Stay out of it,' she shouted as she turned her attention back to Theron. 'Have you ever heard of the Uvalen Code?

Don't you ever do that again?' The Prophet stepped back as she stepped forward, backing him into a corner. Chilcott was about to intervene but the Keep had a mind of its own and blocked him off sealing the corridor. This time it was the Prophet's turn to look surprised, as she waited before continuing. She spoke, 'You have a lot to learn before you become the Prophet your grandfather was.'

Whatever Theron had seen, it had not included this part, as she read the expression on his face, 'Next time say something.'

As the Keep eroded the wall and Chilcott stared at them, Saranon walked past fuming. She was in no mood to stay as Purton greeted her with a far too cheery expression. It was enough time for her teacher to pull her to one side and lead her away to his office. The thought surfaced in her mind to dart the other way, but she would still have to deal with the situation later. At the moment neither option was particularly enticing as she sat down in a chair next to Chilcott's massive desk. 'Do you know what I am going to say?'

'You shouldn't be alive,' Saranon said.

'No,' he replied.

'I'm being serious,' she said. The sorcerer paused as she continued in her pattern of thought. As she spoke, 'He wasn't looking and he only saw the version where you were meant to die.'

Chilcott wore a puzzled look on his face as the conversation dived into an area he preferred not think about. As a solemn expression overcame him, 'Whose idea was it to meld with Indarin?'

Saranon hesitated before saying, 'Mine.'

He sighed while glimpsing the hole in his sleeve, 'So now you are going to leave us with a Prophet who can meld with the Keep.'

In the silence it dawned on her that this was rather unusual, at the same time, she knew that Theron needed to know. It was a sensation that prickled at the edge of her senses and would not leave her alone. She found herself staring at an older sorcerer who seemed oblivious. His pursed lips spoke volumes as she rose in an uneasy deadlock and he spoke, 'Why are you pushing Theron into this?'

'He's already there,' she was in no mood to explain and left Chilcott to mull over his own thoughts.

The hall was dark and distant as she walked along exhausted. Almost tripping over Mitch as she entered her room, he was sitting down admiring the view of the sky outside. The night was fast taking over the day as he stood up, 'There's something I want you to see.'

Saranon was about to argue, but his stare said otherwise and she grumbled to herself as any hint of an early night vanished. He led her down underneath the dragon pens. Into a pile of grimy tunnels marking the edges of the former structure the Keep was built upon. It took a while to register that the place use to be a wizard Keep. She looked at Mitch with astonishment. 'This is why wizards don't like sorcerers in their Keeps,' he grumbled.

The walls still pulsed underneath her touch in a strange embrace, only just audible. The sound was hidden away amongst the calling of Indarin. 'Why would sorcerers want a wizard Keep?' She asked.

'Less work,' he replied.

She had heard and read about the reasoning behind such a move, yet it did not appeal to her. Trading less work for less control of the central core, did not sit well in her mind. Saranon focused her attention on following the energy paths of the Keep. She wondered why it had not been clear before then she had not been searching for the differences.

She placed both her hands to the wall surging out her energy to sense the Keep this time it was easy knowing what to look for. In a small faraway voice Indarin spoke thanking her. It was bitter sweet because there was still much work to be done. She stepped further down, it took her a while to see that Mitch had hesitated at the top of the stairs. 'I won't be following you down there,' he remarked.

'Are you sure?' She asked.

He just smiled and left, he had seen enough of the inner workings of the Keep in the last few days and looked quite content to stay away.

The novelty had almost worn off for her, but she went on regardless, the walls shimmered with a soft light sparkling as she passed by. A small circular symbol lit up on the floor and she followed its path to a large old door jammed shut with age. Saranon used her energy to heave the door half open. It was more than enough for her to fit through the wide gap as a strange sandy smell wafted up in a thick haze. She waited for it to settle before peering down onto the large head of a zennigh. The creature rose, with two gleaming amber eyes rising like two suns above the platform of the walkway. It pierced through the darkness with an ambient glow.

She trembled while standing her ground…the zennigh lifted its wet black nose up. Bumping it with a large dull thud into the railing, as it turned away, lying back down underneath where Saranon stood. She crept over and stared over the edge at the restful giant not making a sound. She stayed watching the sleepy giant cats moving part way down. The one that had curled up underneath her, lied with its head side on to the stairs. She reached out her hand and stroked its soft fur. A clamouring sound jolted through the door. She jumped in her skin as the zennigh remained motionless beneath her touch. Another jolt rattled even closer and Saranon slipped into the folds of the zennigh's fur.

The great creature seemed not to notice as the fur only just covered her. A sound rattled from overhead as she blended into the background. With the mumble of voices further down sifting through the air. In the dimness, if she listened she could make out a few words without giving herself away. It seemed like the perfect hiding place wrapped deep in the warmth of the zennigh. Then something sparked through the folds of fur encapsulating the large open space with light. The transition fell into place searing through the zennigh with such force. The sensation leaped through to meet with her skin.

It sent a sharp bolt of pain through and put an end to

the dull frame of mind inhibiting the zennigh. It bounded to life, pulling her with it. As it ran toward the emanating source she tried to untangle herself from the stubborn reality of being caught in its fur. In the frustration she used her energy and half hurtled to the ground as the zennigh leaped in for retribution. As Saranon steadied herself, she looked up and caught a tiny glimpse of a net. She yanked the zennigh to a stop with her energy. Creating a narrow buffer as the mighty creature stopped short with silent precision. In the glimmer of light from the failed net, she stood defiant. Braxton her old teacher glared back at her.

The zennigh moved its large paw in an unwelcome fashion forcing him to scramble in retreat. Saranon's cold anger hid the fear of standing in the midst of a zennigh den. As the large creature by her side, let out a harsh simmering breath in resentment. As if in unison the zennigh and Saranon peered at one another. For a moment, the creature gave her recognition with its piercing fiery eyes that went on forever. It curled up underneath the stairs in almost exactly the same place. With its front paws stretched out in a display of contentment.

The other path

Saranon trembled as she crept past the sleeping giant. She took care to shut the large door behind her, before rushing off through the dim hall. As she ran, the fear and frustration soaked in as the anger left and now she was desperate to get to the surface. Rounding a corner she almost jumped and only just missed running straight into Mitch. He led her back to his quarters above the dragon dens. He felt her forehead as she slumped in the chair. She had a strange exhaustion creeping up from the edges of her fingertips. 'What did you do, hug a zennigh?'

Saranon blushed and he groaned in acknowledgement.

It was tempting to stay, but she would have to return. Braxton had courted the anger of the zennigh. As she stood, her legs hesitated with weariness and a heavy weight from the contact of the zennigh taking its toll. She grumbled in a bitter acceptance that she would get nowhere without a good night's sleep. Mitch appeared all too pleased to have her close. He had changed after the attack on Indarin and now he was showing signs of eagerness to leave Serenphel behind. If only for a small moment, before she closed her eyes. She drifted off into an awkward sleep with the smell of the zennigh still covering her skin.

A hand reached over Saranon's vision before the light did. Catching her attention in a short gasp, before she realised it was attached to Hailey. Her friend sat beside her, 'You didn't mention Mitch.'

She thought she had, but then she had been focused on training more than anything else. Mitch was not impressed by this new found attention showing few signs in the silence. Hailey asked, 'Why don't you bring him to Armeria?'

She cringed at the thought, but Mitch said nothing at her friend's suggestion. Before she had time to think Hailey dragged her out of bed with great enthusiasm.

For first time since she had fallen into the central core the Keep hummed away to a regular peaceful tune. She breathed a large sigh of relief. It was not the impression she had meant to make so far from home. Todd was waiting outside with two fine dragons ready. As Hailey began to apologise for Katholomu, the enigmatic dragon stepped out from a long sleep. The great beast looked every bit ready, as he rustled his wings half open in the wind that swept underneath rolling along the ground. The grass shimmered in the fresh light of the early morning. Hailey flew up with a graceful whoosh on her dragon putting Todd's efforts to shame. Kat took no notice as he slid into the sky with a great heave, his massive wings powering into a smooth glide.

The almost invisible aura protecting Indarin shimmered as they went. The dragons needed little encouragement to leave the large Keep behind, as they flew into the cool sharp air. Saranon soon forgot the troubles of last night with the large zennigh. The creatures were capable of taking care of their own and so her worry grew distant the further she went. Todd flew his dragon high and turned into a small summersault. Hailey's shouting screeched across the wind, yelling for him to slow down. He smiled and waved back; with Katholomu it was not a wise step to encourage him. She was having enough trouble holding the great dragon steady. With Kat's muscles belaying the itching tension underneath.

Saranon held her seat firm, feeling every slight move and tremor of the dragon's changing mind. Katholomu commanded all her attention as she steered him away from the group, as he wrestled under her weight. The thrusting wings veered off at a weird angle as she clung on, while starting to slip sideways. As she looked over the cusp of the dragon's shoulder, she looked up in time to see Todd's dragon catch the rocky hillside. The beast ploughed down into an awkward summersault throwing her friend clear in a dusty haze. The reaction from Kathomolu was swift as he thumped himself down with the full might of his chest thrust forward. He absorbed the scattered impact of the falling dragon.

Jadaro's head sprang up with a dazed happy relief, the scratch marks lying across the top of his thick hard skin. Kat was less than impressed holding a silent stare back at the younger dragon, as he backed off, giving Katholomu a graceful berth. Saranon wanted to go down and check on her friend. Yet the dragon's muscles lay so tense underneath his arched back she dare not move. If anything she did not want to lose ground if he struck out. Hailey clambered down, rushing towards Todd after waiting for the dust and Jadaro's pride to settle. As she watched on, a wave of relief curled down to her toes and Todd stood up. She was about to breathe out a large sigh, when Katholomu moved his weight, clouting the younger dragon around the ears.

The breath caught halfway and she almost choked, spluttering into the back of the dragon's fur. The reaction was instant as he tilted sideways and jolted her off, before heaving himself high above the ground in disgust. Saranon stumbled, then clambered herself up shouting and running at the same time. Her friends burst out laughing behind her. She turned with such an annoyed look on her face that it prolonged the response. Hailey composed herself and then suggested that Todd could fly with her, which left Saranon with Jadaro. The dragon was large but by no means muscular for a rozzen. She sized him up then clambered on.

He was steady to take off with an even balance, but he struggled in the winds running across. Half way between Armeria and Indarin laid the remains of an old Keep, with the outer edges left to crumble. Escreigh resembled more of a well-kept tomb, than a working Keep with parts left to run down with age. For Saranon it had been an area avoided more out of necessity, to stay focused on her training. The Keep did not have much to offer beyond a simple frame, with the central core having become worn and frail long before. Yet it had taken on a new life with parts still in use. The rest was an untidy rabbit warren with corridors crisscrossing in almost every direction.

The place provided a wonderful hiding ground and peaceful retreat. Hailey ran through it without losing speed. Todd was still a little shaken, with his nerves trembling in hesitation. This allowed her to Keep up as she peered over the ancient scenery. The place had been magnificent in the days of the old Angeon. Zeralden Hadenvar had been the Queen of Darknonia by marriage to the King's second son. The blood line had since disappeared until now. Saranon was still baffled by finding another Angeon in Serenphel. She ran in a rush as she realised she had fallen behind. The ground tumbled and she fell through the floor with a thump. Scrambling to hang on, as the floor she had been hanging onto broke away, before Todd managed to get close.

She tried to soften the blow as one break led to another. Before she knew it she was tumbling way below ground, holding her own weight so as not to land too hard. She finally stopped on a pile of rubble, on top of a dust ridden smelly old concrete floor; she called out to let her friends know she was all right. Saranon peered up and sighed, she had fallen two storeys below and the remains looked too unstable to try and get back out the way she came. Not that she wanted to try that way, as she looked around melting the cobwebs out of the way as she went. The situation only reinforced her view that Escreigh should be avoided as she mumbled under her breath, a large spider ran past.

She was used to dark and dingy places, but she did not like the idea of being stuck somewhere. As she focused her attention on working open an old door. Her muscles ached from the fall, even though she had created a buffer with her energy. A spray of dust blew out as the door sprang open and she stopped it from falling on her face. Inside the room was an old tomb. As she crept past, with common sense telling her that the occupants were long dead, but that did not matter. A light shone down from an opening above and the shock made her jump. Her hand felt something old and creepy as she grimaced, not wanting to turn around. Saranon pulled back and saw that she had disturbed the remains of an old sorcerer. There was an envelope underneath.

Without thinking she took the envelope and went over to the light where she saw a familiar face, as Darren and Todd peered down. Darren let a rope ladder down and she climbed up holding the envelope out to the sorcerer. She heaved herself out with ease at a fast pace, jumping back from the edge, as though it were going to cave in at any moment. Hailey spoke, 'It's okay this floor is quite solid.'

She was not completely reassured as she stood well

back. While Darren pulled up the rope and bundled it away, he spoke, 'I think you should stick to the main paths.'

No one was prepared to argue after and if there was any doubt Saranon's annoyed glare settled the matter. Her mood matched Katholomu's where ever he was. The corridor led to a far grander section still cared for, as Seth greeted them with a stern nod. He looked quite at home in the large area that had been converted into a sizable outpost. She slumped down with relief into a comfy chair before Seth called her over he handed her the open letter, 'It's for you.'

Saranon accepted the small parchment and was about to pocket it as the sorcerer stared at her, then she stopped midway and read it. She almost jumped in surprise the letter was for her, the Angeon.

A small hand written note from a faraway time addressed to the Angeon. It made her wonder what she had stumbled on underneath an old Dreshan Keep. Before she could put it away, Hailey had snatched it and read the letter, she smiled, 'I don't think it's for you.'

'Zeralden had auburn hair,' she remarked.

'Oh,' Hailey exclaimed.

Saranon did not like to admit it but this time she would need to ask Theron. The thought did not sit well and she wondered if another visit into the old Keep would reveal more. Darren eyed her quizzical look, but said nothing in the background as she took the moment to wander off.

The walls did not hum with the same vibrancy as Indarin, but it had been well built and many parts of the building still stood strong. This time she stuck to the more well-used paths, her arms and knees were still aching from the fall and she winced at the thought of another. If anything the place opened up another question, if the note was not for Zeralden, then was it meant for her or Merrick. She was not about to reach out and ask the other Angeon, in fact she had been hoping that Merrick had relented on his current path. A low whistling sound gathered around the corner, blowing a soft cool breeze from the depths below, if anything it was familiar.

The low noise brought with it, a small strange message from beyond it. It filtered through the air holding her attention, as she stood on the top stairs hesitating in mid step. The place lay quiet as she dived into the unknown. The gloom around broke with the small occasional glimmer of light. The energy channelling up from the central core in a last glimmer of strength, in addition to her small light showing the way ahead. A small shimmer waved through the air in a familiar tone reminding her of Odana Temple deep in the heart of the old Zyanthia. Escreigh's walls were coated with a thick layer of dust brushing against her shoulder as she flicked it off. The ancient Keep still had a warm vibrancy running through from a bygone era.

For an old Dreshan Keep it appeared calm and let her wander into the murky depths. The place had been home to Theron's ancestor, Octavious the Prophet, who had been alive in the days of Zeralden Hadenvar. For a mighty sorcerer little was known outside the lasting prophecies that remained hidden away at Indarin. Saranon, the Angeon knew full well from Odana that prophecy had little meaning to an Angeon. Who had the ability to rewrite history, by choosing an unseen path. She had hinted at the prospect to Theron, but he was still absorbed in his textbooks. In an absent minded moment her foot almost went over the edge of the floor which had broken off.

This was no place for scatterbrained thoughts but they were flooding in thick and fast. She tried to find another path. She made it through to the lower level; the old building laid intact, showing signs of weathering around the edges. An old shaft reached down into the darkness where something glimmered from the deep below. A faint movement caught her eye, as the shadow passed through with the beam of light as she threw it into the dimness with a dull thud. The soft sound returned, reverberating up to the cavity above as she peered over almost losing her grip. Saranon groaned as her curiosity sank in and she began looking for a way down.

She secured a rope and used it to lower herself down the columns that still appeared sturdy as she bounced off them. A faint familiar smell wafted up, mixed in with the dry stale air, as the dust resettled beside her hand. Even in Indarin, the great home of one of the most powerful sorcerer clans, all the textbooks she had read, said the same thing, stay away from ockren. Of course there had been no textbook saying this at Zaidek Keep in Normisia which was just as well. It would have mattered not to her decision to ride the great mysterious ockren. That had broken out of the Keep carrying the full anger of the central core.

Now she felt the hairs on the back of neck begin to prickle, as she began to have the timely sinking feeling of being the intruder. The thought did not perturb her as she drudged on with a muffled thud landing in the grubby ground. A sluggish sound rustled from a dark corner of the room. Saranon almost froze to the spot with surprise as a figure moved out of the shadows, with wavy fawn coloured hair. The image of her old friend Tasha transfixed her, as the figure of she, stood close. Tasha held out her hand welcoming Saranon who touched it, the sensation felt real enough. A tear escaped down the side of her face even if the figure was not real it did not matter.

She was about to speak but Tasha spoke first, 'I have been waiting for you.'

The words sent a chill down her spine as Tasha continued, 'You will defeat Merrick, and you must believe that you will.'

'What do you mean?' The thought of another encounter made Saranon's heart sink.

'You are the Angeon!' with that Tasha stepped back into the darkness.

A voice called out from above and she answered, but when she looked back her old friend was gone. As she climbed up the rope, the great golden yellow eyes of the ockren opened into two small faint lines, they shone in the dim light.

As she climbed up Darren grabbed her hand to help her up, 'Did you find what you were looking for?'

She was not sure how to answer; it was not what she

had expected. Tasha's image still played in her head in repetition and she only just caught Hailey's words as she spoke. The confusion rushed in through her ears. 'Are you all right?' Hailey asked.

The relief stretched across her face as Saranon gave a short nod and sat down with all the contentment in the world. Her mind strayed to one thought, the other Angeon. A small scowl crept across the corner of her face. In reluctant acknowledgement of the tension that had grown since her last encounter.

As Hailey grabbed her hand it was a welcome distraction to wander through the outer parts of the ruined Keep. The small group fumbled through the old shell, as she was coaxed into pretending to be a grand sorcerer of years gone by. The sun drew low in the sky as their laughter grew and for a few wonderful hours Saranon let the events plaguing her mind float on the wind. A large thud jarred through the floor as Katholomu landed sideways plunging his claws deep into the wall of the building. He peered at Todd and Hailey with indifference, then leaned forward pushing his head through the open frame.

Before his hand reached over to grasp her, she dodged and climbed up. The dragon was satisfied by the response as he flexed his body, retreating to the outside. He swooped his great wings the full length with an enormous rustling sound against the windows. He heaved himself up into the sky. The enigmatic dragon climbed high into the clouds above. They weaved their way through the picturesque landscape. Katholomu snorted the air out of his nostrils with a stiff blast of hot air, melting droplets in the cold sharp air. His wings itched toward Espony and Saranon held him back, he let out a knowing grunt from deep within the bottom of his belly.

The sound echoed across the sky in stark retaliation. Before finally edging the tip of his wing and turning with a hard almighty swing toward the towers of Indarin. This time it was her turn to groan, as the dragon came into a sudden dive skidding across the open courtyard high above the ground. The dragon held up his claws as he spun around to a stop allowing the momentum to carry Saranon forward. By the time she brought herself to a halt and turned, the dragon stood in complete innocence, with no recognition of what he had done. Without missing a beat, her voice boomed across the open rooftop in a grating tone. Just then the dragon stepped aside revealing Ryan standing behind.

She was about to say something, but she was cut off at the pass with Ryan telling her to leave the courtyard. It took all her energy not to respond, as the haven that Indarin once offered, was fast vanishing at every step. She clenched her teeth before wrapping her energy around her and taking the fast way down melding through the floor. The passage calmed her thoughts until a familiar hand reached out. Larry pulled her over, 'Hello, when could you do that?'

The question felt strange as she had seen others meld through the building before. Larry pointed a finger up, 'That there is sorcerer's stone it's designed to keep people out.'

His words sank in as Saranon peered up at the underside of the courtyard, 'Oh!'

The sorcerer smiled and patted her on the shoulder before walking off with his tools in hand. It was a short but kind embrace, a small gesture of recognition in an otherwise empty room. As she sighed, she peered up and noticed a small leak in the ceiling near the corner of the room. It blended into the dark background. She paid it no more attention before rushing down stairs for a well-earned meal as her tummy grumbled. If there was one thing she hated being late for it was tea. She quickened her pace downward to the large hall and landed on the cold hard floor with such haste that it made a loud thud.

The sound repeated with another thud reverberating through the walls, this time she realised it was not her. The smell of warm potatoes wafted up with the vibrant cooking vapour, as if taunting her as she turned and made her way up. The noise came again flooding through the air with a harsh dull tone as a resonating silence followed. Reaching above into the open wind, Saranon called out as she was greeted with nothing. She popped her head around without a soul to be seen. The sorcerer's stone was carved and worn with age. As she strode across, she breathed and a small sigh of relief escaped from her cold lips, it burst into the sharp moist air. A similar sound echoed through the walls of time and space and she knew where she had to go.

In a glimpse of light sparkling in the haze she moved into a different phase, the only one she was familiar with. A step to the side stood her old friend out of sight, as she turned to face a dark figure leaning over Ryan's wounded figure. The picture made perfect sense as she charged ahead, blocking the figure with her energy. She ran forcing the person to fall back away from the sorcerer. The cloak disappeared and Gwen stood before her. The shock caught her off guard and a great ball of thundering energy catapulted toward her. Before she could retaliate, Tasha stood in front of her and absorbed the blow, Gwen attacked again with the same result.

She sent bolt after bolt disappearing the instant it hit Tasha, it soon became clear that Gwen was tiring and vanished in retreat. Tasha held out her hand for Saranon to grasp, 'This is for you.'

A shimmering glow spread as the energy transferred to her. It dissipated just as the Angeon shone underneath. She peered down at Ryan, before pulling him back out of the phase and into the path of confusion as the sky trembled with a familiar presence. No amount of hiding in the confines of the Keep was going to do now, as the sky clouded in the grey tones of a sorcery deep within.

The enriched energy built up in magnitude, filling the air with a metallic hue. Saranon remained silent, listening in the absence of sound. As a great wave weaved itself back across the sky and the shadows grew even longer. In the distance a low piercing noise carried across the wind, winding itself around the palms of her hands as she flinched. The recognition hurt her ears, as it drummed an age old tone, shaking the foundations of the Keep. One more time she listened, reaching out for the curves in the energy purging out from the source.

The glow intensified in her hands dispersing through the frame of her body as the Angeon became complete. In a terrifying instant an age old prophecy came to life before Ryan's eyes. Only in the tense rumbling, this was not a question Saranon had asked nor had anyone answered. For if there was one thing that she had known all along the future could be rewritten.

CHAPTER TWELVE

The dark haze whipped through the harsh cold wind blowing the hair from her face. Whichever way she scoured the landscape, one thought rang loud and clear. The Angeon was breaking through, a sea of turmoil spun in the sorcery spinning itself around the Keep. The tendrils reached out in a steady motion, as if searching for a source. Sweat shivered down Saranon's spine as her energy surged from within. Only this time it held strong inside her small figure. The energy filled in upon itself, at regular intervals, while staying away from the edge. The smooth silence within created a mirror image of the world outside. Before she knew it, a strange pattern of energy reached out and grabbed hold.

A crack of thunder etched across the clouds heading for Indarin. A great heavy boom reeked through the air, cutting off all sound in its wake. As it ploughed down into the earth, a long glistening arc soared up toward Saranon. She stood in the middle of the sorcerer's stone, held out her hands, as Tasha had done. She began absorbing the energy in massive volumes. For a brief moment it appeared as though the sky were fighting itself with the clouds whirling in ambiguity. In an instant, she held on tight and yanked the energy back out of the ground. She sucked it from the air, before condensing it down into the stone beneath her feet.

In the turmoil a great thunderous sound reverberated. Ripping apart the air, as the outer foundation of the Keep sheared under the pressure. In an instant an eastern tower cascaded down, crumbling in on itself with chunks of the tower flying at a hurtling pace. In the dust that cascaded up from the depths, the build-up of energy relented and Saranon let go. As her hold weakened, her energy boomed across the distance, clearing the sky in a great gust settling the way ahead. The air felt grimy, as the debris cleared, leaving a solemn tone stretching far into the ground. The dying embers of the sparks from Indarin wept over the damaged tower. She searched the sky, but found nothing. It was quiet relief as the calm fell over the land in stark contrast of what had been.

A thought plagued her mind and she rushed beneath the courtyard, as she left, Ryan gave her a stern solid stare saying nothing. The corridors were wild with activity as Saranon grimaced, it could only mean the Keep had suffered damage. She was hoping it did not extend to more than the outside tower. A small shallow blast ran through, knocking Larry over, as he soon scrambled to his feet. He caught site of her reaching out and pointed toward the source. She staggered a moment before pulling a face and stepping in. The fine spray from the hair line breaks, made a light colourful mist of the energy pouring through the Keep. It hung in mid-air applying itself to her clothes as she strode past.

A familiar sound clanked from up ahead, as she caught sight of Purton trying to meld a large break together. The enormity of the task daunted her, as she staggered through, trying not to upset the work that had already taken place. The sorcerer grumbled as he worked handing her a kedril, without losing pace Saranon glanced at its unusual shape. She was about to put it down when he pointed ahead of her. The way was dim but before she could ask Purton, he had moved out of sight. She shrugged her shoulders in annoyance without complaining. As she veered to one side sliding around several small creases, revealing fine breaks. Saranon stepped through the doorway and looked out.

The last remaining pieces hung out into nowhere, as the broken floor vanished into the space where the tower had been. 'Did you want to go out and take a look?' Purton asked behind her.

She glimpsed the open wound below and her stomach churned in an unkind response. She wavered as she leaned over and then an unexpected push from behind, jolted her out into mid-air. Her fall was softened by the pulsing of the energy below, as she found her balance and landed below ground level. As she looked above, Purton's unwavering laugh rang out as he yelled, 'I'll see you later.'

She was caught between a surge of frustration and complete surprise. She wanted to say something, but no words came forth. It was not the way Saranon imagined she would help the Keep. Stuck with a few small kedrils in her hand, peering down at it in disbelief, she wondered how it could be of any use. The debris had slammed the floors together down on the main foundation, that had taken the full force. Protecting the lower levels with dust scattered everywhere. Before moving around, she gathered her thoughts. She cleared the small particles away leaving a clear surface to work with. Tucking the kedrils behind her, she clambered down to assess the base of the foundations smoothing them over.

Indarin rarely saw damage on such a large scale. Yet the tower had been old and further removed from the inner sanctum, the luck had not escaped her. A shadow fell from the side as she peered in the last rays of light, Ryan stood like a calm solid form in the shattered background. The bandages showed in a small slither underneath his cloak. The sorcerer's silhouette dragged along the ground in cold isolation. Saranon braced herself for a stern response, that seemed to hang in the air in anticipation. 'Who is your friend?' He asked.

At first the question drove past her thoughts in surprise at what he meant. The shock written on her face as the bright lights of Indarin came to life.

She sat for moment stumped for words, before Ryan

filled in the silence. 'Very well, if you don't want to tell me.'

'Tasha died in Darkonia,' the words came flooding with a great sadness deep within.

She could see Ryan's expression as he tried to work it out, the sorcerer sat down beside her on the rubble before he spoke. 'You don't do things the easy way.'

Saranon looked around her and answered, 'No.'

The sorcerer stayed for a while before standing in the cold night air that whipped across his face. 'This will be here in the morning, make sure you get some sleep.' he hesitated then turned back, 'Darkonia is lucky to have you.'

She was not sure where his words came from; she had not felt that way in return about the country of her birth. The place had been farthest from her thoughts. As she cleaned up, ready for a late tea in a warm welcoming hall filled with a great many people, staying up late in the night. Mitch's hand reached out and patted her on the shoulder. As he pulled her aside, he still appeared larger than life in a crowded room. His simple shirt showed signs of the dust that had blasted through the Keep. 'I think Theron needs you now,' he whispered in a low tense voice.

Saranon was not about to argue with his stern face, it looked like his day had been as hard faring as hers. She scoffed the remains of her meal down as she nodded in gratitude. She hoped the Prophet's problem would be easier to resolve, than a collapsed tower. The halls appeared silent after the day's events, with the echo still filtering through her head. She darted through and took a step back, as a large man towered before her next to Theron. Armand stood with a straight hard stare, as her friend hung his head saying nothing. It was an awkward moment as a thought dawned on Saranon and she burst out laughing.

She grabbed Theron's arm, 'Come with me.' His reluctance held him back for a moment as she spoke, 'I am going to answer your question.'

'What?' He asked in surprise.

'The one you didn't ask,' she replied.

The Prophet in waiting, gave her a puzzled look, as he moved in a relieved motion out the door.

'Are you feeling all right?' Theron asked.

'So you want to know why you have difficulty seeing me in the future,' she remarked.

The sorcerer stopped and glared at her as he whispered, 'How did you know that?'

'Odana Temple,' she replied.

The Prophet pursed his lips in a state of partial frustration. He stood in silence contemplating the conversation. Saranon took hold of his hand, yet the sorcerer stood where he was. 'You wouldn't want to miss this for the world,' she spoke.

A tiny glimmer warmed in Theron's expression. As he let go of his staunch pose, he still wore a look of uncertainty, as she asked him to hold on. With a dry gust of air rushing over the tunnel's edge, she pulled him over before he had time to let go. The might of the Keep hauled them down at an intense pace, with the giant drone of Indarin echoing around them. Theron clung on so tight, she could feel her fingers going numb under the pressure.

The regular pulse of the central core vibrated through the walls. The energy increased in strength, as they hurled deeper into the Keep. The Prophet had his eyes closed in anticipation and Saranon smiled as the energy bore down on her, while she shielded him from the blow. As the tremors grew louder, she could feel the time for her old self fraying away at the edge. A glow shone through from beneath the surface, as the Angeon wrapped around her outer form, in the darkness. The Keep's energy surged toward her sealing the transformation in an intricate mould. It created a shallow buffer as they descended.

Small shards fractured off the opening in the central core before them. It pulled the two down with a renewed force, sealing the gap without a trace. Theron gasped in the absence of a steady gravity, as the central core whirred below. Before he had the chance to gather his senses, Saranon lead him down further. An opaque shape glowed in the hollow light, bouncing in a hazy glow. She was certain if it was anyone else that had been with her, the reaction would have been far from calm. As it was, Theron remained in a curious state of awed silence, glimpsing down at the object below. The object was held in a giant dark silhouette forking out of a magnetic whirl wind of static clouds, held in an eternal cycle.

The sorcerer reached out, placing his hand through the soft glowing mass, pulling out the object held inside. A giant rumble headed up the dark spine from below as the Angeon lifted the Prophet up. A hike in the energy spored towards them as Saranon catapulted the Prophet out of the central core, before it reached them. The impact drilled searing pain into her head as she held herself against the flow. She stayed for as long as she could, as she transmitted the energy back into the Keep so that it could heal itself. The glow burned bright beneath the ground intensifying in force. This time she stayed in the form of the Angeon, letting the energy of Indarin pass through.

As the central core increased its capacity, she waited in the darkness. She projected as much as she could, back into the Keep. The sensation washed over her, the Angeon recognised it. As she felt it surge through immersing herself in the transformation. She magnified the energy upward, rebuilding the fallen tower as she went. The Keep embraced her sorcery flowing above. The warm sensation of the glow magnified in completion. The full transformation of the Angeon wrapped completely around her soul. Saranon was no longer bound by the confines of the Keep, as she reached upward flowing in an internal glow. She broke past the surface in a fiery blast. The rip melded, healing itself behind her as she landed beside the Prophet in waiting.

The Angeon held out her hand and he held out his in return as he smiled. A voice cut through the courtyard in front of the new tower. As Armand and Ryan ran toward them, in an almost frantic panic, as they stopped short of the barrier around the pair. Saranon waited in the calm of the buffer, but for Armand it was too late, his son had already melded with the Angeon. A low tone rang out piercing the night sky as Indarin glimmered in the darkness. The dull noise pulsated through the walls of the Keep as it shimmered with delight around the two. It brought Indarin into perfect alignment with the Prophet. As the Angeon let go, ending the peaceful connection the glow of the Keep stayed resonating with the Prophet's energy.

Saranon relinquished her role, returning to her old self as she stood back. She almost tripped over Mitch who beckoned her away from the gathering crowd. He had the tiniest hint of a smile curving the edge of his lip, 'You don't do things by halves.'

She was about to reply, but he turned the other way. As they stepped into the dragon pens with the giant Katholomu curled up on a pile of blankets. The dragon watched through a shallow slit below his eyelid, as the magnitude of the night set upon her. Mitch leaned a shoulder to lean on, before she thudded on top of her untidy bed. He sat down as though waiting for something to happen, at the end of a long day, all Saranon's weary body wanted was to curl up and sleep.

The shadows played on the ceiling as her heavy eyelids closed. The peace was broken by a soft noise as the wizard left the room and she smiled in her sleep. The first light of morning streamed in through the curtain, far too early. She remained oblivious to the outside world. A faint shadow appeared to block the light, as she jumped at the sight of Theron waking her up. 'Father wants to see you,' the sorcerer spoke.

She took a while to focus, then shooed her friend out of the room, before tripping over in her haste to get ready, grumbling as she went. She rushed out of the room and almost ran straight into Armand standing tall. As she searched the space she caught sight of Mitch sitting down.

It was not the sort of greeting she had expected after such a tumultuous day, and Theron offered no clues. The daylight splayed across Armand's face. He spoke in a firm and rational manner with the weight of the past days showing beneath his eyes. An awkward silence hung in the air, as Saranon pieced together the meaning of the conversation. A loud gasp escaped her lips in recognition of reading the information that Odana had left her and Jedd had translated. The shock did not appear to catch on to the Prophet standing before her, as Theron watched on. As soon as Armand stopped, she let out a bold laugh, 'That is not what I was expecting.'

By the look on the sorcerer's face her reaction had not been expected either. Yet it did not matter, after all as Saranon smiled she saw the clear picture. Merrick had not progressed to this level and the Prophet had let her know. As she pondered the thought, she spoke clear and precise, 'Theron I think you need to let your father know.'

The room fell silent in the space that followed as Theron stepped back, 'I thought you knew.'

Before Armand had time to lose his calm expression, Mitch stood up, 'I think what Saranon meant to say is, she knows she can return home now.'

'What do you mean?' Armand stood back in confusion.

'I am complete,' was all that Saranon said.

'No, I didn't say that,' Armand still looked confused.

'I'm afraid you did.' Theron spoke, 'Odana told

Saranon the signs to look for and you confirmed it.'

'No,' Armand was still in disbelief as he shook his head, 'It takes years, you misunderstood.'

'I knew before you told me but I thank you for the confirmation,' she smiled.

Armand stared at Theron hoping for support. Yet Theron offered none, 'I told you, but instead you believed Braxton.'

This time it was Mitch's turn to speak. 'We will stay until the end of the term, that should give you more than enough time to sort out Indarin.'

Saranon could not help feeling empathy for Theron. Something had gone astray in the lines of communication. At the end of the day she had to remind herself she had only come all this way for one reason. Whatever problems lay at Indarin these would need to be dealt with by the Armythral.

As Armand realised he was in the middle of a losing argument. He gathered his composure and left her standing with Mitch close by her side. 'I can see why Captain Mirshendy feared you,' the wizard spoke.

'Are you serious?' She asked.

He did not answer her question. Instead he hesitated near the door, 'Make sure you have your bags packed, we may have to make a quick exit.'

Saranon did not doubt his words as they resonated in her head, he had been quiet at Indarin, but he was no fool as he kept out of the way.

The day was off to a strange start as she gathered her

thoughts for the evening lesson. She liked Anne and the idea of having to say goodbye hurt inside, as she closed her eyes before bounding out the door. The day still streamed down a bold ray of sunlight through a clear blue sky. The cool wind that whipped at her feet belied the hint of the last days of winter. She was pleased not to be in Serenphel long enough to experience a hot summer. Todd stood with a satisfactory smug look at having beaten everyone else to get ready. Saranon scrambled to catch up dropping her bond-breaker in her haste, as it sliced a third of the way into the rock beside her.

Todd shook his head at his friend, as he walked off to be the first to try firing his energy out in the open. They had practised many times before, but the Keep had always provided a mental wall of safety. She wondered if her friend would be so keen out in the open air. She clambered on a ledge over to the side with a good view along the valley below. Wedged between arrays of rocky hills, it was a perfect platform that showed years of solid use. A small gesture showed Todd's nerves under his thick outer edge, as he steadied himself with Anne waiting by his side. The first blast veered to the left catapulting off the rocky side before fizzing out in the middle in a plume of smoke.

Todd steadied himself with some reassuring words. The second blast hit straight with a high arch that landed short of the goal. Theron clambered up beside her as they cheered the sorcerer on, for his third try. The effect was massive this time, the blast shot low and hard. It managed a fair length of the valley before disintegrating in the distance. Todd stood back to a barrage of loud applause as Theron skimmed down to take his place. The Prophet stood solid and true with three impressive blasts across the valley, but none came close to Todd's final mark. Todd gave Saranon a gentle push down, 'It's your turn,' he said with a friendly smile.

She had been so caught up in the moment, that she forgot and hesitated before reaching Anne who was waiting. She steadied herself taking a deep breath, surveying the valley below. From where she stood, it appeared so much larger and she could feel her nerves creeping in. Saranon focused her mind on the open target, letting her strength gather and well up inside, until it began reaching out. The sound of her heart beat ached in her throat, as she opened her eyes and let go. The cataclysm pulled at the edges as the sound followed in the gap left behind. The blast seared both edges of the valley and flew straight to the end without losing speed.

In the silence that followed a solitary voice rang out, it was Theron shouting for her to do it all over again. She let the build-up continue, before letting it fly with ease and accuracy across the valley, two more times. One after the other, straight as an arrow, all three shots hit the end of the valley. The sound echoed outside the valley in a sweeping gust of intense energy, roaring through, ripping the air apart as it went. Saranon smiled in acknowledgement, if there was any doubt that the Angeon was whole this plummeted the idea deep into the abyss. This time the Angeon rose, as she flew above and catapulted one final blast, as proof of what she had become. The sound roared in agreement back across the valley.

It took a while before she returned to her old self. As half the population of Indarin had gathered to watch after the first boom shattered the peaceful sky. Theron rushed down to greet her as they walked back, the sorcerer could not wipe the smile off his face. This time Saranon let it go, she had done what she set out to do and in the short space of time she had grown. Even Todd was lapping up the excitement, he held his head high as the crowd parted, letting them through. Theron paused at the sight of Armand peering down from the balcony. She gave him a small nudge, as she whispered, 'He'll have to get used to handing the reigns over some time.'

Theron gave her a side-ways glance and spoke, 'I'm not ready.'

'You were ready before I came,' Saranon exclaimed in a loud voice that hurled above the breeze.

Todd laughed, 'I wouldn't argue with her she's the Angeon.'

The group stopped then laughed as Hailey met them for a well-earned hot meal in the large hall. As the sun sct on a peculiar day, she could not help but wonder what had happened to Merrick. Not a word had been said and this only played on her mind as she dabbled in her tea.

If it were her she would not have given up, the burden plagued her mind as Hailey distracted her from her gloomy thoughts. It was the second time her friend had asked her to describe what it was like to blast raw energy across the valley, but she did not mind. Anne had helped relieve a great deal of stress from her shoulders. She gave Saranon the opportunity to announce to Indarin the magnitude of her ability. Anne's warm smile shone through, her teacher was always straight forward.

As they entered their apartment Hailey had an inquiring look on her face as if she had been holding something back. 'What did the note say?' She asked.

She knew what her friend meant as she unfolded the small note and handed it to her. 'Is that all?' Hailey exclaimed.

'You don't need to say much if you use the right words,' Saranon read it aloud, 'To the dark haired Angeon, look after my heir. Octavious.'

CHAPTER THIRTEEN

Time for dragons

The sun shone bright as the morning warmed and the air filled with a fresh breeze. It had been a long tiring week and she was readying herself for a weekend at Armeria. Kathomolu snorted near the window in agitation, making it appear as though he had been waiting for hours, instead of minutes. Hailey tapped and opened the door to the veranda, 'I don't think your dragon will wait much longer, unless you want to fly with me?'

'I'm coming,' Saranon shouted as she peered out at Kathomolu as he curled his head over the railing and she climbed on. 'I'll meet you there,' she shouted and they were off.

The dragon wasted no time launching full pelt into the sky as the breeze flowed underneath his wings. If she did not know better, she would have thought he was running away as Kat gathered speed along the way. It was just as well with the activity below as a great many dragons took to the sky in all directions from Indarin. The great Katholomu grunted his preference to stay far from the crowd. It dispersed into the air sending all manner of colourful dragons streaking across the morning sky. A small shadow broke free as Levette; Hailey's dragon skimmed, gaining speed. Saranon's dragon pretended not to notice the elegant lady as she flew overhead.

Jadaro lagged behind in comparison, the medium sized dragon not yet grown. The dragon was dwarfed in the experience and speed of the other two. She thought he and Todd were well suited, though she did not like to say so. They glided back and forth among each other in the crystal blue sky as the warmth of the day broke over the land. Katholomu edged ahead as he dived down, dragging his heals across the ground in a sudden halt, as he closed his great wings behind him. The dragon kicked sideways at the last minute and Saranon clung on with both hands, so as not to fall off. This last offering had become Kat's new trick as he took pleasure in catching her off guard.

Hailey had already landed as she walked over trying not to laugh. Katholomu curled himself up in a tight ball with his back absorbing the full rays of the bright sun. The three were glad to be back at Armeria with its timeless atmosphere and the waves crashing in the distance. The faint smell of sea spray wafted through the air filling their lungs. Seth greeted them as they ran through the old gates at the edge of the garden before Saranon stepped inside. A flash glimmered to life in the protective markers surrounding the garden. Before she could ask, Hailey had spoken and Seth fobbed it off. She stared at her friend sharing an uneasy look, then went inside.

The old Keep still worked well and hummed with an unusual vigour underneath her fingertips. She brushed them against the wall. Whatever it was, Hailey had also noticed the change through the place. For the moment she followed without saying a word as she kept a watchful eye. She caught up with Darren and Rory, the pair were at a peaceful ease, calming her suspicious mind, as the thought passed. Rasputen filled the courtyard with his giant frame as she stepped out. She had to negotiate her way around the dragon that was just as stubborn as hers. As Saranon moved too close she trod on his tail, the dragon arched his back in an unimpressed response.

The dragon remained unwilling to move, as Hailey and Todd found their way around the giant who flared up his mane. Seth tried to sooth his beast, as Rasputen half stood, his wound showed underneath. Hailey gasped in horror, 'What happened?'

Darren did his best to skirt around Hailey's bold stare without answering the question. It created an awkward impasse, before Seth asked the three to leave the courtyard to allow the dragon to rest. Before anyone could argue, her friend tugged at her sleeve and they dashed away from Seth and Darren.

The strange mood followed them through the Keep, clinging like a stain in the air as they went. Hailey showed signs of being unimpressed by the response, but neither was about to annoy Rasputen. Saranon followed her friend down to the cool shore's edge as the sun shone down. She peered back toward Armeria which shone in the warmth of the day. Whatever had bothered the Keep appeared to be far gone, she ran along as she realised she had been left behind. The wind blew deep off the water's surface, sending a chill down her spine. She looked back over the water and thought there had been something there, but no trace remained. She ran almost clambering into Hailey who stared down at the ground. Revealing massive scorch marks running parallel along the earth.

The scorched path continued off centre towards Armeria and disappeared without a trace near the Keep. The three stood in silence as Todd reached down rubbing his fingers in the charred dirt, while Hailey remained frozen to the spot. The thought made Saranon giddy as she stood on the spot where Seth and Rasputen had defended Armeria. Hailey ran home with a look that concerned her, as she ran after her. It did not take long for the shouting to start with Seth standing next to his wounded dragon. The outburst made her cringe and before she knew it, her friend had dragged her into the conversation. 'Tell Seth he just can't go around taking on an attack like that on his own,' Hailey spoke.

She could feel her face go red with embarrassment under the stern eye of her friend. Unfortunately Saranon knew it was not that simple and offered Hailey no relief, as her friend stormed off in a huff and Todd ran after her. She sighed and grumbled to herself as she stared at Rasputen bathing himself in the warmth of the sun. The sanctuary of the garden felt awkward with the large dragon curled up in a restless mood. He stiffened his claws scraping them along the ground in a grating tone, as he lowered his head further down. It was a peaceful moment, before Seth urged her away from the sleepy dragon. The sorcerer made no attempt to convey what had happened, other than the wounds on his dragon.

The silence hung in the air as Saranon passed through the narrow corridor. Up to where Hailey was searching through the draws of an over-sized desk. Before she had time to ask anything, Todd held some papers up behind her. Hailey reached over and snatched them from out of his hand with a satisfied smile, as she flicked it in her hand. Footsteps sounded from nearby and she jumped. While her friend stuffed the papers away and pretended not to notice, as they dashed out of the room. She caught site of Darren before they fled down the stairs via a second staircase. Hailey stopped to catch her breath in the open doorway as she glided through.

She grabbed Saranon's arm with a jolt and whispered with a sweet determination, 'Come on.'

As she peered up Todd had already raced ahead. She let out a small groan and ran after them while a hundred small thoughts flittered through her mind. Almost every one of them, ending in a place called trouble. Levette and Jadaro were easy to find. They played with Katholomu who relented to the two younger dragons chasing each other in the long grass. Hailey climbed on Levette beating Todd who had been given a head start.

Before Saranon had time to think Katholomu decided that he would close the distance. He lifted her up on his head and shoulders, while showing off with a long smile. The dragon flexed his head to reveal his sharp back teeth, before bunching himself up for a massive leap into the sky. The wind swept across her arms in an agitated tone as the sun warmed the air. The bright light shimmered across Katholomu's dark body, as he swept his wings to go higher. She found herself looking down upon her companions, as they sped inland. Hailey swooped ahead and down into the crux of the valley, Levette landing on the steep incline.

As Jadaro matched the daring manoeuvre his foot gave way on the ground and tumbled. She watched with a bubble of air caught in her throat. Todd managed to jump clear but the dragon tumbled further down the hill. He cascaded into a mass of greenery, flattening a path before diving into the undergrowth. A horrid sound roared up from below, bouncing off the rocky incline and echoing with a deep grumble through the entire valley. The sound swept away all of Saranon's thoughts in a heartbeat, all except one Ferridge, the dragon of the other Angeon. Jadaro's screaming echoed across far too clear in the still air. Katholomu had not yet landed as she looked on with a steady sinking feeling.

Todd made it to Levette, but as the dragon launched Ferridge lurched out of the depths with Merrick in clear view. Without so much as a prompt, Katholomu veered in sideways, locking his claws around Ferridge's. Bringing the dragon down hard with a mighty crash, as Levette needed no encouragement making a mad dash out of sight. Saranon braced herself as she struggled to get some distance between her and the fighting dragons. For a moment she lost sight of Merrick and a deep rumble flew above her head, hitting the rocky edge behind. She would have to leave Katholomu to fight his own battle, as she ducked half slipping down the slope.

A warm haze heated up the air as she made her way to the bottom of the valley in the distance. It became clear she had stumbled into so much more. As she stared across and into the bulk of a massive construction site, a thought rushed into her mind. The other Angeon had begun the early stages of building a central core. She did not have time to think, as a thundery bolt flashed across the sky. Leaving her only just enough space to block the hit, as it sent sparks cascading out from the impact. Saranon could see several figures in the distance rambling together and deep inside, her heart hit rock bottom.

She had come so far and she did not know what giving up meant, when there was no way back she would just have to move forward. The decision brought tears to her eyes as the reality meant facing another Angeon. She held her breath deep inside as she cried, she wanted to scream out as she stood on the verge of frustration. The air stemmed up around her as she took on her true form. The pure elegance of the Angeon long trapped inside her fell into perfection as the paths within her lay complete. She floated in the air with the sheer force of the energy holding her up as the attempts the other sorcerers made melted away from her being.

The energy spawned within searching far into the ground in the shallow edge of the deep ravine waiting for a new central core. Merrick responded with a cold hard bolt searing through the air. It exploded into a multitude of shards above the gaping hole in the depths as Saranon stood her ground. The fierce intensity of the energy below began to rise as Merrick pushed the massive force towards her from a great well of strength. The ferocity of the onslaught caught her off guard. As part of it trickled through at the edged sending a searing pain deep into her lungs. The sharp exchange sent shards of light and energy catapulting in all directions. In the tiny fragment of calmness that followed she held her grip.

In a moment between her breath and the solemn sound of her heartbeat she returned fire. The blast struck deep and hard cascading into the ground and across the land with a spray that cut so fine as the ash of charred dirt fell. The hole collapsed into a molten dark mass beneath her. As Merrick fled and any sign of other life soon disappeared in the panic to escape the rupture in Tordoren. The molten lava ran hot and fluent creeping into the deep cracks eating away at the valley. She sent a chilling surge deep into the earth pummelling down the rising disaster as it leaped to the surface.

The sheer pressure strained the edges of her being as the land shuddered with the competing forces. A last defiant rumbling tremor stretched across the depths and beyond the valley. As Saranon landed on the solid edge of the hillside looking down a familiar figure wandered over inspecting the site as he went. Theron had flown up to meet her dragon curled away from the damage. 'I don't think I need to tell you my father won't understand,' he spoke as he surveyed the valley.

'No,' she replied.

'Good then I won't,' the sorcerer gave a faint smile as they stared in awe.

She shook her head in disbelief. As Katholomu shook himself out of a large clearing and curled up beside her without any sign of his latest struggle. She dared to think how the other dragon had fared. As her eye perused the valley it focused on a sobering sight as the fallen clump of Jadaro's dead body peeked out from behind a clearing. She was not sure how Todd would react but then it had been inevitable. Katholomu leaned over his head and brushed it sideways against her. As a tear ran down her cheek but in her heart she knew it had all been too late.

The Prophet glanced out surveying the view before adding, 'You do know if you can break a Keep you can also make one.'

'Is that a hint?' She asked.

Theron laughed at her response and went to leave. 'Oh no, you're helping me with this one,' Saranon said.

Before the Prophet had time to respond, Seth landed with the wounded Rasputen and Darren with Colderay right beside him. The remaining four sorcerers in the group were quick to follow, as Seth glanced over the edge and into the remains of the valley below.

'Just a normal day really,' she said trying to make light of the situation.

Theron kept a straight face beside her, 'It's a good thing I didn't ask you to show off.'

She kept back a quiet laugh that ended up sounding more like a snort as the sorcerers surveyed the damage in silence. Darren kept a serious tone as he spoke first, 'Seth told the Eskardy, that he hoped their new Keep, would fall into oblivion.'

'That's the polite version,' Seth commented.

'Yes I know that,' Saranon spoke.

They gazed on in silence as Seth clasped his hands on his hips staring down at the mess, 'Is there anything left of him?'

'Who Merrick? I think Theron could answer that one better.'

'I would prefer not to,' the Prophet spoke.

'He's still around,' she said as she looked over to where the sorcerers had fled. 'So who's going to tell Todd about his dragon?'

'You can, in fact you can help clear this whole thing up,' Seth spoke in a disgruntled fashion.

'Seth!' Darren chimed in.

'No, if he's going to start an argument he can wear it,' Saranon spoke to Darren before she turned her attention square on Seth. 'If you had been honest with me, this would've been different.'

Theron broke in, 'She's right.'

'Thank you,' Saranon answered.

'But it would have been the same outcome,' the Prophet finished.

'Thank you,' she spoke a little louder and glared at him.

Seth changed the subject, 'I'll tell Todd about his dragon while you two sort out this mess.'

'Me?' The Prophet exclaimed wide-eyed.

Katholomu lifted his head and yawned at the commotion. As his empty stomach let out a loud growl, that reminded her it was teatime and the thought of food was too hard to resist. The dark sky blanketed the scars in the earth below, as they made their way back to Armeria after Theron had gone. The sticky sweat from her dragon saturated her clothes, as she clung on until they arrived to a quiet Keep.

The silence hung in the air like a dark cloud around her, before Seth broke the atmosphere, 'It's good to have you back.'

Darren smiled and then shook his head. They ventured inside the dim hallway with the warm smell of a large feast filling her nose with a deep breath. It was not until Saranon had entered the room proper, that a wide-eyed familiar face popped around the corner. Hailey gave her a big hug, filled with relief as she exhaled a breath full of tension and her shoulders finally relaxed. 'I'm sorry,' her friend whispered in her ear.

'Don't be, next time your brother should speak up,'

she exclaimed.

Hailey let out a soft laugh that took the edge off the silent vacuum in the room, 'That's a tall ask.'

It was with some delight that the two friends found ways of annoying Seth across the table. The turmoil of the day built up in Saranon's head. Her eyes grew tired and she tiptoed from the room as the hour grew late and her arms grew heavy. A few hollow sounds stemmed indoors through the gaps, but as her head hit the pillow, none of that seemed to matter. A hand crept across her vision in the morning light and she woke staring out at nothing. The image stayed with her as she bounded down the creaky stairs.

The murky start to the day as the clouds gathered outside, did not appeal to her mood. She entered the outer yard to find Katholomu in immaculate condition. He looked every bit the pure thoroughbred in his fearsome prime. As he arched his back casting a faint shadow on the ground as the wind picked up. She hauled herself up on his hard shoulders. As the dragon leaned down and bounded with magnificent force into the open sky. The clouds parted as though in anticipation, letting the great dragon pass. The immense scar did not take long to find heaving up from the ground below. No amount of denial could hide it as the sunken dirt revealed the cataclysm of destruction.

The broken, dying signs of an ambitious dream held up for all to see in a dismal embrace, as the ground still trembled in the eerie silence. A small gathering on the hilltop viewed the damage. As Saranon recognised Theron and brought Katholomu down close by. Not a word was spoken as she landed and met the group while Chilcott peered over the edge. 'You have an unusual way of doing things,' the sorcerer remarked.

As they watched, Levette brought Hailey down by their side, the smaller dragon was quite nimble and did not miss a step. 'Well, I think we have everyone here,' Chilcott spoke with a firm certainty in his voice.

Hailey stood surveying the scene, for the first time her mouth gaped in awe. It was greater than she had imagined, as she stepped behind Saranon not wanting to get too close. Chilcott did not appear to notice, as he held out a small glimmer of light, that shot out to stretch like a thin spider's web resting with great care over the valley. He motioned for Hailey and Theron to follow suit as each mesh crisscrossed and reinforced the last. The fine lines sparkled under a shady sky, holding under the soft breeze as a chill ran up her spine. She stepped forward feeling a small surge grow stronger. As the power stirred within, as if knowing the moment had arrived. Still she hung back waiting for Chilcott to prompt her as a moment of uncertainty swept over her mind.

The Angeon dived forward embracing the web and sending a massive surge melding the energy deep into the damaged ground. The sorcery removed the last signs of construction of the central core forming the earth as the energy saturated through. The last rays of sparkling light from the faint web disappeared as the great scar healed through the valley floor. A shallow mist rose up covering the surface of the valley as Chilcott looked on. The sorcerer gave a long worried gaze over the valley, before returning to his dragon. For a moment he hesitated and then thought better of it as he launched into the sky.

Hailey rushed up to her side, 'He knows something.'

'I think a lot of people have,' Saranon responded.

Hailey stared over at Theron, who was pretending not to notice, the Prophet remained calm in the light. Katholomu grew impatient, as he came over beckoning her as she replied. She climbed on his back before they flew into the grey sky. A cold shiver ran through her as she realised she had not seen Todd in the distance. Indarin grew larger as she made her way, swooping down to the dens. The pavement was scarce of dragons on what should have been a busy day.

Instead of stopping in the courtyard Katholomu veered his head in the dens. He angled his body inside the large opening taking care not to scrape his wings. As he did so, Mitch came out to greet them, holding up his hand to help her down, as she slid off the side of the dragon's shoulder. He looked as though he had not slept at all, but the shabby appearance suited his rough features. He whispered in her ear, 'The sooner we get back home the better.'

Saranon wanted to believe in that thought. Yet with Merrick still out there and without the beginnings of a new Keep, a sinking feeling made her doubtful.

In stark contrast the great halls of Indarin were filled to the brim with the usual hub of activity. The Keep showed no sign of the drastic events outside. She almost wanted to scream out in protest and instead settled for a small grumble as she sighed. The end of the term was fast approaching and she had so much to do before then, as she rushed off into the busy hallway. A small solemn figure sat in the apartment as Todd waited for her arrival, Saranon closed the door. His drawn face appeared pale in the afternoon sun, as it streamed through the large windows decorating the room. She could feel the space grow tiny as an awkward silence clung to her throat.

Todd smiled, though his eyes were filled with a deep sorrow, as the two embraced in a warm hug. The sorcerer steadied himself as he pulled himself together with a deep sigh. 'I've got another dragon, Hailey picked him out.'

She could not help a muffled laugh, if Hailey had anything to do with it the dragon would be built for speed. 'His name is Kadvere,' Todd stated.

The name sounded familiar, as a thought fled through Saranon's mind, it was good to see that he had another dragon to care for. Her friend was attached to the great beasts. With an insatiable love for flying whenever a spare moment presented itself.

CHAPTER FOURTEEN

Vision Eternal

The storm hit the Keep hard, as the rain wiped out any memory of what had been. Mitch stood like a dark silhouette peering out across the courtyard. As the smell of damp wet dragons wafted through the air, she realized the horrid smell was coming from Katholomu. The dragon had moved himself into a corner and no one was game enough to confront him. Mitch pretended not to notice until a voice echoed across the distance. Hailey's words cut through the air, 'Saranon, that dragon stinks!'

'I think you'd better clean him,' Mitch added.

She had been avoiding it because every time she had been about to clean Katholomu, he had gone out into the rain again.

The dragon eyed her with a knowing stare as she went up to him. His dirty grubby skin needed a wash. As she sighed in defeat and called him, for a moment she thought he would not move. At the last minute his tail lifted and he stretched, flexing the might of his muscles. As Kat strode over he flicked something heavy near Saranon, it clanged and rolled out of sight before she had a chance to see what it was. Mitch picked it up. 'You can look at it afterward,' he spoke as he wondered off, without giving any hints away.

She grumbled as she started scrubbing the dragon that was easy to bathe when he was in the mood, but it took longer due to his size. She watched as the miniature mountains of dirt came away from his feet and claws and wondered what the dragon had been doing. Katholomu always loved the feeling of being dry again. He purred with a loud rumble of satisfaction revealing his shiny teeth. The dragon wasted no time heading straight for the opening again, dashing outside as Saranon shouted after him. She stopped herself from going after him and stared at Mitch who smiled in return. 'Here, you might want to look at this,' he said smiling as the faint musty smell of wet dragon left the air.

She had almost forgotten how annoying Mitch could be, as she stared down at the remains of a seal, for which the image had no meaning. Now that the dragon had made himself scarce Saranon was left holding an awkward puzzle. The weather eased with a fine rain spraying through the opening with each gust of wind. She held the seal in her hands and she realised she had seen the pattern before. She fled down into the depths of the Keep, as the small lights lit up along the corridor penetrating the darkness.

She pursed her lips as a cold wash of anger fleeted through, scowling across her brow. Saranon kicked something small in the dim light as she made haste and swung back to see the small object tumble beside her.

The tiny object looked like a broken kedril, as she rolled it over in her hand she was about to fob it off. A small glint caught the corner of her eye, it was not the type of tool she was used to and she knew why. The path led to a few different tunnels which did not make much difference. She just needed to get down as she let herself slide through the floor. Falling down as she slipped, half catching the floor below. Before meeting the harsh familiar stare of two piercing yellow eyes lighting up the large room. The elegant ockren stood far too close, for comfort. She peered beyond it to the open door containing the other part of the seal.

The great magical beast created by the Keep itself, showed no shyness in the faint glimmering light. Saranon stood in a slow steady motion as she stared at the creature. It wrapped itself around as it brushed past with its skin tingling at the touch of her hand. It whipped its body round to face her at an angle, shining its eyes past her soul. The path to the door way was now clear, even though she hesitated with her heartbeat resounding in her throat, as she made small slow steps. Her fingers touched the edges of the frame and she yanked them back with the shock of pain. The charred remains of the blast still clung in the air with the seared end of the door showing.

The amount of energy spent for such a feat did not make sense. Then Saranon had to remind herself she had an unusual way of gaining access to the Keep, one that was not open to others. The seal, the remains of which she held clumped in her fist, would pose an obstacle for a majority of the sorcerers she had seen at Indarin. She stuck her head around the doorway and jumped in surprise, almost hitting her head on the frame, at the sight of Purton staring at her. 'Most people usually don't try and walk away from the prize,' the sorcerer said.

'Pardon?' She asked.

'Go look behind you,' he pointed.

Saranon gave him a puzzled look after staring out at nothing, behind the ockren, 'I don't…'

'Look harder,' Purton suggested.

She was beginning to get annoyed and fumed with a deep sigh let out underneath her breath. In stark contrast the ockren smiled baring its teeth. Purton pointed at the altar not straying far from the doorway. It took a moment for her to recognise it since it had been so long. Without hesitating she walked over to the altar running her hand along its edge. The image of Antavagon ran fresh in her mind as she took a step back.

A moment of silence hung in the air before she raised her hand to the open doorway. With all her might she used her energy to rebuild the door with a new seal sturdier than before. She took one small look admiring the new frame before she strode through the closed door. She appeared next to Purton who had been waiting on the other side. 'What did you do that for?' He asked as she appeared astonished.

'No good will come of anything behind that door,' Saranon spoke as she strode up the hall.

Purton was about to say something, but thought better of it changing his mind mid-way. 'There will be repercussions,' he spoke.

'Mm…' She was caught in thought as she turned to face him.

At that moment a flurry of activity fell through from above as several sorcerers, including Braxton, rushed past. They started with a barrage of verbal grievances at the sight of the sealed door. The only words Saranon waited to hear, were the assumption that the Keep had foiled their efforts before leaving. Purton's mouth dropped in silence as he followed, saying nothing. Waiting until they were well clear of the commotion.

'Are you going to tell them?' He asked.

'There is no difference between me and the Keep unless you want to?' She eyed him.

He backed away from the question as he whispered, 'You really are playing with fire.'

'Is that warning meant for me or them?' Saranon spoke, as she left Purton with that thought.

The recognition of the altar stirred back a range of vengeful feelings creasing though her skin and shaping her brow. It was a sight she had blocked, out to such a point, that she had only just noticed the altar's existence.

A myriad of tones from the past, flashed over, her making her mood even darker than before, as a fork of lightning boomed across the open sky. A thought entered her mind and she knew where she had to go. Her old friend Tasha would be waiting in the place between time and space. The one person she trusted more than anything. Tasha had seen the altar before the one that linked the phases, but that path was not one she chose to venture, she would have to find another way. She darted into her apartment making a mess, while trying to find one thing. Corsavere, the bond-breaker was easy to lose track of.

She had not worn it for ages. As she looked up, Hailey peered at the mess and moved a clump of clothes, revealing the smooth dagger still hiding in its sheath. Hailey's words hit hard as she spoke to them, 'I'm coming with you.' Her friend continued, 'This isn't just about you.'

Saranon felt as though she had missed the first part of the conversation, as she stood in bewilderment at the statement. Todd peered around the corner, 'I'd like to say the same but I think I'll leave this one alone.'

'Theron said you mended the seal,' Hailey explained.

'Theron talks too much,' she grumbled aloud.

She was not so sure about having company, but Hailey was not about to give in and Saranon knew she would need help. She handed her friend Tellembre, the bond-breaker was well designed and easy to use. A smile lit up her friend's face in acknowledgement, if anything went wrong Hailey would need to defend herself. A sad thought, which did not let go as she tried to shake it off. The shadows grew deeper, as the light faded with the culmination of clouds sweeping up what was left of the delicate blue sky.

They rushed off to find a weakness in the frame of

light shrouding the Keep in a fruitless task. As the light outside gave way to the genuine darkness of night. As the last glimpses of sun shot through the sky splaying across the open floor of a narrow corridor, a tiny glint sparkled. Saranon held on, dragging it to her holding her breath in excitement and with a small nudge a door way opened. Before she could speak Hailey had rushed forward, gone in an instant with her following close behind. A shear shrill met her ears, through a stifled strain, as the phase settled itself with two new occupants. She could see Hailey up ahead as far as the eye could see, they were the only two people here.

She moved down towards the seal, to be certain it held just as well in this place. Her friend followed with her hand near the hilt of Tellembre in anticipation. The eagerness glinted in the corner of her eyes as she walked on. As she approached the seal in the dismal silence, she held out her hand and touched it, the binding held strong as she sensed it. The look on Hailey's face was clear disappointment, as they searched around finding nothing. She stayed a while managing to convince herself that they had done enough. While feeling as though there was something left undone. As they made their way back, it was far easier to break out of the phase, with a breath of relief as they stood in the real world.

A sharp pain stretched across Saranon's vision as it slammed into her body. Hailey wasted no time making ground to hurl Tellembre in full display. Hailey struck the blade hard up against the might of Braxton's bond-breaker.

The effort gave her a moment to steady herself, at the sight of what had just happened, taking it in with every breath. As she gazed into the background, she saw what she was looking for, as Tasha drew her finger with such smoothness under her chin and pointed. Saranon knew what her old friend wanted her to do and she raised Corsavere drawn in the form of a sword and brought it down. In the last instance Braxton twisted and braced himself. He held his bond-breaker against the steady force.

For a moment they were interlocked as Hailey's screams cut deep through the air, she clung on in a cold grip. Her eyes were cold with the knowledge that the sorcerer would not live. She arched her arm under, in an all mighty swing and the blade hit true underneath as Braxton's body fell to the ground in a still motion. His robes covered the wound as he went. The shock reverberated up her spine as she let the sensation pass over her and let the bond-breaker down. Ryan came rushing to watch the last of the devastating scene, as he covered the body and stared in shock at Saranon. She did not flounder under the strain of his eyes, as no amount of pressure would have prevented the inevitable.

She clung to her bond-breaker as the sparks of heat from the clash of sorcery simmered in the air, the embers fading to the floor. If it was not for Hailey standing between them she would not have been so calm in the failing light of the evening. Ryan glared at her before turning away; it was a hollow defeat which she knew remained unresolved. The energy inside her settled as the immediate danger, now lay in a heap on the floor. She could not help but wonder who else had been involved. She did not expect such a blast of the seal to be done by Braxton alone. The thought weighed heavy on her mood as she retreated to the sanctuary of her small apartment, with Hailey staying close to her side.

A rattle ran across the window making Hailey freeze to the spot, as a familiar voice soaked through the wall. 'Well, are you going to let me in?' Mitch wasted no time summing up what he saw.

Saranon's bond-breaker filled the narrow coffee table in its full sword length. He picked it up admiring Corsavere's blade with a keen eye. He gave no inclination of relinquishing the prize as he looked up at her. 'I haven't seen it close up since you've always hidden it away,' he exclaimed.

Leaning over to take Tellembre as Hailey stood back in a silent response. Her friend handed the bond-breaker back. It appeared small in its dormant form as Mitch eyed the second prize in Saranon's hand. He swapped the bond-breakers over as she placed Corsavere away. Mitch held the bond-breaker for a while. Before asking the question that had been plaguing his mind, 'Which one did you use at Antavagon?'

'Neither, Pennie has one and Clara has the other.'

He smiled as Hailey spoke first, 'You made others?'

'I don't know what Ryan was more concerned about, you or the bond-breakers?' Mitch interjected.

Both sorceresses looked puzzled. 'Why would he be so interested in them?' She asked.

'Because he can't make them,' he replied.

Hailey stared in disbelief as the thought crossed her mind. Ryan was powerful and the inability to make a bond-breaker would not go unnoticed. Saranon was not convinced, but Mitch did have a point, Ryan had been staring at the bond-breaker and not her. She did not feel at all like settling for the night. As Mitch strode with her through the corridors, he had his own bond-breaker which he wore at his side. The dull brown glint and rough edges belied a sturdy blade, she was not so keen to parade hers about.

There was one place she wanted to revisit, a place where she could let her thoughts run free. Mitch had spoken of a memory she had kept silent deep inside. One she still struggled with, as she reached the door grabbing his hand as she went. The place was as she had left it, the eastern tower which had been rebuilt. It felt smooth and cold to the touch as she knelt down in the courtyard remembering Tasha, as she had seen her friend last. She could feel the anger build up as the memory of blood staining the floor welled up inside. Mitch placed a comforting hand on her shoulder. It was not a perfect night as the faint drizzle and grey clouds blocked out the clear moonlight.

Random patches broke through the sky as the wind whistled past enveloping her warm cloak. It did not take long for a call to carry thick across the breezy air with a harmony that rang true. Saranon broke from her silent stare and turned upward to face Ryan across the courtyard. The sorcerer stood tall with a firm determination as he faced her in the cold night air. The only sound came from the external draft wrapping itself around the tower as the two met in silence. Mitch stood close by, in a reassuring stance, not far from her side. The cold wind divided them as Ryan spoke, 'You have no idea what you've done.'

She stood a moment, before answering. She was in no rush as the words left her cold lips, 'Protecting the Keep, which is what you should have done.'

The sorcerer glared at her and was about to say something. As Saranon interrupted, 'The Armythral have allowed their own to harm the Keep far more than Merrick could. There is no reason you can give to justify those actions, none. So do not stand there and tell me otherwise. I have seen the results first hand, with the death of my friend Tasha, whose spirit still walks Tordoren. The seal remains.'

Her chest heaved with the strength of her words as they resonated through the air. She was prepared to fight even if it was not what she wanted. A figure grew out of the shadows not far from where they stood, as Anne slipped away, the hood of her cloak fell as the wind caught the edge of the material. The older sorceress stood between the two facing Ryan as she spoke, 'You knew there would be consequences now let Saranon be.'

Ryan could see he was getting nowhere and with one last hesitation he left into the grey dark night. It took her a moment to recover from the encounter and calm the flow of the fiery sensation inside.

The energy continued burning strong as she turned to

meet Anne's sorrowful eyes gleaming in the darkness. The wind whipped across the surface of the ground. The older sorceress faced her and sighed with a deep and meaningful purpose, before suggesting they go inside. The walls of Indarin hummed with a quiet satisfaction. The lights beamed overhead as she strode onward. Mitch fell in place by her side as her mind ran with a torrent of dark images from the depths of her past. The seal had been broken in the Keep. It did not feel like Saranon had seen the last of the turmoil that had encapsulated Indarin. The mood scowled a crease across her brow, as it darkened her frame of mind.

Her pace quickened with a sharp edge as she headed closer to Theron's quarters, the sorcerer sat resting as she entered. It took a moment for her to realise they had been expected, the thought annoyed her as she gazed at her friend. Mitch found an excuse to leave and she envied his ability to fade into the distance. The skill escaped her the more she tried, though it had not stopped her trying. The Prophet asked, 'Is there something you want to know?'

'No,' she replied.

He appeared astonished at her response before she continued, 'I know where this is going to lead.'

Before Theron had time to answer after his bewildered look, she interjected again, 'I think you're in danger.'

'I know,' he said.

Saranon was not satisfied by such a quick response. For a Prophet Theron had a habit of jumping to conclusions, which frustrated her, as much as it reminded her of herself.

There had been a time when she would have let that be without a response, but the memory of Tasha lay thick upon her mind.

She grumbled to herself when she realised that the Prophet would not budge. She swept out of the room and marched down the hall. In her haste she had left her coat behind and muttered under her breath before turning back. The small oversight was the last thing she needed at the end of a long and arduous day. Without thinking twice she slammed the door backward almost taking it off its hinges. A hard dull thud sounded instead of the deep whack of wood on wood. She swung Corsavere out in an easy grace far too quick as it came within a hairs breadth of Ryan's nose. The blade flashed in front of his horrified look as he stepped backward.

The sorcerer regained his composure and half threw Saranon's coat at her, 'Leave.'

'I think you misunderstood,' she placed her coat back on the chair. 'This is my place.'

Theron who had waited without saying a word spoke up, 'This is her place.'

Ryan looked at her and then at Theron with a cold gaze. He left without uttering a word with the other sorcerers in the room. In the silence that followed the Prophet spoke first, 'Nice blade.'

'I think so,' she said in an inquisitive tone with a question trapped at the end of her tongue.

It was not the first time the Prophet had neglected to mention the current situation as she grumbled to herself in deep thought. 'You realise you will be expected to stay the night,' Theron spoke.

Saranon had no time for mind games, but there had been something going on and she was intent on finding out more. She eyed the Prophet as he proceeded to prepare a spare bed for her, 'You can be inconvenient sometimes.' She commented.

'Really,' Theron answered in an amused tone. 'I thought you wanted to visit?'

The idea had crossed her mind, but the Prophet tended be get on her nerves after a while, as she gave him an annoyed stare in response.

'Is this your way of saying you're scared?' She asked.

Theron returned her annoyed look, as he threw a pillow in her direction. She had more than enough to worry about. Yet wherever she went, somehow she ended back at the same point, with the Prophet at the centre. 'What do you know about Ryan?'

The sorcerer went silent, 'I thought you were not going to ask that.'

Saranon corrected herself, 'I meant you know him, not everything is about what you see.'

Theron looked a little hurt. For all his secrecy he prided himself on his ability and the sorcerer made a point of not wanting to be interrupted by glimpses of the future. Her friend sat and spoke in a reminiscent tone. She listened while checking over her bond-breakers and belongings with small relief. Ryan sounded as much ordinary as any powerful sorcerer could be, in a place like Indarin. Theron gazed into the rays of light beaming through Corsavere, 'Your father carries a blade like that.'

'I thought I said… Oh never mind,' she grumbled.

She only had vague memories of her family and with a common surname she had not had the best of luck finding any leads, even with Pennie's help. She handed over the bond-breaker for Theron to have a closer look. He appeared to want to say more, but instead kept it to himself. Saranon began to wonder if she could keep from clouting him over the head, if he continued to pull irritable faces. He hinted at something then changing his mind. She sat making herself comfortable on the chair opposite. The Prophet handled the elegant bond-breaker.

He stared at her with a quiet gaze, 'What was Odana Temple like?'

'Magnificent,' she exclaimed.

'You do know, Odana never fell,' Theron spoke referring back to the days of the Dreshan Occupation.

It took her a moment to realise what he was saying. If Odana Temple had withstood the invasion, it held an unbroken history of Zyanthia, including the Angeon.

CHAPTER FIFTEEN

Final Hurdle

A tiny thought entered Saranon's mind as she hurried down to the dragon pens. The morning was cool and brisk running goose bumps along her skin. Katholomu was panning his tummy to the first rays of light breaking through and warming the hard surface of the courtyard. She sat close to his warm thick skin as the dragon purred away. His belly rumbled with a low deep sound, reverberating through her hand as she stroked him. She fumbled around until her hand touched the circular talik. Thanks to her friend Jedd she had been able to make a slow and steady start on reading the information it stored. Odana Temple, the great Keep at the centre of the old Zyanthia had transferred portions of what it knew. Now in the grasp of her hands it seemed even more real.

If there was no need to search any farther than what

she had, then in theory the small device held the key to the door that she had been looking for. Saranon closed her eyes in excitement, which she held back. For what she had already read did not make sense and the Keep was not human, the way it saw events would not be the same as she. Katholomu pulled his head around on his long arching neck, rubbing his ear on her back. He poked an eye around staring and pretending not to notice. The dragon flopped sideways curling his tail around in front of his mouth in a sleepy stretch. Unfortunately the more she searched, the less she found, which gave any hint about why there would be two Angeons.

She thumped her hand up against the dragon in irritation and he gave a short grunt of annoyance. At least for now Saranon would have to concede that the world had granted two Angeons. The thought did not rest easy, even though part of her liked the idea of not having to be alone. The sky fast reached the middle of the morning, when a voice stretched across the open air. 'There you are, I thought I'd find you here,' Hailey spoke as she grabbed hold of Saranon's hand.

Her friend showed little fear around the large marmoz dragon as she patted his long nose, Kat moved his head.

They rushed in just before the class started. An air of anxiousness continued to cling around her as the dust settled with Braxton's death. Her friend Hailey had been taking the liberty of helping to fill in the gaps in the short space of time thereafter. Still it did not rest easy on her mind and dragging a friend into an old score linked to her past, was not the most comforting sensation. She had seen the fallout in her past and was not convinced her friend knew the type of consequences involved. She managed a meek smile as Hailey caught her looking her way. For his part Chilcott remained completely focused on the task at hand.

After a brief moment she did the same, either way the quickest way to end the mess would be to finish her lessons. A small spark flicked across her desk as she looked up to Hailey's smiling face. She sighed to herself as the class finished and a familiar tone rang out just as she was a step away from reaching the door. 'Saranon we need to talk,' Chilcott could make the simple sentence send a chill down her spine.

He was like a gentle giant lying dormant and no one had the nerve to annoy him because he had the ability to back up a threat. She tried her best to appear at ease in his presence, but the attempt required some effort which showed on her face.

'Mitchell tells me you dealt with a similar matter in Darkonia,' Chilcott spoke while tapping his pen on the desk.

Saranon was not used to anyone calling the wizard by his full name. She was even more surprised that he had taken the time to speak with Mitch. All she could manage in return was a blank expression. The subject was one that she kept hidden deep within her mind. Chilcott continued, 'If you wave that bond-breaker near me you had better have a good reason.'

'Yes,' she spoke with an exasperated shrug as she stood up.

'There were other ways to deal with Braxton,' he said as he eyed her.

She stopped, placing one hand on the desk. While peering down at the old scar that creased along Chilcott's arm only just poking out of the edge of his sleeve. 'I wish there was but I think you know that,' Saranon spoke as she left.

The conversation had placed her in a rather foul mood as she stormed off without hesitation. The lack of seriousness conveyed to the broken seal brought an old anger from deep inside. The memory of Tasha had haunted her dreams. Chilcott was a sorcerer who could take care of himself. Still she wondered if he knew the depths of the darkness which lay hidden in a foolish desire.

Hailey beckoned her out of her momentary pause with the memory fading, as they headed for the dragon pens. Her friend grasped Levette, her beautiful rozzen dragon, as she made her way onto her shoulders. It was a temporary sweet relief that Saranon allowed herself to be drawn into, as she climbed onto Katholomu and they swept past the old courtyard. Her dragon knocked several garden tools before launching high into the air. She cringed as a few faint shouts followed in the wind. Kat was not one for delicacy although it was more for display to show off his enormous size. She let out an all too familiar sigh as they flew across the sky.

In the distance Colderay and Rasputen flew with pure

elegance. Holding their riders high as Hailey waved to her older brother. Katholomu saw it as a signal to show off and immediately flew close to Rasputen as the dragon growled and snapped at Kat's wings. Saranon just managed to stop Kat from taunting the other dragon again, as they flew within a tight formation. She continued to struggle as Seth shouted out for her to hold on. As she was almost ready to take her dragon down, he settled as though nothing had happened. They glided a moment before coming to rest down in the valley. The damage still showing in creases along the ground, the only remnants left from where Merrick had been.

Darren landed Colderay much closer than Saranon would have liked, as the sorcerers showed no fear from what lay beneath. Hailey stayed near the edge with Saranon who had no desire to be nearer. The memory had been set aside after the discovery of the broken seal which continued to plague her mind. It filled her dreams with a misty darkness. A small section of the ground crumbled under Darren's foot and Hailey jumped where she stood. The sorcerer stumbled before regaining his balance on the uneven earth. 'What will happen when Merrick returns?' Hailey asked.

Her mind was far away, the thought had not been her main concern and the question drew her into a different direction.

'I don't think the Armythral are ready for him,' she spoke with deep honesty.

Her friend responded with a knowing silence. It was the answer Hailey did not want to hear, the unspoken fear that had spread through Indarin. She figured it had been there long before she had arrived, if Chilcott's scar was anything to go by. What seemed like a pile of rubble and dirt held Seth and Darren's attention for a long time. Although the sorcerers refrained from asking questions, their glancing eyes spoke otherwise. Saranon stood near the edge. The dragons were in a world of their own as they exchanged snorts and grunts before appearing silent.

A jarring sound cut through the air. Katholomu sent Colderay shoulder first into the rocky hillside, followed by a horrid screech. She scrambled onto Kat's shoulders climbing over his left wing and holding on as hard as she could. She jolted the dragon sideways with her movement and clung on tight as a shallow scratch mark appeared on his right arm. For all his temper Katholomu was reluctant to lift a finger unless taunted. Colderay nursed a massive bruise down his left side before scampering backward. Her dragon raised his chest in triumph and let out a deep growl of satisfaction. She clung on gripping the mane around his neck.

Seth and Darren wasted no time darting along the rugged ground to help calm the giant dragons as Katholomu gave them both a stern stare. The slitted eyes of the great dragon shone through in a menacing tone. He let out a muffled grumbling that bellowed through the harsh cold wind. Before another word was uttered, Hailey had taken Levette into the air and away from the disgruntled male dragons. Darren showed great ease in calming Colderay down. In an all too familiar manner which suggested this had happened before. Katholomu sat letting the chilly air run through his thick coat cooling his sweaty skin.

Saranon dreaded the thought of having to wash him again. She wondered if it would have been simpler to have a female dragon that had an aversion to rolling in the dirt. Just as the idea entered her mind, Kat wiped his sweaty shoulders along the ground. He gave little time for her to change sides. She let out a small grumble which went completely unnoticed. As the great smelly dragon now covered in patches of dirt launched into the air and headed toward the dragon pens of Indarin. Katholomu stopped in the courtyard, flopped out his legs, and bent his head over. He drifted straight to sleep as she tried to nudge him awake. She did not want to leave him all dirty and smelly, but the dragon had relaxed giving all his weight to stay in place.

A small crowd of wizards watched, hovering around the doorway of the pens. Saranon gave in as she left the smelly snoring heap of a sleeping dragon to clean up. Mitch stood near her as she rinsed her hands, 'You do realise you're going to have to clean that in the morning.'

She gave him an annoyed stare, 'Yes, why, are you volunteering?'

He did not look impressed, 'It's your dragon. How are you going?' He asked.

The question seemed odd after everything that had happened. 'Normisia is looking really good right now,' she replied.

He smiled, 'I wouldn't bet on that.'

Mitch had a way of saying a great deal with few words, the eagerness to return to his home land shone in his eyes. It was the only sign he displayed as he left her alone. The warmth of the large dining room shone bright, it was nowhere near the size of the great hall. Yet, what it lacked in grandeur, it made up for with a welcoming atmosphere and a view that spanned out over the resting dragons. The last rays of the fading light melted with the glowing lights to create a vibrant glow as Saranon ate after a long day.

She waded through the flowing corridors to find herself at the front door of her apartment. As she opened the door Todd opened it from the other side. He shuffled her into the room, 'Have you seen Hailey?'

'Not since this afternoon,' she replied.

'She left a strange message with Seth and he hasn't been able to find her.'

Saranon woke from her tiredness with a start as she realised Hailey could have been missing for hours, 'I have to go.'

The thought crept in and once it was there she was unable to shake it. Hailey would be ideal for the one thing that the Armythral had allowed to go too far. She ran then with a mighty leap transformed as she fell through the floor of the Keep, dropping several levels as she went. She slowed to a halt just missing an ockren, as she fell into the darkness underneath the great Keep. The course hairs of the creature rippled across her skin in an unnatural motion. As she peered around the seal was still intact, but the eyes in the ockren spoke of unease. The Angeon searched, finding almost no sign running her fingers over the wall and then a faint murmur tingled through to her spine. A hole had been blasted through the wall hidden by layers of sorcery.

She traced her way back to the sealed door. The one sealed by the Angeon which she could pass through, just as she took the first step, a weight tugged at her jacket. Saranon turned to see the ockren pulling her back and pointing its head in another direction. A part of her knew the ockren was right, whoever was in there would know that she could walk through the sealed door. She drew Corsavere, taking it from its sheath, as she closed her eyes, drawn in the depth of the memories that lay just beneath the surface. In full flight she swung herself through the wall, as it faded around her with ease. The bond-breaker rose without hesitation, as she drew Tellembre from its hiding place.

Two sorcerers fell, hitting the floor in unison, as the sparks began to unravel. An all too familiar scream cut through the air followed by the next. The Angeon moved on, without as much as a glance toward Hailey screaming at the sight of her own blood. As the last sorcerer hit the ground, the Keep moved like a living being pulling the remains through the floor. No sign was left except Hailey and the Angeon. Saranon hid her bond-breakers before kneeling down to embrace her friend. She allowed her sorcery to weave its way through. Healing both Hailey and the Keep and she wiped away the last signs of blood from her friend's hands.

In the calmness that followed, a sound crept in from

outside. She stayed silent as voices raised shouting through the still air. To her surprise the Keep refused to let anyone in as Hailey gathered her composure her face belied the fear in her eyes. A shattering motion broke through the wall. The sorcery from outside found its mark in the damaged wall breaking through the Keeps defences. Indarin howled in anguished pain at the intrusion. Its voice no longer silent, as Chilcott came face to face with Hailey and Saranon. The fierce look in his eyes said he was in no mood to be messed with, as he examined the room and a few small remnants left behind.

Before the sorcerer had time to say anything Seth managed to break through with desperation. As he hugged Hailey in his arms and she began to cry. Darren moved a little slower behind him gazing over the sight and taking every care to help Hailey as she left with Seth. A small movement caught Saranon's eye along near the altar. The Keep was beginning to retaliate against the intrusion. 'Go, go now!' She shouted to Chilcott and Darren, 'Just go!'

The older sorcerer took a moment to react, as Saranon looked him in the eye, 'It is not your time to die.'

He was about to say something as she cut him off, 'I will see you again.'

Just as the two sorcerers left, the surge of energy from the Keep reacted to the intrusion like a virus spread around the altar. It hesitated then spread through the whole room. Then it reached the Angeon and she hoped that she was right as she held her breath. The energy spread through her joining her with the Keep, but then she had met the Keep before. In the exchange of the raw energy surging between her and the Keep, the pulse cut through. It disintegrated the last remnants of the ill-fated attempt to take over the Keep.

Indarin's anger spilled forward as it sealed the room anew. The Keep hurled the Angeon out before the last part of the ceiling hardened with a new seal. The thrust catapulted her back to just outside her apartment. The Angeon slipped away and a familiar voice carried across the corridor. It was then that she remembered Chilcott had an apartment close by, as the sorcerer's firm, still voice cut through the air. Saranon turned around to see the early rays of the morning sun shining through the window. 'I said are you coming to class?' The sorcerer repeated.

She took a moment to realise her perception of time had been distorted. As she followed Chilcott spoke in a straight tone, 'We missed you in class yesterday.'

'What?' She gasped as her teacher smiled.

She ran to catch up as the sorcerer strode on and stopped as she noticed Hailey sitting at her desk. As she sat down her friend leaned over and whispered, 'You've been gone three days.'

Saranon grumbled at the thought, it was not what she had expected. The time lag made sense as Indarin reeled at a repeat performance. The Keep had showed little sign of its deep seated anger at the betrayal of a hand full of Armythral. The intense ferocity of its determination belied its mood. Three days lost meant Indarin had made the seal well and it would only take a short time before reality sank in and someone noticed.

Part of her could not wait for the class to finish, as she rolled the pen over in her fingers. The agitation showed plain on her face, as Hailey smiled in recognition. On another occasion her friend would have laughed. Yet the jovial mood had slipped away from her eyes replaced with a quiet sadness. A rush of stomping came from behind the door as Ryan slammed it open, staring straight at her. 'You!' He shouted.

An immediate reply sprang into Saranon's mind. She remained tight lipped at the sight of the exasperated sorcerer. Before he had a chance to step much closer Chilcott grabbed his arm from behind and yanked him back.

Ryan swung at his opponent as the class fell away, trying to avoid the fight, Chilcott managed to pin the sorcerer down. Hailey made for the door after the other students and motioned for Saranon to follow. As Chilcott shouted for her to stay she shot him an irritated glare. Before the sorcerer could say anything she spoke, 'You seem to be doing that a lot lately.'

He looked up as the two men broke up their arguing, neither one appearing a winner, 'Yes.'

Ryan steadied himself as he realised he had chosen the wrong time and place to take out his frustrations.

It was not the ideal meeting place but she knew that with Chilcott there, it would be safe. The underlying tone of Ryan's voice cut through the air, 'You planned to seal off the altar.'

'Indarin planned to seal it off, are you going to go after her?' Saranon added after a moment's silence, 'I would have done the same.'

She was about to say more, as a scream resonated behind the closed door. The sound curled down her spine as she recognised who it had originated from. Chilcott allowed her to pass unheeded, as the sight caught her off guard.

Sandra, a solitary figure, held Hailey close to her blade. The bond-breaker was raised within a finger's width of her pale, white skin. The Angeon reached up inside and the dagger flew, like metal attracted to a strong magnet, across the void. Sandra stood in shock, before she scrambled out of sight and her friend fell in an exhausted heap, before Seth ran to pick her up. Saranon held out her free hand to Ryan, 'Come with me.'

To her surprise the sorcerer did not hesitate as they slipped out of phase with the real world. Out in the courtyard a lone figure wrapped in silken white stood in silence. Tasha's beautiful warm hair flowing around her face, the figure did not move. 'This is the result of the Arthrose, it will wound your Keep more than my mirror image can,' Saranon continued.

She held up her hand reaching out to Tasha's hand as her old friend did the same. They clasped hands as Saranon added, 'This is not what the Arthrose had planned.'

As she spoke the words, Tasha combined her energy with the Angeon. The strength of the meld rippled out as the Keep responded in kind and they returned leaving

Tasha behind. The energy still pierced the air and the sound of Indarin rang through the air. Saranon spoke, 'This path is not for you.'

She relinquished the Angeon and the Keep settled, as its hum blurred into the background. Ryan stood quiet, before Chilcott swept him to the side with a friendly seamless motion of his arm. He left her in a mist full of cloudy dreams, merging into the edges. It was not the response she had been looking for. Yet, at least the sorcerer had taken it in, a small consolation as she trudged to the small apartment. The door opened as her hand reached out and Seth's face appeared, with a weary look, similar to her own. His presence gave her a start, even though she half expected to see the sorcerer. Saranon glanced around for her friend, who had gone to sleep. Darren's eyes followed her around the room, as she shut the door. He was sitting without saying a word, but it did not stop the feeling that there was something he wanted to say.

As she walked past Seth pulled out a chair for her to sit down, 'We need to talk,' he spoke as he sat nearby. 'I am hearing two trains of thought, one says that we lost our best chance to protect Indarin and the other says we almost lost the Keep. In three days the Keep has been sealed far stronger than any of our best and the only form of sorcery intertwined with the Keep is yours.'

Saranon knew it was not the outcome she had hoped for, as it left little hidden from view, even though it meant Indarin had been healed. She would have preferred the cover of secrecy which now seemed to be seeping away with every moment.

A hand reached across near her shoulder. As she looked up to see Hailey who had woken with the noise, 'Why are you persecuting my friend?' She stared at her brother.

Before Seth spoke she did, 'I lost an old friend the same way, the path led to ruin and it would have been no different for Indarin.'

She could sense Hailey flinch at her words, as her face paled and she left with Seth following shortly after her. Darren asked, 'What happened?'

'Antavagon wanted revenge and I was only too willing to give it. It wounded the Keep and I wounded the Arthrose.'

The sorcerer sat in thought, before he spoke; 'Now the stakes are higher.'

Saranon knew what he meant with the other Angeon so close, it was not what she had expected to find in Serenphel. The room grew silent when Seth re-entered with a sorrowful stare, hidden deep within his eyes as he sat with his head bowed. 'When I first saw you I did not think you were able to kill a sorcerer,' he spoke to her.

'I saw my world fall apart, I do not want to see it happen again,' she replied.

'What are you going to do when Merrick comes?'

She had hoped that day would not come before she left, even though the time was fast approaching, it did not go fast enough.

CHAPTER SIXTEEN

Time to stand

The morning sun broke through the narrow slit between the curtains. Marking a golden crease across the sheets as Saranon tried to sleep in the early dawn. It flittered along her fingers as she raised her hand before a shadow faded past. She startled as Mitch's face became clearer into view. He was a solid figure who managed to achieve an awful silence when creeping into places. She remained reluctant to leave the cosy warmth of the blankets wrapped around her as she stared in annoyance. 'Ryan wants to see you,' he spoke.

She was in no mood to face him, but if she managed to find an excuse to avoid him, it would only prolong the agony.

Mitch ducked his way out of the room to wait in her tiny little apartment which appeared rather crowded.

She peered around the corner before shutting the door. She scrambled together a few things, almost forgetting Tellembre. It sat on the table in a dull frame, its pearl white finish gleaming just below the hilt. He was well dressed in comparison as she eyed him, thinking of how shabby she looked. It was not the start to the day she had been expecting and being outdone by a wizard in even simple matters brought a crease to her brow. He nudged her out into the corridor when she did not move fast enough, 'Have you forgotten?'

'What?' She snapped back.

He gave her a wry smile as he fell in step beside her, 'Your exams.'

'Don't be silly that's a week away,' she responded.

'You lost a few days remember.'

'Oh…' The thought did not sit well in her mind even though she had studied.

It was not the first time she had lost track of time and he revelled in the opportunity to remind her. Even though she had studied, the idea rattled in her head as it signified the passing of time and the reality of returning home. The Armythral were engrossed in the second Angeon albeit one not to be over looked. She had been far more concerned about the reception waiting for her in Normisia.

For all Mitch's steadfast commitment, the initial welcome had not been warm. Hence staying there was bound to be problematic. The thought stuck, shading her mood on what by any account should have been a tremendous moment. The excitement bubbled in the air from hundreds of sources. The next generation of sorcerers prepared themselves in anxious anticipation. Saranon groaned as all the activity seemed to slide off her when all she could think about was Normisia. She turned to Mitch, 'I suppose you will be happy to be home?'

He showed no expression as he moved along the corridor, 'We have a long way to go yet.'

He gave a short bow as he turned leaving her at the door. The small gesture was a little out of place, amid all the frenzied excitement. She breathed a heavy sigh as she knew it was now all down to her, all this way for a few tests and it would be over along with her time in Serenphel. She reached up and touched the door. It opened and she took a deep breath and entered the room. The air was dark and chilly, she knew it to be an illusion but the steady heartbeat pumping through her chest said otherwise. The energy seeping through the walls, electrified the corners of the room, intensifying as she moved forward. It was a simple, yet elegant test 'just reach the other end of the room'.

Hailey's words still clung in her head, an idea she had not yet fathomed. She had fobbed it off while trying to hide the seriousness of the matter. The first barrier passed through her with only a flitter. As she moved forward she held out her hands for the next, making her stomach queasy, as she pushed through. The fine array of the flows of energy glinted off her hair in a faint enigmatic glow. The third and fourth barrier held a little stronger than the last, still they did not bother her any more than the second. Saranon stood before the fifth barrier and reached forward. It felt sharp to the touch as a prickling sensation ran through her hand, but she was not swayed.

She did not come here to fail and with a mighty effort she forced her way through. The barrier stung with precision as she passed through. The sweat clung to her skin as she remembered to breathe and opened her eyes in preparation for the next one. The touch of the sixth felt like ice, as it sent sharp cold shivers in a needle like fashion down the length of her spine, but she was not deterred. Saranon was no stranger to the feeling of pain and she pressed on as the icy barrier pressed against her heart and then let her pass. The seventh barrier showed no mercy, as the razor sharp edge stung to the bone. Clinging, before letting go, as the searing sensation flashed through her mind.

She stood at the far end of the room with her eyes closed from the memory of pain, a voice shouted through an open door at the end. 'You know you don't have to go through them all,' Chilcott stood in front of her holding out his hand.

She took a moment to steady herself before following the corridor, it felt like a breath of fresh air. She inhaled its welcoming warmth as it wrapped around her. The intensity of the moment passed as she peered at her lecturer in stone cold annoyance and grumbled as she left. Saranon only just made it around the bend as Hailey leaped out, almost knocking both of them to the ground. 'So how did you go?' Her voice was filled with excitement.

'I think I over did it,' she spoke.

Hailey broke into gales of laughter, 'We were

wondering if there would be anything left of the test after you went through.'

She was not sure how to respond as Hailey moved her along, 'Come on.'

She felt like saying something but the words appeared all jumbled inside her head, as she ran to catch up. As she ran an image grew out the window to her left, it struck out behind the clouds, then as she peered again it was gone. The image played in her mind as though it had been pulled from her imagination. Her friend would have to wait as she turned off toward Theron.

The Prophet had been silent since Hailey's rescue, far too quiet for her liking as she sensed him avoiding her. The sorcerer had sat his test early, not that it mattered with the amount of training he had been given. She held her hand up to knock as a voice spoke from the other side, 'Come in.' Theron spoke.

It was not the sort of reception she had expected as Saranon entered the room to see the sorcerer gazing away. 'I think I just had a vision,' she spoke.

'What?' The sorcerer asked.

'I was looking out the window to the north and I saw a large grey blob heading this way.'

As soon as the words had left her mouth she realised how silly it sounded, but the Prophet was not laughing. Theron turned toward her his face, pale and drawn in the light, 'I think you know what it means.'

'No, but I can improvise,' Saranon did not like riddles at the best of times and his response annoyed her even more as she stood to look at him.

'If we're in danger you're supposed to say something,' she retorted.

'Are we?' He asked.

'You're not helpful,' she said as she walked away stopping mid-stride at the door.

'Oh, when are you going to tell Hailey?' She asked.

'Tell her what?' Theron hesitated.

'That you like her,' she replied.

The surprise spreading across Theron's face said it all, as Saranon smiled with glee. Her friend may be a Prophet, but he was still hopeless with girls. There was one name that escaped a mention, the other Angeon. The thought filled her with a twisted dread even though there had been no sign of him. For the moment at least he had stayed away, she felt so close, yet so far, from returning home.

It remained on the edge of Prophet's lips as he refrained from talking, when his eyes portrayed his thoughts. After their last encounter she was not looking forward to dealing with a sorcerer whose past she did not understand. The Armythral had been careful when discussing the other Angeon. The gaps in their conversations spoke more than their words. 'If you are expecting Merrick, I have a right to know, he is my kin,' Saranon exclaimed.

'You have a strange way of referring to the other Angeon; he does not share your sentiments.'

She sat down staring at him with open arms, 'I met his sister, what makes you so certain?'

'You will fight,' Theron was not used to being

questioned.

'I have fought with my best friend, is that the only thing you see?' She enquired watching him.

The Prophet hung his head saying nothing, as though in shame before continuing, 'He wants you dead.'

'Who doesn't?' She asked.

'No one here…' The sorcerer began.

'Look around you, I am not what people expect and I am not to be tamed,' as she spoke the words, Theron's legs gave way as he dropped to the floor.

She knelt and held the Prophet as his eyes went cloudy the great swirls revealing the essence of time. The whole event did not last long as he stared at her and whispered, 'You know.'

It was not the answer Saranon had been looking for as she grumbled underneath her breath and left.

Still she was not about to argue with the Prophet she had not asked much of him. Yet if Merrick did return Indarin was at greater risk with her presence. Two Angeons in the same place made for a difficult task for any Keep, no matter how great. With any luck Merrick would not appear, even if the image suggested otherwise. For now she had other things to focus on, as Mitch greeted her near the dragon pens. 'If you are looking for Katholomu, he's been gone since the morning,' he said.

He had an irritating habit of reading her immediate thoughts. 'Besides I thought you would be getting an early night ready for tomorrow?' He continued.

'I made it through today,' she exclaimed.

'Don't be too confident,' he spoke as if staring would somehow make her go and rest.

Mitch could be annoying at times as she relented and let him be, as she made her way up to her apartment. A barrage of shouting hit her like a wave, as she opened the door. Seth stopped as she entered the room. 'Did you know about this?' He asked in a hoarse voice.

Saranon looked at Hailey's sullen face. She wondered if it had anything to do with her conversation with Theron, before she could respond Seth answered for her. 'A storm is coming and the only one the Prophet told is my sister.'

She was relieved after having misplaced her assumption. 'It's about time he had a girlfriend,' she remarked.

Hailey's cheeks went bright red. 'That still does not excuse what happened,' Seth spoke.

'No, and I'm sure you would know what it's like to bear a great burden upon your shoulders,' Saranon said with a hint of sarcasm.

'The Prophet is not there to tell all, when there are some things better left unsaid. If I have to make it clear Merrick is mine to deal with,' she stared up close at Seth who was much taller. 'Not one of you is to get involved understood,' she spoke with a firm grace.

Seth hesitated a moment before responding, 'If that is your will, but let me know if you change your mind.'

'Do you really think you can defeat Merrick? He has more experience than you,' Darren raised the question that Seth did not ask.

Saranon breathed a heavy sigh before she responded,

'Is that what bothers you? You see a girl, when I have spent many years fighting for my life, I am as ready as I will ever be. Now I think you owe Hailey an apology.'

Seth's stubborn eyes did not sway under her glare at the feeling of being left out. He frowned as he shook his head. The inability to help played on his face. 'Take care,' he said as he leaned over and gave her a short embrace hugging her in both arms.

The warm gesture caught her off guard; she was not quite sure how to react as he laughed. Hailey gave her a small smile of approval as her face looked more relaxed.

'I'm sorry,' Seth said with a genuine vindication to his sister.

'Now that's resolved, Mitch expects me to get some sleep,' she spoke with relief.

'Merrick is going to come for you,' Hailey said with an urgent tone.

'Yes, I know.'

Saranon would have preferred to be gone by the time Merrick arrived, she started packing the last of her belongings. Yet the hope of avoiding the other Angeon was starting to dissolve before her eyes, as the light dimmed outside. She held Corsavere in her hand. The memory of Odana Temple stayed with her as she touched the smooth edge before hiding it away.

The temple plagued her dreams even as far as Serenphel with the image of the central core greater than any she had seen since. The blade felt cool underneath the soft caress of her fingers, a reminder of her stay. The ancient Keep of the Angeon of old from a country long since gone and only remnants remained. At least for now Odana would have to wait with her time at Indarin drawing near. The place was not as she had imagined, but she had persevered for her own sake. The place grew quiet as she peered at her talik, fondling it in her hands. It had been a while since she had heard from Pennie. Her friend limited their lines of communication while she was in Serenphel.

A quiet knock sounded on the door as it opened to reveal Mitch, 'I think you should come with me.'

'What happened to an early night?' She shouted as she caught up to him.

'Things have changed,' he spoke as he opened a door in the exam area. 'You will be doing the test early.'

For a moment her mouth hung open in clumsy astonishment, it was not what she had been expecting, as Mitch disappeared. Her long drawn out sigh filtered through the air, as she held out her hand and stepped inside. The darkness engulfed her, as she plunged and slipped into nothing when the floor gave way.

The hard surface vanished into the walls as if it did not exist. For a moment the fear rose up into her dry throat, with her voice caught in mid-stream. The ice-cold water wrapped around Saranon as she sank deep below a vanishing surface. The impact came down hard upon her body, chilling her heart and crushing the air out of her lungs. The sensation spread like a sharp pain, as her toes began to numb in the darkness, she tried to reach up and hit a solid surface with her fist. The panic rose inside her, followed as she hunted for a sign of a way out. Just then something rose from beneath her, gripping her leg and pulling her down.

She tried to concentrate so she could breathe underwater. Yet her technique was still clumsy and the creature pulled her down too fast. She tried to start again, but the cold filtered through to the edges of her mind as she tried to stay warm. With an almost angry reluctance she gave in, transforming into a mermaid. The grip of the creature below slipped as it slid into the depths and she grumbled at having to move forward in another form. As she rushed through the depths of the tunnel, her lungs pumped the oxygen through her body. Her mind returned to a calmer state even though she was still trapped in the swirling dark depths. She had been unwilling to transform and the mere fact that she had been forced to use it, placed her in a murky state of mind.

She managed to find a small pocket of air, before plunging down in the depths of the unseen. A faint light glowed out of the corner of her eye, as she rushed towards the first target with a cranky determination. The sooner she was away from here and on a dry hard surface in the warm open air, the better. The icy darkness played host to an obscure obstacle course, which only blackened her mood the further she went. One of the large grey creatures, a gentle giant of the murky depths with incredible strength, brushed too close. As Saranon bounced off the quadmar's fin like arm, it turned staring at her through piercing eyes showing no emotion. The look was cold grey, as they locked eyes for an instant, then it moved out of reach.

It made her mermaid form pale into insignificance as she quickened her pace. A faint glow lit up from below and she groaned knowing that it would mean travelling deeper. She edged her way between two of the creatures as they swam by angling down to pick up the target. As her hand reached down, she felt something pass near her side. She swallowed as she turned to see a quadmar blocking her path, its great tail masking the way out. She froze, still not making a sound, as the shock of her predicament tingled through her spine. The thoughts racing through her head, as she tried to distract the graceful beast without bringing it to temper.

She flicked its fin and the quadmar moved a little sideways, yet it was not enough. She waited, trying to gather her thoughts, then with one quick move the great creature slid clear. The exit was in sight and she wasted no time darting through as the quadmar's tail fin swished higher. The impact catapulted Saranon forward and upward before her head broke the surface of the underground cave. She leaped out, while transforming back into her real self and her soaking wet clothes. She edged her way a short distance from the murky, marble edge. Breathing out her exhaustion as her excitement floundered. She preferred to admire quadmar from a distance and on dry land, rather than a step away.

As if in mocking the creature closest moved and made her heart miss a beat as she held her breath, before letting it escape. She smiled in a quiet relief with no desire to move and dried her clothes with the warmth of her energy. It did not take long for the warmth to wipe away the ice cold memory of the dark pool that lay beside her. As she turned peering down with satisfaction at the thin cylinder targets clumped on the ground. She stood up with a slow stagger catching her breath as she peered at the water's edge. The time below had passed with great reluctance, making just a few hours feel like a whole day had passed in her absence.

Saranon looked around her. The place remained silent as she strode away from the murky pool. Her hand took hold of Tellembre at her side, as she peered around the empty rooms, when the area plunged into an eerie silence. The only sounds emanating from the water and echoing along the cavernous walls behind her. The corridor felt like a hollow tomb, as the walls gave away nothing in return to the soft touch of her fingertips. As a stranger, the Keep had spoken little with a wave of small gestures, but not even that sprang to life along the stale surface. It was not the greeting she had expected as she searched around, not even the Keep gave an answer to her inquisitive mind.

The quadmar stared back from a watery grave as she contemplated going back the way she came, but the water was not appealing. A quick flitter of movement rippling along the liquid surface only confirmed her thoughts. Saranon used her energy to call out but no reply came as it struck out to meet nothing in the dim light. Off in the distance of the darkness a small faint tone ignited a familiar spark inside. As something deep within recognised the source and her energy grew flaring to the surface. Still no other sign came and she wondered if it had been a mistake, as she returned to the sound of the dark pool of water.

The quadmar making tiny ripples, her only company in the vacuum of silence echoing throughout the Keep. The strange sensation sent goose bumps along her arms as she looked upward hoping for a response in the void. A voice cut through the air with a harsh undertone. 'In our mind we fear what we most dread, but you are something else, it would have been better if you had not been created at all.'

Merrick's soft tone filtered through every direction.

His voice touched her ears, as though he were standing right beside her. Saranon's senses had gone numb as she stood not far from the icy water, not knowing which direction to take, as the voice gave no sign.

A cold rush of air swept past from above. She looked up to the open door, when it creaked, echoing through the underground chambers of the Keep. The air wavered around her as the light from Indarin shone down the walls. For once the quadmar remained silent in the dark pool. As Saranon peered into the murky depths a hurtling force of energy shattered the moment in an instant. She dived for cover as it just missed. With the heat narrowing down on her back, radiating with ferocious intensity from the source. The impact hit hard as she clung on to solid ground. She tried hard not to breathe in the fractured shards of energy catapulting off the edges of the blast.

In the frame of the vacuum that followed, she lashed out from an awkward position. She fell back near the water's edge with the blast from her own energy. 'Surely you can do better than that,' Merrick's words rung in her ears with a mocking grace.

An array of light broke the surface, glittering in a needle like fashion along the walls of the building. Growing in magnitude as it ripped through. She dove to the side only just missing the second blast, as it melted through the wall behind her, leaving a horrid mark. She swallowed, as the sweat poured off her skin and she managed to send a resonating blast back through the open tunnel. The sound speared out in a spiral, caressing the walls and leaving charred marks as it split the air.

It took a great deal of strength and she was losing ground. Saranon bent down to the icy pool and as the next blast thundered through, she dived. The icy depths greeted her with its chilling tone, as she transformed for the second time in the same day and the thought made her cringe. A voice rang out loud and clear sending a chill, filled with darkness, from above. 'You were not meant for this world!'

Merrick's words resonated even through the water as she darted away. She was running out of time, but she needed to find a more suitable location to take on the other Angeon.

CHAPTER SEVENTEEN

When the end turns anew

Saranon clambered into a quiet place to transform back before climbing up and away from the dark pool. The walls of the Keep, still gave no sign of what had taken place. Indarin felt like an icy tomb with no sounds of life emanating through its corridors. It chilled her to the spine, as the silence followed, cutting through her senses with a sharpened edge. In the end, the message was still the same. A dull numbness returning nothing, not even a peep as she ran through the emptiness. She searched for a glimmer or a hint of just a glimpse, to guide her, as she sank in the realisation that she was alone.

If the other Angeon had succeeded in one thing, it was finding her. Then she had been here before with Antavagon in her past, waiting just below the surface. The images hidden under all the layers, that had been placed with care, as Saranon had merged out into the world. The Keep waiting deep in Darkonia, with the hope that one day she would return and if not Antavagon had exacted his toll in a fearsome rage. As he let the Angeon loose on the world in a defiant form of retaliation, before returning to a quiet state, away from prying eyes. As the window of her past played in her mind in a rhetorical form, she listened for any sign of Indarin, as she moved further in toward the heart of the Keep.

If the other Angeon was looking for someone easy to prey on, he had sent her back to where her journey began. She saw the images flooding back, the memories that told her the Keep was there, waiting for her. No matter how much she wanted to pretend. Underneath the surface, lay a predator forged from the coldness, similar to that of the other Angeon. Merrick had control of the Keep but the image he had created was too smooth. It slid into the background with a perfection the Keep did not possess. A shadow of the character held within the structure of the building, belying its natural being.

As she touched the surface running her fingers along the wall, the old memory prickled up her spine. Antavagon the prison in her homeland, had held years of anger waiting to be released. In comparison Indarin was so much larger and so much more, even for an Angeon holding such a Keep, would be short lived. An echo of a whisper ran down the windows shattering the peace, with a hollow sound resounding at the source and she knew what had to be done. As the soldier inside took over, she raised Tellembre in her hand. The bond-breaker sang a sweet faint song filling her head through the empty madness. In a slow subtle form, the fierce brutal flow of the Angeon ran seeping in and saturated her skin through every edge of her being.

The pale blade of the bond-breaker shone with the impact of the first silhouette of morning. Breaking over the horizon and etching its way along the land. The immature light revealed an intense calm in the centre, void of its ferocity in the absence of the Keep's ability to fight. Her steps penetrated the awkward silence spilling down the halls in every direction. For a moment Saranon fooled herself into thinking she was alone, when she was far from it. The false image mattered not as she made her way knowing the path well. Her blade sang with a metallic chime the only other sound to cut the air.

She headed down, turning her back on the sun's golden rays of light, that broke through the windows giving a false glimmer of hope. When the real light lie deep within and now Saranon had to fight, as she broke the plain cold seal, from the old gateway to below the Keep. The path to the old source of power where others feared to follow in the footsteps of the great, and now it would know the Angeon. As she strode in the darkness of the mighty Keep, it laid dormant, she had one mission to make Indarin speak. She pummelled through the underground passages. Each time she hurtled herself forward at the next barrier.

The iron grace of Tellembre breaking deeper with every step as Saranon lashed out with a cold embrace of the energy inside. This time she would not sit side by side within the central core, this time she would give it a voice. The thought held her in a clumsy trance as she lashed out with hard intent. Small sounds scratched the surface of her attention as she turned around and held so tight onto the Angeon within. As she peered around, she stared straight into the eyes of Purton lying curled up and in pain on the floor. It was not what she had hoped to see and it made her hesitate as she took the image in. The sorcerer gave her a rough smile through his pain, as he lay half stretched out near the wall.

The memory of him stayed with her, as she moved on with a purpose as the picture of his face played in her mind. There was only one way out and that path lead down as she drew on her energy intensifying its strength along the way. The power of the Angeon reeled within writhing in wait as the sensation of the central core became stronger. The two sources whispering to each other from afar as the barriers fell away. The distance shortening as she managed to reach the place near where she and Theron had melded with the Keep. It appeared cold and grey almost lifeless to the touch. The stale air wept with the stains of moisture dripping down along the surface of the walls.

Saranon reached down with a power untold, ripping the floor beneath her as it melted and cracked under the pressure of such force. The seconds passed like hours before a mighty roar filled the vacuum. The stallic energy poured out with a trembling thunderous blast, flooding all the way from the core. The energy enveloped her soul mingling with her energy, before it took her whole, into the deep. The blast that followed was enough to shatter a million minds. It took hold exploding through the Keep like a fireball raging through its connections. The intensity took Indarin by surprise as it succumbed to the overload. The raw energy pulsated throughout, wrapping around the edge of the Keep, with a flood of renewed strength.

The clasps holding the Keep to silence melted away as the energy flooded through at a mighty speed. Crackling along the conduits and saturating the building. An intensity engulfed Indarin, a great power combining with the core. As it climbed, it let out an unwavering source, giving the Keep new life. In the darkness of the depths, Saranon held on for all she was worth and more, as she pushed herself to the limit and then further. She grabbed hold of every essence that made the central core move, driving it harder and faster, washing away the pain of the Keep as she went. In the only reality which was hers, as she held on in the darkness.

Shining bright beneath her like a sun in a black sky. The charge spurred onward and upward strengthening Indarin as it surged through. A glimmer came from the distance, a hazy shimmer she recognised, the other Angeon. In the darkness, through the pain, she cried tears for everything she had been through, she was not alone. Yet the world had condemned her to be that way and she knew it would have to be. Whichever way, there was one thing she held certain for all she was worth, Merrick could not escape, not this time. A great surge from beneath inside the central core fired up skyward taking the Angeon along with it and out into the blood red sky.

The flames mingled with the early rays of a sunset filled with the rage of the Keep. It gave the sun a hot orange glow burning its way across the land. A mark deepened on the horizon, a blemish on an otherwise golden image. Penetrating the auburn colours of the setting sun in a cold embrace as it shifted across the sky. Saranon regained her composure long enough to stand facing the other Angeon from afar. If not now, then time would not present it again as she held on to her source. She drew down upon the Keep's energy and steadied herself as the energy raged within waiting to be let out.

A numb hollow sensation wrapped around her as she grasped out searing through the pain. The blast of her sorcery impacted with a deadening blow. Catapulting across in a great wide arc as it melded with a force just as strong, striking out, slicing hard as it cut through the air. The pressure crackled sending out sparks across the sky. It hit the ground with a deep roaring anger, thudding into the surface of Tordoren. She held on in the intensity as the energy ignited into a hurtling torrent, as it pounded with shear force, creating a cataclysm across the open sky as Saranon held her ground. Standing with all the strength she could gather from within and hoping that what she had done would be enough.

The great roar from the Keep below, filled her ears as it held on gathering speed. The charge flowed out in an ever widening circle filtering through the air as it reached her, holding her up strong. With Indarin fierce as ever she aimed all she could. Concentrating on Merrick as the fragments from their energy sparked across the sky. Her hands throbbed with the impact of the force as she crept closer in a steady stance moving forward. It was not the way she had wanted it to go, as the other Angeon held his ground. It would have been better not to take the sorcerer on, but the choices had already slipped away. This time it was not so easy to leave and the thought of losing her friends compelled her to go on.

She had held her ground, before the other Angeon and the pain was no stranger as it sank in. The only time Saranon had known the full extent of her power. As she faced a bleakness which overcame her, when the ground she had gained, diminished. The arc bowed off centre as the two sources of energy missed. Merrick's energy hit the Keep with a thundering impact, rocking the ground and hurtling her to the side. The momentary shock ran through her as she peered upward. She moved without hesitation steadying herself on the uneven muddy surface.

The glimmer of hope faded into the deafening roar heading her way. The energy struck through the vivid sky lighting the way with a deadening brightness. Consuming the background noise in its wake as the world grew silent. The pressure hit her on impact as it shattered through the air. Blasting its way around, shrieking past her ears, as the time drew near and Saranon knew she had to choose. The anguish rattled through her mind as the pounding force stemmed up from the depths. A blinding premonition from a time long since buried in the grave. The flawless energy flowed from her deep into the ground as it hurled outward crashing through the earth. Her energy locked around the other Angeon in a cut throat embrace bringing the sorcerer ever closer.

A harsh cold edge ran across the torrid sky as the air filled with a blinding rage colouring deep into the cuts carving up the ground. A harrowing howling stifled in an intermittent sound as it broke through the hurtling wind. It took every moment to strike out against a merciless hold grappling through the rubble. The intertwining of the forms of energy melding as she held out, as Merrick struggled at every turn. The ground of Tordoren rumbled as she dragged the other Angeon closer. The earth before her crumbled, spreading out, as it went in a steady cascade, plummeting into the waiting dark as she used her strength to stay in place. As the widening crevasse travelled toward her, creeping ever further along the open field.

The other Angeon lashed out as he stood near the other side of the crevasse. The blow caught its mark as Saranon faltered on the edge of the pummelling chaos beckoning for her to fall. Merrick rose in the haze with a vicious grin reaping the reward of his success as he gained ground. She stared in a cold, unforgiving manner across the divide. She clung onto the edge as she flailed over nothing before steadying herself. The other Angeon grasped the moment of his strong hold, as he rose widening his arms in a cold embrace as he seized control. She bit her lip from the shear grit of her teeth as she held on and then let go leaping into the void. The jolt ran like a shockwave wrapping around

Merrick's legs and dragging him down with the force.

His rage howled, cutting the air, as he catapulted off the edge and into the writhing darkness. The other Angeon's cries pierced from above. Screeching through in an anguished and unrelenting tone, before the earth absorbed the sound. As the outer form slipped away Saranon became the Angeon of old once born again, but alas it came too late. For all she could do now was the one act she would see through to the end, as she took hold of Merrick in a final embrace. His screams arched upward to the sky beyond, as she took him down into the darkness inside Tordoren. The Angeon of old clasped on with all her strength in the shimmering light as her energy burned bright and beyond.

She held on in a tight embrace taking the other Angeon down deep into the ground, as the energy carved its way through. The heat pounded through her body with a vibrant flow, keeping Merrick's attempts at bay as he struggled. The harsh determination stayed in her mind as he struggled. For now the fighting seemed useless, as her sorcery held in place, not letting go from the path she had chosen. Any sound from without soon evaporated, as they fell further down. The noise which encroached around them resonated from her sorcery. The grip grew tighter as they went deeper into the darkness.

Her energy broke through the bonds and tore through the other Angeon's skin in a fine array as it held in place. Merrick gasped in shock as he could scream no more and the earth began to shatter in around them in a torrent. As the tendrils of Tordoren wrapped around them, a grip from the darkness half woke her from the hypnotic trance. A grip so strong, it bound around her, hauling her upward as the ground caved in pulling with a heavy grace. The last rays of a crimson red dusk spread across the land sweeping the ground in a shadowy silhouette. Saranon blinked in the light as the dragon's great wings carried her above the whirling turmoil and her body cried out in pain.

CHAPTER EIGHTEEN

An elusive Prophet

Chilcott watched as the dragon lay Saranon down as Kat stepped back curling his tail half around letting his wings drop. The wind raced howling in a cloud filled sky as the darkness of night washed the ground, racing at a heavy pace. The sounds of life began to emerge from deep inside the Keep as he waited, but no movement came. The winds beckoned low across the tower trickling the light bearing of rain, faltering as it swept across the land. Chilcott walked toward Saranon as the dragon lowered his head and nudged it to the side, beckoning for her to wake up. No sound came from her as the dragon stayed waiting in the evening light fast fading into darkness. Katholomu let out a mournful sound as if knowing the exacting cost of the attack.

Chilcott waited acknowledging the dragon's pain.

Kat stood so close his mighty claw tapped the stone, but a hands width from Saranon's flowing hair as it soaked up drops of rain. He leaned over sheltering her body from the burdening storm as he arched the tips of his wings out as the rain pooled. The echo of voices carried through the air as Chilcott stood beside Katholomu. The great dragon peered up without moving. Hailey's voice rang out behind him. 'Saranon!' She screamed.

Chilcott remained still as he held out a hand only to halt Hailey from rushing in, 'But we have to help her.'

'Go back inside,' he commanded.

Hailey hesitated in the dark and a silent tear escaped down her cheek, as she realised what had been said. In the dying light of the sorcerer's gaze as Chilcott stood in the still night air, the breeze whimpered to a halt. A heavy thud grew louder from the open door as Mitch made his way rushing past in the late night hour. His sleeve caught on the dragon's claw. As he stooped down underneath Kat's great wing and reached out taking a moment to lift her from her place of rest. The bond within him held a glimmer of hope inside as he paused before Chilcott. The sorcerer made no effort to move, as he guarded the dark open sky, waiting for the turmoil to ease in the field below.

Katholomu lifted his head after Mitch had darted from view. As he took care to curl up near the sorcerer's side peering out into the distance. Chilcott raised a hand brushing the dragon's soft leathery skin. The flames of light around the perimeters began to light up the Keep, with an eerie glow, bouncing shadows off the walls. Kat arched his head as faint noises flared through the still soft air and the sorcerer bade him to stay. The outer skirts of Indarin came to life with a reassuring surge of activity bellowing through the fragments of light. A few steps carried their sound across the open air as the sorcerer turned his head with a great reluctance.

He sighed in silence as the young Prophet joined him on the outdoor terrace overlooking the land. 'At some stage you will have to own your decision,' he spoke in a rough round voice to the Prophet.

Theron peered out over the wall's hard edge, unwilling to provide a reply to his teacher's advice. Chilcott strode to his side with a firm stance as he peered into the darkness. 'There is no room for complacency at Indarin, for whatever reason you had now is not the time to hide,' he spoke.

Theron swallowed as he closed his eyes, 'I did it for the Keep.'

He laughed, 'You are a braver man than I.'

He patted Theron on the shoulder before taking his leave to the well-lit halls inside. The echo of movement rallied down the long sweeping corridors amid the sorcerer's presence. It caused a stir in the murmur of voices as he travelled past. The sound of chaos gave way to a practical vibrant tone, as he ventured below to the medical area. He stood, closing his eyes for just the whisper of a moment, in the silence between the rushes of noise. He held his hand forward moving the door as he went. Purton's friendly smile peered up through a crowded room, as his friend waved, but it was not who he was searching for in the wake of the turmoil.

He strode past with a purpose to every step, as he moved forward through the fray. A small gathering of whispers passed near the door as he opened it ajar and peered in to see the pale image that lay waiting. Chilcott knew that every moment from here in, counted as Anne remained calm with determination. Mitch waited saying nothing at the scene playing out before him, as Anne and Rasine stabilised the Angeon. He began to ask, then hesitated in the moment, as Saranon opened her eyes peering at nothing. Mitch sat beside her, but she did not utter a word in the soft surroundings. Chilcott moved a little closer and her eyes stared straight at him piercing through his soul.

'How did you survive?' Saranon spoke through a dry swollen mouth.

He knew she was referring to the scar on his arm a reminder left from his encounter with Merrick, 'He missed.'

Chilcott held her hand. It was cool and clammy with little strength left. Yet she held on with a stubbornness that shone through. As he left, Purton joined him in the hall looking half his old self, 'There's no use worrying about Saranon when we've got a Keep to sort out.'

'That is not what concerns me,' he replied.

Purton looked into his friend's troubled brow, 'You mean Theron, don't you?'

It was not like Chilcott to keep secrets, though he was one to leave out words. The ones he was thinking in the foremost of his mind as the hours bled into the long night. His eyes grew tired, but the power of sleep evaded him in the dim light as the Keep fell into a familiar hum. The purr of the great centre core filtered up through the tiny vents to wash away any fear left in the hearts of the Armythral. Every sense that fled along his old bones told him that there was a business left undone. He peered into the soft lamp light flooding over a cram filled desk.

The Prophet had given no sign away, as the end drew near and the Keep along with its occupants had been unprepared. Regardless of the merciful outcome the lack of foresight was obvious. The gaping void plagued his mind, as he rubbed his brow in irritation. A soft knock woke him out of his thoughts as Anne beckoned for him to follow her lead. A rush of shouting pounded through the great hall as they entered. It broke a sultry deadlock when Armand and Elliot backed down. 'How did I know it would resort to this?' Chilcott spat the words out in distain.

'Theron needs to be punished,' Elliot rasped with conviction.

'There will be no passing of judgement until the job is done. If you are not resting for tomorrow's shift, there is plenty of work around here. I will hear no more of this,' Chilcott's voice shouted echoing off the ceiling, as it boomed through the air.

He waited to see who would stay for the night shift, with few rising, to the awkward challenge. As Armand stayed behind, his face filled with a heavy weight. The sorcerers worked through the night and into the first harsh rays of dawn. A golden glimpse pierced the crisp air to creep across the land. The sun reached out its insidious gaze, stretching upon the fierceness of the battle, raking a path toward the Keep.

It echoed the call of a lack of sleep among the weary eyed in the face of the grim task ahead. Indarin held well its own, in the morning light, with most signs of damage proving to be superficial. A small blessing, as the peace filtered through with an eerie groan, as the wind wrapped itself around the Keep. Theron stayed close by his father's side, with every attempt to remain out of the way. It only made the obvious more abundant as he attracted the attention of others. At first Chilcott saw no reason to question the young man. As he had seen many a young sorcerer make mistakes, but as the tension grew, his thoughts turned. Armand was an old friend and he had known Theron well. 'You may have kept a silent air, but all those faces out there will expect an explanation,' Chilcott spoke.

Theron peered over at Chilcott with knowing eyes, 'I will not shy away from what I did.'

Armand stood strong as he spoke to his son, 'You need to reach out, and hiding behind a righteous tone won't find you any friends. You will speak in the great hall when this is done.'

The sorcerer would hear no argument after his decision was made, at some stage his son would have to grow up and defend himself. Now, would be as good a time as any as the day grew strong and vibrant around him. A distant tone called out across the open sky harrowing the mournful end of a plagued era. As Chilcott tried to forget, the scar on his arm, would not let him. His eyes caught Theron's as he looked up and the Prophet said nothing, as the sorcerer gave him a firm stare.

The weariness was settling in on Chilcott's shoulders, with no good reason to stay longer, he made his way back to his apartment. Anne had placed a large warm breakfast on the table in anticipation and he smiled, she knew him too well. As the afternoon sun raised its head through the slit in the curtains, a thud and shouting reverberated into the room. He dashed out to the commotion. The sound blasted into the corridors as Todd pinned Theron against the wall amid Hailey's screaming. The scene appeared familiar as he stood between the two and bellowed in a deep low voice, as Todd backed down. The Prophet left in the moment with no need for any further encouragement.

He faced Todd with the signs of a skirmish showing on his face. 'You have lived with Saranon for months. You know Theron was not involved.'

'But he could have done something?' Todd exclaimed.

Chilcott let out a bellowing laugh, 'I don't see anyone here brave enough to tell the Angeon what to do, now clean up those marks. Don't make the same mistake I did.'

He uttered his last words with a solemn tone as a bitter warning. The day was almost gone and he meant to check on the Angeon before the day was through. It was a sobering journey down to the medical area, as Mitch sat in silence watching over the sleeping sorceress still as pale as before.

It was too early to tell the damage done, as he held her hand in a loose grip. He waited, without wavering, in trust which was more than he could say for himself. The Armythral believed that the Angeon were just another form of sorcery. Yet his instinct from the first time he had met Merrick as a boy, told him otherwise. For all the talk of the other Angeon's death he was not so convinced. He knew only too well that a sorcerer who does not want to be found can disappear. Only time would tell as the evening passed. The voices for Theron to answer to the great hall, haunted every step growing louder into the night.

For all he was worth the Prophet had stayed out of the way as if avoiding the inevitable, before being thrust to centre stage. For now, the matter grew far from Chilcott's thoughts, as Purton caught sight of him and handed him his set of tools. In a Keep this size there was always work to be done, as he smiled to his old friend. It would be a comforting relief as they walked into the deep stretches of the building. The pleasant sound of the humming Keep ran underneath the caress of his hand. It offered a small relief to calm his thoughts. He laid his hand into cleaning out the gunk that had matted along the conduits, filling the grates.

Purton chuckled, behind him in a familiar setting, he was quite at home in the bowels of Indarin as he hummed in tune with the Keep. Chilcott frowned without uttering a sound or losing pace with the work at hand, as his friend continued smiling even more. In the midst of the moment a sharp rush of footsteps raced towards them. As Anne almost threw herself into Chilcott's arms, 'Theron is missing.'

Purton sighed as he packed up, 'It's started,' he exclaimed.

He had been hoping and his heart sank in the recognition of the impact of Anne's words as she spoke them.

He strode up above, quickening his pace toward Armand's chambers where his friend greeted him with a solemn stand. 'They took him, Ryan has him and I want him back. I've called a meeting in the great hall and I want you there.'

Armand did not need to ask, he had supported Theron from an early age. It was not the form of resolution that he had been hoping for, but now the path had been taken he would stand by the young Prophet. The decision had spurred the Keep into action as the details spread rife. Armand was right to call a meeting so soon, even if it meant little preparation, as he gathered a few belongings.

Chilcott's bond-breaker Shehoarth sat in its case in silence, a token of his youth now gathering dust on the shelf. His own energy might have been more than enough to see him through the years, but he was no fool and wiped off the dust as he held it. The great irony of having to defend himself from his own clan, did not rest easy on his mind. The room lay clear, as he stood for a time waiting for the great hall to fill, before making his entrance. He had earned a great deal of respect and there was no need for grandeur. A small hand caught his attention from the side as Rasine beckoned him closer, 'It's Saranon, she's missing and so is the wizard.'

'What?' Chilcott whispered in disbelief, 'Let me know if you find anything.'

The astonishment drained from his face as he entered and sat near Armand. He said nothing in a room with abundant ears listening for the slightest sound. Armand was a grand speaker who took his time. Armand captivated the audience, holding back great strain and the love for his son to emphasise his point. As Elliot stood opposite and began, a slow yet steady cheer crept into the crowd. Chilcott knew he had made the right decision to bring Shehoarth. The mood told him it was going to be a long night as he clenched his fist out of sight. Elliot's furious tone cut deep as Armand demanded to see his son and Ryan standing by Elliot's side finally relented.

As he took his leave, the silence clung thick with tension pounding through the air. It was not an easy task as a few from the audience beckoned and jeered. The great hall was familiar with the peace and quiet of daily business. Yet the unusual events made the undercurrent electrifying with intensity among the clan. A shaken pale face emerged as a band of sorcerers kept a close circle around Theron, who held his head to the ground. He stared at his feet as he walked. The pain shone in Armand's eyes, as the ferocity of his emotions pierced his lips.

In the moment Ryan smiled, knowing the impact cut deep as the crowd responded in a loud roar and Elliot spoke strong. 'We were placed in harm's way because a Prophet, a boy, would not share his knowledge. This Keep has suffered at the hands of a fight, which does not concern us. People have lost their lives, when we had the ability to prevent it. Instead we are left with a child who thinks that playing with people's lives, is a game.'

The words cut deep, but the growing support in the crowd cut deeper still. Chilcott began to wonder if the chance had been lost to get Theron out unscathed. Anne gave him a worried, knowing glance as if reading his thoughts.

He grimaced as Elliot went on and Ryan chimed in with a lashing tone before Armand could stand his ground. At best, Theron would have to be reprimanded in the strength of support and any ground lost, could not be regained. It would be held against the Prophet forever more and with his youth that could well be a long time. Armand held his ground rivalling back a slow growing support, but it was not enough and he carried on. He looked at Theron but the Prophet hung his head not looking him in the eye. If anyone was going to save him it would be Theron himself and now was not the time to play the victim.

Chilcott lost track in his own thoughts as Elliot's words caught his attention. 'What have you to say in all this Mr Chilcott?'

He stood up and took the stand with a firm vibrant tone. 'I remember finding a sorcerer trying to drain the energy from an Angeon and when I went to intervene I was prevented from doing so. Yet when that Angeon broke free, that sorcerer screamed for help and his screams rang out through the lower levels of Indarin. You created a monster and now you want to blame a boy for the consequences. If you want to talk about punishment I would start with you,' Chilcott spoke with conviction.

Elliot's face burned bright red with anger, as he shouted, while Armand smiled in response. Elliot's fury showed in his words echoing across the great hall with a bitter rasp. Chilcott's speech held ground as Ryan and Elliot worked hard to regain their support with a waning crowd. He would not admit defeat, even if it meant, reaching a compromise. Either way Chilcott had hit his mark and returned to his chair with a knowing glint in his eyes, as his achievement took on a life of its own. In the long rain of events, a change so discreet occurred, it was almost lost in the array of words. The person presenting themselves as Theron stood up and transformed.

***

Saranon, the Angeon, rose in her full glory with a small smile of satisfaction creeping across her face from the looks of surprise. The change was so subtle it caught the sorcerers around her off-guard, as she used her energy to move them aside. She took her place at centre stage for all to see, as she set her tone hard against the background. She had no fear of the Armythral in the midst of the damage done. The only feelings running through her head all led to loss and pain. In that moment Elliot uttered unfathomable words, 'You should have died with Merrick.'

'I did not kill him so pray tell me, how is he dead?'

Saranon shouted with some bemusement to Elliot in the great hall before lowering her tone. 'After what Chilcott said I doubt the other Angeon will ever stray far from you. It is a pity, I always wanted a brother.'

She almost stated the last sentence through mocking eyes as Elliott grasped the meaning of her words. The Angeon spoke as she stood in the centre of the great hall first turning to Armand. 'Theron is safe, but this is not his fight and I told him not to come. Now Ryan you have something that belongs to me and I want it back.' She spoke as she stared right into the sorcerer's eyes.

Elliot turned to Ryan, 'What is she talking about?'

Ryan began to look worried as the meaning of her words sank in, he tried to run in a mad dash that came to a sudden halt, as she reached out. The panic in his eyes was visible, as she held him down and out of view of the crowd that were now standing on edge. As Elliot looked on in horror he realised that Ryan had stolen part of Saranon's energy. He looked like he was about to jump, but stayed almost captivated not able to veer away. Ryan breathed his last breath, before she covered his face, she peered up at Elliot. 'I hope you choose your friends more wisely.'

She continued. 'Now I have a different kind of score to settle, as I said before and I will stand by my word Theron is your Prophet now and in the future. His ability to keep silent saved many of your lives and many more including Indarin. It takes a brave man to speak the future and a true Prophet to know when to remain silent. Theron has done this and more, you have Indarin, the other Angeon is not in the position he once was and I will return to Zyanthia. May Odana help anyone who stands in my way.'

The Angeon stared around the room to a sea of faces in open silence as Armand stood, 'I think I can speak for all here, when I say you have our leave.'

As one group, all the sorcerers in the great hall in unison, rose as Saranon walked toward the door. Mitch released the handle from the other side opening the doors their full length to reveal one lone figure. Theron stood smiling as she approached. He held out his hand in recognition. 'You have my leave and my gratitude, if you ever come this way again you will always be welcome at Indarin,' Theron smiled.

A loud cheer echoed through the hall as Armand rushed to greet his son in open arms too scared to let go in the moment. She looked at Mitch's wide grin filled with excitement at the prospect of returning home to Normisia.

It had been a long time and the thought of being among wizards was appealing after being around so many sorcerers. With any luck Pennie would have made progress searching for her parents. Something which had plagued her so far from the country she had still not reconciled with. It was tempting to think that when she returned that would somehow change, but inside, she knew the damage lay too deep. The wounds along her back, a constant reminder of a childhood lost in the dark void. It had been left forgotten in the edges of Darkonia and the gaping memories of a life before. She did not anguish at her lack of knowledge of the past, for she had not been the only one to feel the spiteful wrath.

As she stood in the courtyard looking back at the majestic Keep, standing stronger than ever. The wound running along the earth caught her eye, as she gazed over the land. 'I hope I do not have to do that again.'

He stood by her side, 'You are the Angeon, I don't think you get to decide.'

She looked at him knowing the truth of his words. It was not what she wanted to hear. Then Mitch had never been one to soften the blow when he spoke. 'How did you know about Ryan?' He asked.

'It took too long to recover,' she smiled as she beckoned him to follow. 'Now where did that dragon go?'

Mitch smiled as he strode toward the dragon pens. He still managed to be annoying in subtle ways. She hesitated before following. The yard showed no sign of Katholomu. She peered around the corner to see his great paw sticking out sideways, as he slept curled up near the open door. The large opening revealed his head just inside, completely relaxed as Saranon walked toward him. She felt his coat; it was smooth and soft and smelt fresh, Mitch smiled beside her. The dragon moved with a calm resolve as his head came close to hers and he looked straight into her eyes.

'What do you think?' Hailey's voice sprang from behind the dragon's head as she beamed from ear to ear. 'We thought we would help and I don't think anyone could stand the smell any longer.'

'He looks beautiful,' she replied.

'I'm glad you like it, Seth and Darren helped, and I

just wanted to say thanks.'

Saranon patted Kat's head as he raised his shoulders. He stretched his muscles and hind legs before shifting his weight and lowering his head to step outside.

He glimmered under the early evening sky as the wind caught his wings and he bent his head back waiting. She clambered up his side, sitting herself close to the top of the dragon's shoulders. Mitch followed, placing himself into position. Katholomu lifted his great form up to meet the night stars shining down. He motioned for the dragon to go. Kat heaved up into the dark sky, swooping up in a wide arc, turning mid-air. Then flying up at a great height leaving the Keep Indarin far behind.

ACKNOWLEDGEMENTS

Life has been a journey filled with many challenges, and the people I would like to thank would not fit on this page. To everyone out there who has been part of this incredible journey thank you, your support has been appreciated.

– Please Leave a Review –

For all the wonderful people who have read the book it would be fantastic if you can leave a review, this helps other readers find it. Thank you.

BOOKS

The Legacy of Zyanthia series:
Made in the Image of the Goddess
Running through the Rising Tide
Deep in the Shadow of the Fallen

AUTHOR

If you love fantasy with adventure and a hint of the unexpected the quest is about to begin. Escape into fantasy, and the mystical world of magic mixed with adventure. You are in good company although chose your company wisely. There are anti-heroes, wizards, and a range of chaotic characters ahead. Not to mention dragons. A fantasy world set in an ancient mythical world has to have dragons. Tales of sword and sorcery captivated Chantelle from a young age. Reading until all hours of the night to find out what would happen to the characters. There was just one problem the story would finish far too soon.

Hidden away in the distant past the life of a fantasy writer began. The real life struggles have been a saga all of their own for author Chantelle Griffin. Originally known as Chantelle Lowe and born in Tasmania, Australia. Her dreams haunted her from an early age. Vivid tumultuous dreams carrying adventure and danger. It took the author into a fantasy world filled with sorcery and treachery. The story continues to captivate her writing. If you love fantasy with adventure follow the Legacy of Zyanthia series.

www.chantellegriffin.com

GLOSSARY

ANGEON: 'The Angeon is Darkonia's answer to the Oracle, a sorcerer born with the ability to break down all defences and render a civilisation powerless.' There had been no Angeon since shortly after the Dreshan Occupation ended over 200 years ago with Zeralden Hadenvar the last Angeon who ruled Darkonia (as Queen) by marriage to the King's second son.

BOND-BREAKER: A weapon made by sorcery when dormant resembles a dagger, when activated resembles a sword it acts as a catalyst to magnify and aim the user's energy and can be used equally well by wizards as well as sorcerers. 'The most feared swords a sorcerer could use made of heart stone a melding of the elements to form a solid material that resembled crystal and sharp enough to cut through stone.'

CENTRAL CORE: The working core mechanism which powers the Keep, usually hidden away deep within the earth. It is a large engine created by sorcery which then continues to thrive on a combination of energy drawn from deep within the earth and sorcery. The combination creates a very raw and powerful energy which is difficult to manipulate.

DEAD ZONE: This is created when part of the Keep is not receiving energy from the central core or when energy has been diverted.

END NODE: Last outpost of a Keep's main energy source located at semi-regular intervals around the perimeter.

FERMADICIDE: Dark skeletal creatures.

FIRE MARK: A mark on the right shoulder to, the symbol of the fires of chaos given to the Issola in the camps.

HILAZEN: Bonded wizard.

HOST: Wizard joined with a Keep, it takes 60 hours to complete a union.

HYRIK: Restraint on sorcery, like a collar.

IMBENIK CHAMBER: Near the central core within the Keep, in between the indolin chamber and the central core it contains alters where a sorcerer can meld with the Keep.

INDOLIN CHAMBER: Inside the Keep, in between the habitable area and the central core.

KEDRIL(S): Tools to fix a Keep.

KEEP: A building protected by a central core powered by sorcery and energy from the earth. The tunnels led down to the primary systems and the central core that transferred energy from far below the ground into the core and turned

into a usable energy source. Most central cores were located deep in the ground where the temperature was constantly warm…'
KULTIER: Long giant cockroaches.
LAY-LINE: Fast method of travel.
MAZETTE: Small (bird size) dragons.
MISQUEW: Riding cat.
NEFRELLE: Small creature (cat size), part human with very sharp teeth and claws.
OCKREN: Big cat, the soul of the Keep.
PALAFON: Tiny dragon.
QUADMAR: Aquatic creature from the murky depths, larger than a mermaid.
SACRA SEAL: Small, can hold it on your hand.
SHEAL: Liquid inside the Keep, very potent compressed raw energy.
SKADA: Small mechanical creatures that help maintain the Keep, they resemble a large spider.
SOVA BAG: A deceptive small light pouch that can become an enormous bag and hold a lot of objects, it will not hold living things.
STALLIC ENERGY: Energy from the Keep.
TALIK: Communication device. 'The sorceress held up her talik a small round disc that could open small enough to fit in the palm of her hand and placed her thumb on the centre of the outside…'
TRIDEN: Giant crab/spider, dark brown.
UVALEN CODE: '…A complex masterpiece describing the natural laws that governed sorcery.'

ZENNIGH: A large cat that normally lives within a Keep, they are too big to fit in a house but that has not stopped the occasional one from trying and getting their head jammed in the doorway.
ZYANTHIAN REGION: Armedicia, Taria, Normisia, Darkonia and Alveron were formed from one country called Zyanthia.